SALT GIRL

SEAHOUSES MYSTERY

KATHERINE GRAHAM

This is a work of fiction. Any similarity to actual persons, living or dead, or actual events, is purely coincidental.

For all the teachers

CONTENTS

PROLOGUE

Then

The night is quiet. *Deathly still.*

Those words come to me – it must be a line from a poem, or perhaps the lyrics of a song – and I instantly regret them, pushing them from my mind. I force myself to think happier thoughts. *Positive mental attitude.* That's what I need right now. Positivity.

The gravel crunches under my feet. I tread as lightly as I can, even if it slows my pace. In the empty silence of the night, my heart is hammering.

The last bus left a couple of hours ago. The timetable is folded up in my pocket, even though I know it by heart.

I was supposed to be on that bus. No worries. I always have a plan B.

I'm out. *I'm getting away.* That's all that matters.

Hitchhiking is not ideal, but I've been mentally preparing myself just in case it came down to this. I'll have to take my chances. There's no other choice.

I'd hoped to leave earlier. Typical that on tonight of all

nights, they were glued to some stupid old film. The music from the closing credits floated up the stairs while I watched the clock, picking at a cuticle until it bled.

I was forced to bide my time, listening until the tread on the stairs had faded, until I'd heard the flick of the light switch and the creak of the bed, then waited another half hour for good measure. No one heard me leave. I'm good at going unnoticed. Let's face it – I've had plenty of practice.

It's cold out here. It's already March, but winter has yet to release its icy grip. My breath mists in front of my face as the chill begins to bite. I pull my scarf tighter around my neck.

There are late trains from Alnmouth and Morpeth. In my head, I repeat the timetable I've spent weeks learning by rote. I could even sleep in the station and wait for the morning train. That's OK. I can do that. There's a fleece and a couple of cereal bars in my backpack. I like to think I'm well prepared.

You can't hear the sea from here. I'm on the path that runs between the houses, a cut dissecting two rows of back gardens. There's barely even a breeze, but the air carries the scent of a log fire and I find it comforting, reassuring. It's a homely smell.

I don't know why I think that. I've never lived anywhere with a real fire.

The windows of the houses are lit up. Little squares, like an advent calendar. Some people haven't closed their curtains. They don't expect anyone to be out here, not at this time of night. It's why I chose to come this way. Besides, why would they worry about someone seeing inside? It's not like they have anything to hide.

I got out.

I need to get to Newcastle. This time, I'll tell Dawn the

whole story. Once she knows the truth, she'll cover for me. Not like before.

That's if anyone even comes for me.

It's only two months until my eighteenth birthday. I'm hardly worth the effort now. If I ever was.

His words replay in my mind; a scratched record. *You can't leave me.* I mute his voice.

The light from the windows doesn't reach the path. The gardens are blanketed in darkness. Shadows pool in the corners, swirl at my feet. I don't even have the light of the moon to guide me – it's a sliver of silver, hidden behind a veil of cloud.

It's fine. I know where I'm going.

Dawn is going to be livid. Like, nuclear explosion-level furious. But we'll get through it. We've been through much worse, me and Dawn.

The thought of her makes me want to cry. I won't, though. I need to stay level-headed. There'll be plenty of time for tears later. Right now, I'm in survival mode. *Fight or flight.* I chose flight.

Besides, there's no fight left in me. I just need to get away from this whole mess.

And what a mess I've made.

Against the darkness, I hear a noise. I freeze, holding my breath.

But there's nothing; only the thundering of my pulse in my ears. It's just me, spooking myself. I exhale, long and slow. Willing myself calm.

From here, I can see where the cut ends, the point at which it meets the street. There's a lamppost, the orange glow casting long shadows onto the road. I focus on that streetlamp. It's not too far away, and from there it's only a short walk to the middle of the village. The arcade, the pubs. People.

I'll flag a car down, ask for a ride. I have a whole story worked out. I'm going to tell them I'm a student at Newcastle University. I came to Seahouses for a weekend with my boyfriend, but we had a row and now I need to get home. Everyone always says I look older than I am. Anyway, it's dark, and people who give lifts to strangers at night presumably don't ask too many questions.

I hear something. Definitely something this time. I scan the path behind me, the way I've just come from. There's nothing but blackness.

What was it? A bird? An animal?

A person?

It can't be. There can't be anyone out here at this hour. Not anyone creeping around, at least. Except me.

My phone is in the side pocket of my bag. I could get it out, but it would cost me precious seconds. Besides, there's no one to call. I'm on my own.

I pick up speed. *Just keep going. Almost there, now.*

There's a sharp whack to my shin – it comes out of nowhere, and the shock delays the pain. It takes a second to hit, but when it does, it's excruciating.

It feels like another entire second before I realise I'm falling, tumbling forwards. Slow motion.

My hands hit the gravel first, my palms searing in agony. My scarf falls off, my backpack slides from my shoulder and lands beside me with a thud. Did I trip on something?

I was tripped.

I've been caught.

I know it before my brain can process the urgent need to scramble back to standing; I know it before I've even righted myself on the ground. My attacker has not yet stepped out of the shadows, but I already know who it is.

I didn't make it. I didn't get away, after all.

I don't even make it to my feet. Then there are hands around my neck; I claw at them, desperately. I can't breathe. They tighten, pressing against my throat with a sickening urgency.

I can't breathe.

The gravel is sharp beneath my knees as I drop again. My arms flail, purposelessly, pathetically, grasping at the night. Something kicks in, adrenaline or instinct. I try to prise the hands off my neck, fighting with every remaining atom of strength, but they're squeezing.

The fight is being squeezed from me.

I'm so tired of fighting. I've been fighting my entire life.

Why didn't I wait until tomorrow morning? Or next week? I could have taken the bus to school and simply vanished, slipped away in plain sight.

I wish I had screamed for help just seconds earlier. I wish I'd punched or kicked. I should have run for my life while I had the chance.

It's too late now.

To run. For my life.

Our eyes meet and I see pure hatred and, beneath that, something more fragile. Something maniacal and – even more frightening – a frantic and despairing hopelessness.

There's no hope for me, either.

The world is spinning. Black spots cloud my vision, the darkness seeping inside me. The last traces of air, of life, are being squeezed from my body. I'm fading.

This is it.

Will anyone miss me? Will anyone even notice I'm gone?

I'm afraid of what comes next, of what awaits me on the

other side, that eternal unknown. Infinity. But the fear doesn't have long to take hold, to tighten its icy grip on my consciousness. My conscience.

The last of my light fades, and there's nothing but the darkness, swallowing me whole.

1

Now

Izzy watched as Finn brought the sledgehammer down. The concrete cracked on the first blow; the noise sent a shudder through her.

She leaned against the doorframe. 'Coffee?'

He glanced up, noticing her. His face was streaked in dirt, sweat. 'I'd love one, please.'

She slipped her flip flops off, allowing the cool of the kitchen tiles to soothe the soles of her bare feet, and snapped a capsule into the machine. He'd need water, too. It was thirsty work and today was one of the hottest days of the year so far.

These tiles, they would be next. Who chose brown for a kitchen, anyway? Then the bathroom. And then the master bedroom, and the kids' rooms, and the living room. The garden. She mentally ticked through the renovation projects in her mind.

The conservatory had nudged its way to the top of her list after a storm three weeks ago. Izzy had woken in the middle of the night with a start, the dregs of a nightmare clinging to her. Reeds around her ankles, threatening to pull her down.

A crash. For one horrible moment, she wasn't sure what was real and what wasn't. Her mind raced with potential catastrophes: the children. *Amy.* Those terrifying seconds stretched on, reality suspended between this world and the next.

But the noise. That had been real.

They'd seen the evidence for themselves in the morning. The roof of the conservatory had almost blown clean off and the west-facing window had collapsed inwards. They tore the structure down, only to discover an uneven foundation that would have to be replaced before rebuilding could begin. Izzy had wanted to cry. It was just one more thing on top of all the other things.

Hilariously, Jake thought they could tackle it themselves. He'd convinced himself after watching a couple of videos on YouTube and had even gone as far as buying a sledgehammer. Izzy had tactfully suggested that one of the labourers she worked with needed the money.

At the thought of Jake, she fingered her engagement ring. Even after three months, it still felt too big, too clunky. A weight she couldn't quite get used to. She blushed whenever strangers' eyes rested on it and had taken to hiding her hands in her pockets.

She took the coffees outside and handed one to Finn. Further cracks had appeared in the concrete now. Even the most solid things can be destroyed if you know the weak spots.

He took a sip of coffee and wiped his brow with the back of his forearm. 'I saw the plans for the new conservatory. It'll look canny once it's finished.'

She resisted the temptation to correct him. They weren't getting a new conservatory; it was an *orangery*. 'Maybe that storm did us a favour, after all?' The coffee was too hot, scalding her tongue.

Finn set his mug on the ground and picked up one of the smaller chunks of concrete, the muscles in his arms growing taut with the effort. They'd managed to wedge a skip into the cut at the bottom of the garden, and now it was almost full. Shards of PVC, Perspex, and plasterboard stuck out at ugly angles.

Izzy shifted her weight from foot to foot. Should she be helping? Finn had worked for her on a couple of projects, those interior design commissions that called for a little more muscle than she could muster. She tried to think of something useful to do.

The water. She'd forgotten his water.

She padded back into the kitchen and ran the tap, enjoying the kiss of the cool water on her hands. There were emails to be sent, invoices to be filed, and she needed to finish the proposal for the Fletcher property. The kids were staying with them this weekend. She had to order groceries, plan meals, coordinate with Jake about what they would do to keep them entertained. Tasks, demands, *things* piled up in her mind. Life had been so much simpler when it was just her.

Finn had hauled more pieces of concrete to the skip. The ground was emerging where the conservatory used to be, its foundations now reduced to boulders. Pebbles.

Everything could wait.

She sank into a chair, one of six around a faded wooden table on the deck. This would also be replaced, eventually. But with what? Her sketch book was full of doodles, unfinished drawings of incomplete ideas.

She looked up at the house. *Their house.* Grey stone, two-storey, four bedrooms and three reception rooms. A steal, until you costed up the amount of work that it needed. But that's what Izzy had wanted. Wasn't it? An opportunity to show off her skills as an interior designer. A blank canvas, something she and Jake could put their stamp on. A home they would create together, just for them. If only she could figure out where to begin.

The sky was cornflower blue, cloudless. She closed her eyes, feeling the warmth of the sun on her face.

Three months since they had bought the place; three months since Jake had gone down on bended knee and asked the question she instantly knew the answer to. So why her hesitation now?

It wasn't him. It was *here*. The village she had yearned to leave, yet it had pulled her back. She was a fish snagged in a net. Seahouses had been the last place on earth she'd thought she'd put down roots, if she ever did.

Finn was clearing the ground with a shovel now, filling the wheelbarrow with smaller pieces of concrete. The patch of sweat on his back darkened, a V blooming in the heat. He probably would have taken his t-shirt off had she not been there. Effortlessly, he steered the wheelbarrow down the path to the bottom of the garden.

Izzy adjusted her thoughts. Mindfulness, that's what it was called. Instagram was full of it these days, not to mention her mother. Wheelbarrow half-full, rather than half-empty. See? It was just a question of perspective. But busy was good. Busy filled the days. Busy kept her mind from wandering, occupying the space that might otherwise fill with doubts...

In the distance, she heard the latch of the front door.

Jake.

'Out here,' she called.

He appeared at the doorway, blinking in the bright sunshine. No court today, which meant jeans and a cotton shirt, now folded back on his forearms in acknowledgement of the great weather. It had taken a lot to coax him out of the tweeds he was so fond of wearing when they first met. His mahogany hair, streaked with grey, gleamed in the sunlight. And those arms... She caught a glimpse of the soft down that ran in a ridge to his wrist, and her stomach twisted.

He smiled at her, creases appearing at his eyes. That grin he kept just for her. 'Looks great,' he said, without taking his eyes off Izzy.

'Guys...' Finn interrupted, shattering their moment. 'There's something here...' There was a question in his voice, unsteady, wavering. Uncertain. His brow knotted in a frown, his hairline sodden from the exertion. She really should have given him more water.

Izzy walked over to Finn's side, peering into the shallow trough he had excavated. 'Looks like a ball.'

But she could already see a hole. *That was all right*, she told herself, even as her heart fluttered. An old football with an egg-sized hole in it. Nothing more.

She took a steadying breath.

Jake crouched down for a closer look. 'Pass me that trowel, would you?' He didn't look at Izzy this time.

He gently scraped back the earth, revealing more of the ball. There was a second hole, mirroring the first. Izzy's stomach knotted.

'Is that...?' But Finn didn't finish his question. He doubled over, dry heaving.

She could see hair now. A football with two holes and hair.

Jake exchanged a glance with Izzy, a frown etched on his face. A bead of sweat rolled down his temple.

'Darling,' he said, doing his best to keep his voice steady. 'I think you'd better call the police.'

Izzy dialled 999, her hand shaking. From the garden, she could hear the muted discussion between Jake and Finn. She told herself it was better to wait in here, by the front door, ready for when the cavalry arrived. Inside the house it was cool, but her skin was clammy, sheened in sweat. Panic rose in her chest. She fought to keep it down.

She sighed in relief when the knock at the door finally came. It was a familiar face on her doorstep, and Izzy watched as Detective Inspector Pamela Bell registered the connection, the detective's expression softening as she eventually remembered how she knew the woman in front of her.

It had been two years since Izzy's sister died, but there were moments – like this – that dredged the memories back to the surface and opened the wound afresh. A scar, never to heal.

'Izzy Morton. Good to see you again.' Bell's voice was flat. 'You told the dispatcher you'd found something in the garden?'

The lines in the detective's face had deepened, but her eyes were just as bright, as piercingly inquisitive, as Izzy remembered. At her side stood a younger male detective, freshly shaven and clean-cut. A guy who might have been Izzy's type, a decade ago, with broad shoulders and a crisp white shirt. He peered over Izzy's shoulder into the house, seemingly eager to get started. Wordlessly, Izzy waved them inside.

'We're doing work on the place; you'll have to excuse the mess.' She instantly chastised herself. As if the partially-stripped walls and bare floors would bother anyone when they had just unearthed a skull in the back garden.

Possibly a skull. Izzy forced herself to keep an open mind, as much as she could.

'This is Finn Hanlon, our builder, and you already know Jake Ridley.' She didn't introduce him as her fiancé and wondered if Jake would be irked.

'Jake, of course. Hi.' DI Bell's tone was cool, but Izzy heard the familiarity.

The law enforcement and legal community in this corner of the country was small and consequently tight-knit, with frequently blurred lines between correct and proper procedure and the personal connections that facilitated shortcuts. As the partner of a local solicitor's firm, Jake had regular dealings with the police, but Izzy had never dared to question if he ever ran into the detective who worked on Amy's case.

They'd covered the hole with a tarpaulin, and Izzy was grateful she didn't have to see the football again and wonder what it might be.

Who it might be.

Jake dragged a hand through his hair. 'We did the best we could.' He looked as if he might throw up. 'As soon as I realised what it was – what it *might* be – we stepped back and did our best to preserve the scene. Hopefully, there's not too much contamination.'

DI Bell nodded towards Finn, who was still unsettlingly pale. 'I take it you found it?'

'Yeah, I suppose. Although I couldn't tell what it was, at first.'

'We were all here,' added Jake. He gestured to Izzy. 'My fiancée and I, we were present when it was found.'

Izzy purposefully avoided the detective's glance, her hands fixed behind her back.

The sun was high. Midday or thereabouts. Izzy thought back to that morning, when Jake had mentioned he might come home at lunch and work from here this afternoon. She couldn't understand how he could concentrate, how he could focus on cases and legal procedure among all the mess.

Lunch. She hadn't even thought about eating. Anyway, she'd lost her appetite now.

'Let's have a look, shall we?' DI Bell draped her blazer over one of the chairs. 'Step back, please.'

Izzy averted her eyes as the young police officer pulled back the tarpaulin. 'Jesus,' he muttered under his breath.

'All right, Rich. Let's radio it in.'

Jake's hand on Izzy's waist made her jump. 'Are you feeling OK? Do you want to come and sit down?'

Izzy shook her head. Her mouth was dry. A radio crackled to life, and she tried to tune out the words. *Human remains. Burial site. Crime scene.*

DI Bell folded back the cuffs of her shirt sleeves. All business, now. 'Forensics will be here soon. In the meantime, DC Denton and I need a few more details from you. Shall we go indoors?'

Izzy led the way, thankful to get out of the heat and far away from whatever *that* was.

'Make yourselves comfortable,' Jake said, gesturing to the battered leather sofa. He took an armchair and Izzy perched beside him, craving the comfort of proximity. She chanced a glance at Finn, who was still pale.

DI Bell eased herself onto the sofa, laying her jacket

carefully on the seat beside her, smoothing out an invisible crease. As if there was no rush.

'How's your mother?' she asked.

Izzy sighed. Her mother was one of the reasons she hadn't wanted to come back to Seahouses in the first place. And after Amy's death, Izzy's family drama had been laid out for everyone to gawp at. *Again.* The people in this village loved to gossip. She had learned the hard way, twice before. It would be a bloody circus, now.

'She's fine.' It was all she could manage to say.

'Tell me about the house,' said Bell. 'You haven't been here that long?'

Jake cleared his throat. 'We bought the place three months ago. Izzy and I, that is. She's a fixer-upper, all right. Quite the job!'

He was babbling, betraying his nervousness. Izzy placed a hand on his shoulder and offered a reassuring squeeze.

'And the previous owners?'

'It had been on the market for a while,' Izzy mumbled.

The amount of work required had put many people off, according to the estate agent who had showed Izzy and Jake around.

'An elderly couple lived here before.' Jake sounded calmer now. 'Well, just the wife, at the end. The daughter sold it.'

DI Bell nodded. 'We'll need to speak to her.'

'I have her details, somewhere,' he said.

'Will it be on the news?' Finn blurted out. 'I mean if it does turn out to be... what I think it is?'

He was already thinking about his role in the press coverage, Izzy could tell. About being on TV and the stories he would be able to tell his mates down the pub. She imagined the events of this morning growing more dramatic, gorier, with each retelling. She couldn't blame Finn; not much happened in Seahouses.

'One step at a time,' said DI Bell.

The other detective – Izzy had already forgotten his name – consulted his notebook. 'I noticed there's a lane at the end of the garden.'

'Yes.' Jake nodded. 'It's a cut that runs along the back, all the way to Seafield Road.'

The man nodded. 'So anyone could gain access?'

A knock at the door interrupted them before either could respond, and Izzy made a mental note to add replacing the doorbell to her list of priority projects.

'That'll be forensics.' DI Bell nodded to her colleague. 'Get that for us, would you, Rich?'

This is how it starts, thought Izzy. Already, it wasn't even up to her to answer her own front door. Once again, their lives would be available for public consumption, a buffet for strangers to pick over. The circus had come to town.

From the armchair, she watched as people in white suits and heavy boots trudged through her home. Moon men. More arrived, using the cut at the bottom of the garden for access.

A white tent appeared where the conservatory had stood, and Izzy observed with detachment as a dog handler encouraged a German Shepherd to sniff around the flowerbeds she was planning to landscape. They wheeled in a generator and rigged up lighting.

At some point, Jake told Finn to go home for the day. Izzy didn't say goodbye.

The day turned from cornflower to ochre, pinks and lilacs streaking the sky as the sun began its descent. The police continued working as darkness finally fell.

'What a mess,' said Jake. 'Perhaps you should stay at Mike's tonight?'

Izzy shook her head. She didn't want to impose on her brother-in-law. She just wanted this to all go away.

'They'll be out there for a few days,' he said softly.

'The kids.' There was no way they could have her nieces and nephew hanging around with all this going on. 'I'll ask Auntie Sue if she can have them this weekend.'

The advantage of the whole family living close by was that the children always had somewhere to go. Between Izzy, her mother and her aunt, there were enough people to make sure Mike got a break from parenting single-handedly.

But she'd have to tell them about this. Tell them what they'd found.

'Who do you think it is?' She allowed herself to voice the question that had been plaguing her all afternoon. Jake folded her in his arms and she leaned into him, inhaling his familiar scent for comfort.

'Who knows? Could be linked to the old owners. They'll check the missing persons' register to start with.' He sighed. 'They'll know more in the coming days.'

The whole village will know more in the coming days, Izzy mused.

They were interrupted by DI Bell. 'That's us done for now. The forensics team will keep working through the night. We'll keep an officer stationed at the access point, just in case.'

She didn't need to explain that it was a necessary precaution to stem the inevitable tide of rubberneckers that would arrive by morning. News of a body being found would already have spread, and Izzy knew that the more inquisitive locals wouldn't be able to help themselves.

How had someone managed to bury a body without

being caught? The garden was visible from at least a dozen houses. Hadn't anyone questioned why their neighbour was digging up his lawn?

There were shadows under DI Bell's eyes now. Presumably it wasn't every day that she uncovered human remains in a back garden. As a detective covering a largely rural beat, she was probably more used to dealing with missing pets and speeding drivers.

Except for that one murder case. Amy.

It struck Izzy, then, that she was the common denominator in this. Perhaps bad luck was following her around.

Or perhaps it was Seahouses? For a village where everyone knew everyone, people seemed to be remarkably good at hiding secrets. Or at least, burying them.

2

IZZY CRADLED THE STEAMING MUG IN TWO HANDS. HERE, IN the sanctuary of her mother's kitchen, she found she could at last breathe. The tension she had been holding in her shoulders all morning started to melt away.

'It's been three days. Don't worry, they'll give up soon enough,' her aunt Sue said, biting her lip.

This past weekend, the story of a body found in a Northumberland coastal village had dominated the news agenda. The police held a press conference on Saturday, confirming the victim had been a teenage girl.

The forensics team had uncovered a quantity of salt in the shallow grave, inspiring at least one of the tabloids to bestow a nickname on the victim. Izzy shuddered as she recalled the headlines. *Salt Girl.* The broadsheets had run with it, and she'd even heard the presenter on *Sky News* reference the moniker. A wave of nausea rose in her chest.

One paper had disclosed the name of Izzy and Jake's street. That had been enough to attract a gaggle of reporters to their front door, including two crews who turned up in satellite vans with blow-dried and coiffured presenters. Even now, a knot of press remained encamped on Izzy's doorstep.

Emily, her aunt's partner, joined Izzy at the table. She and Sue were a study in contrasts: while Sue was curved, solid – Izzy liked to think of it as *huggable* – Emily was slight, with skin that bordered on translucent.

In the early days of their courtship, Sue had admonished Izzy for referring to Emily as her girlfriend. *Partner* was indeed a far more appropriate term – and not just because both women were well into their fifties and possibly beyond the bounds of *girl*-anything. No, it was more than that. *Partner* perfectly captured the nature of their relationship: a balance between two equals. They shared the work of supporting the family, in particular Izzy's mother, who required more support than most.

'Did Jake hear anything about missing persons?' Emily asked.

Izzy shook her head. 'Not yet.'

Jake had explained that the police would initially search for reports of people who had gone missing from the surrounding area. Although the net could widen, it was unlikely that someone had disappeared from the opposite end of the country and ended up here.

He had reeled off figures that made Izzy's head spin: someone is reported missing every ninety seconds in the UK, eighty-five percent are found within two days, only one percent of missing people turn up dead. He meant to reassure her, but she saw it as further proof of her appalling luck: one of the one percent had been buried under their conservatory.

Thanks to Jake's personal contacts in the police force and at the pathologist's office, they were being kept in the loop. Izzy wasn't sure if that was a good or bad thing.

'They're going to make another appeal at today's press conference, apparently.' The beginning of a tension headache flared, a dull pain in Izzy's forehead. She kneaded a knuckle at her temple, willing it to subside. 'At least the forensics team should be gone this morning.'

Izzy had spent the days studiously avoiding the clinical white structure that dominated their garden and devoting all her energy to not thinking about what was going on inside.

On the advice of the police, she and Jake had strategically made themselves scarce when the body was eventually removed. They took the children to the beach as a distraction, seeking some fresh air to take everyone's mind off the horror that was unfolding at home. Izzy and Jake had trailed in the wake of her nieces and nephew, holding hands and saying very little.

Telling the kids had been torturous. Izzy had agonized over how to shield them from the hideous truth, but try as she might, could see no way to sugar-coat this one. Better that they heard from her than their friends in the playground, she reasoned.

She had sat the three of them down, fighting against the urge to cry, and explained the gruesome discovery the best way she could. She remembered the tremble in Lucas's tiny body as she held the three of them close. Even now, she imagined she could still hear the breath snag in Hannah's throat.

'How were the kids this morning?' she asked.

Sue sighed. 'Hannah's still following the whole story online. I suggested she avoid reading too much of the detail, but you know what she's like.'

Izzy understood. Hannah was inquisitive and intelligent and had been through much more than most sixteen-year-old girls. And the victim was a young woman around her age. It hit close to home.

'And Betsy? Lucas?'

Sue and Emily exchanged a glance, and Izzy recognised that her aunt was hesitant to tell her something. 'Betsy had another nightmare last night.' Sue shrugged. 'It's normal – she's only ten.'

Izzy's heart sank even deeper. The house was meant to be their forever home, not just for her and Jake, but for the kids, too. Would they ever feel at ease again, be able to sleep soundly, with the ghost of the body under the conservatory haunting their dreams?

'And Lucas had a lot of questions about the salt.' Emily stirred sugar into her tea. 'We tried to give him the child-friendly version.'

Izzy sighed. 'I just don't get it. I mean, I read the papers; I know the theories. But why would anyone do that?'

It had baffled the police as well as the press. Izzy had done her best not to read too much of the speculation.

'It could have been to prevent someone from finding the body. The salt would keep animals away. I imagine if you buried a corpse in your garden, you wouldn't want a fox digging it up,' Emily said matter-of-factly.

It was hard, Izzy guessed, for a scientist's mind to not go there. She swallowed against the sudden tightness in her throat and tried not to think about foxes.

Sue considered it for a moment. 'I suppose that's why the conservatory was built in the first place. My guess is that it went up not long after she died.'

'It is interesting, though.' Emily sat back in her chair, a frown of concentration meshing her brow. 'Salt would preserve the body. That's why the ancient Egyptians used it in mummification. But it would also preserve evidence.

Presumably, someone who buried a body would want to avoid anyone finding out how it got there?'

Izzy nodded glumly. Jake's friend in the pathologist's office had shared more or less the same conundrum. At least well-preserved evidence might help the investigation, which had so far drawn a blank.

The previous occupants were deceased, but the police had interviewed the daughter. According to Jake's contact at Northumbria CID, the woman had not only been distraught, but quite insistent that her parents couldn't have had anything to do with it. The evidence might suggest otherwise, of course, in due time...

'It's the ritual.'

None of them had noticed Izzy's mother enter the room. Anne was wearing a full-length black kaftan, her hair wound up in a chignon on top of her head and secured with a red silk scarf, creating quite an arresting sight.

Satisfied she had their full attention, Anne continued. 'In lots of cultures, people bury their dead in salt. It's an ancient practice seen all around the world. My theory is that whoever buried the body was performing a ceremony. Giving the deceased burial rites of some sort.'

Theory. Izzy didn't like it when her mum developed *theories*.

'Well, let's try to focus on happier subjects, shall we?' Izzy met her aunt's eyes, and they exchanged an uneasy look, an unspoken concern that this topic – like so many – might be upsetting for her mother.

Izzy pushed away the cup of tea that she hadn't been able to stomach. 'I'd better be going, anyway. Hopefully, the press pack has moved on now that the police are finished.'

She doubted very much that the media appetite for the story would diminish any time soon, but she couldn't face listening to her mother spiral off into one of her episodes. Her mother required a level of energy that, today, she didn't possess.

Izzy strolled along King Street and onto Main Street. A coachload of schoolkids snaked in a line behind their teacher towards the harbour, forcing Izzy to wait until they passed. The warm weather was set to continue for at least another week. Great news for the local businesses that relied on a thriving tourist trade and had lost so much income during lockdown. Indeed, Main Street was already packed. But were these visitors drawn by the appeal of a day by the beach or the grim headlines? Izzy suspected it might be the latter.

Last night, she had asked Jake if he thought they should move. How could they stay in their house after this? She could have sworn she saw his heart break at the suggestion. *Give it time,* she told herself. Sooner or later, the articles labelling their forever home as a *house of horror* would become too much to bear, even for Jake.

Izzy turned onto their street. Sure enough, there were four figures waiting at the garden gate. She drew a deep breath, steeling herself. Only once she got closer did she realise one of them was familiar.

Diana Wheeler seemed to get more petite every year, as if she was shrinking piece by piece, which made Izzy wonder if she might one day disappear altogether. But she still had the posture that Izzy remembered from her schooldays. Straight-backed, head held high, just as she had been when she stood at the front of Izzy's classroom all those years ago, with that booming voice and piercing stare. And despite being well into her eighties, the old lady remained a force to be reckoned with.

Diana had experience in dealing with the media. It was, in her eyes, a profession that had been respectable once upon a time. Goodness knows what her Lionel – the late, great Lionel Wheeler, onetime Deputy Editor of the *Newcastle Evening Chronicle* – would make of today's contingent.

Well, perhaps they weren't all that bad. This charming young man from the *Chronicle* had seemed quite interested when Diana informed him of her links to the newspaper, and the reporter from *The Sun* had been ever so polite, even after Diana told the girl that she wouldn't deign to clean her windows with that particular publication. According to the young lady, it had all changed now, and there was a new female editor in charge, which Diana thought was most impressive and quite the indication of progress. Perhaps she should give it another chance after all.

She was enjoying their discussion so much that she didn't see Izzy approaching.

'I said we've got no comment,' Izzy mumbled, avoiding eye contact with the reporters.

Diana offered them a sympathetic shrug. She hated to think of the hours these bright young things had wasted, although they couldn't say she hadn't warned them.

In a somewhat contrived display of solidarity, she spoke loud enough to ensure Izzy heard her parting shot. 'Now do please naff off.'

She had always wanted to use that line.

Izzy closed the door behind Diana, bolting it for good measure. She and Jake seemed to have made little progress since Diana's last visit, although the wallpaper in the living room had now been removed. Presumably, Izzy hadn't been able to tolerate that ghastly paisley print a single day longer.

Diana chanced a glance in the direction of the garden, her eyes alighting on the freshly-dug earth where the conservatory had once stood. *What a terrible mess.*

And Izzy looked wretched. Diana noted the dark circles beneath her eyes and the fingernails bitten down to the quick. She couldn't help but draw comparisons with Amy, Izzy's darling sister, who – Diana had little doubt – would have taken this upset in her stride. Of course, she would never say as much.

'Shall we have some tea, dear?'

'God, yes.' Izzy raked her fingers through unwashed hair. 'Excuse my manners. Coming right up.'

Diana followed her into the kitchen. Perhaps it was safer that they spoke in here, as far away as possible from the garden. 'I imagine you've been having a frightful time of things.'

Izzy set out two mugs on the counter. Not like Amy, who had always brought out a china tea set for Diana's visits. 'I assume you've been following the news?'

Diana had, although only to confirm what everyone in the village already knew. Most of them seemed to have more detail than the BBC, although who could say how reliable any of it was? Diana wanted to hear directly from the source herself.

'It was a girl. A young woman,' Izzy corrected herself. 'A Jane Doe, so far. They're looking for a match on the missing person's database.'

Diana cautiously regarded the young woman in front of her, wondering how much to tell her.

She thought back to the first time she had laid eyes on

Izzy Morton, then still Isabelle – a gangly but confident eleven-year-old on her first day at secondary school.

Diana had watched her grow, nurturing the girl's love of words and storytelling, and had been one of the first to notice something was horribly wrong in the weeks after Izzy and Amy's father died. Of course, she hadn't understood just how pear-shaped things had turned out – how could she? But she had done her best to protect the girls and shield them from further harm.

Teaching girls was like that, she mused. Imparting knowledge wasn't the half of it. It was about training them to think for themselves and to see the world with courage in their hearts and goodness in their souls. Rallying them to succeed in a world in which the odds were often stacked against them, while protecting them from the evil which resided within it.

Her mind, as it often did, flitted back over the years. Forty years of girls' faces crowded her memory, jostling for her attention. Try as she might, she struggled to remember the names, these days. But the personalities – those stayed with her. Like colours, music. Abstract and yet tangible, each with its own melody and rhythm. They came to her in her dreams as well as in the long days during which her memory was her sole companion.

The news last week had been a dreadful shock. And, as the days wore on, Diana found herself thinking: could the unfortunate dear be someone she had known, once upon a time?

She had spent the past five days raking over the faces in her mind, panning fragments of memories, waiting for a crumb of gold to catch the sunlight. And, eventually, one face had come to her.

'My dear,' she said, her voice faltering. 'I have a dreadful idea of who it might be.'

Izzy ushered Diana to the small kitchen table, urging her to sit. Her old teacher seemed to be burdened by this knowledge, and the last thing Izzy needed right now was for Diana to have some sort of *episode*. The woman was almost ninety, after all.

'There was a girl...' Diana trailed off, as if contemplating where this story truly began. 'She joined us for sixth form, just a few years before I retired. You were off at university by then.' Her eyes came to rest at a spot on the floor, and Izzy noticed those normally sparkling sapphires were misted with a sheen of sadness.

'A bright girl. Brave. Wonderful sense of humour. There was one time—' Diana stopped, dismissing this vignette with the wave of a hand, and started again. 'She was in foster care. A rather challenging home life, as I recall. Not that she let it get her down. Quite a determined young thing. And a high achiever, academically. Well on her way to university.'

Izzy nodded, saying nothing. Her heart fluttered as she did her best not to connect the girl in Diana's story with the grim discovery in their garden.

'She was living with a foster family in Seahouses. She was here for a year or so, settled in well at school, and so forth. Good grades. But then something started troubling her. It happens, sometimes. She became withdrawn.'

Yes, that sounded about right. Izzy remembered how hard it had been to focus in the classroom while her entire life was crumbling around her.

Diana sighed. 'And then she simply vanished. Never to be seen again.'

Izzy pinched her nose between a thumb and forefinger. 'If she disappeared, surely her family would have reported her missing? Or even the school?'

'Of course they did. I met with the parents shortly afterwards. The foster parents. Social services seemed powerless to do much about it, apparently. Young people in these situations frequently run away. And she was almost eighteen. The Barretts – they were the foster parents – were deranged with worry. But I received a call from Maeve Barrett a short time later. The girl had been in touch. It seemed she had run away after all.'

'So, she ran away. What makes you think it could be her?'

Diana glanced up, their eyes meeting. 'My instinct? My gut? We simply accepted the story without questioning it all those years ago. But now...' She smiled, smoothing down her skirt. 'It's foolish, I know. Probably just the wild ramblings of an old lady, over-thinking things.'

Izzy knew that Diana considered herself to be many things, and foolish wasn't one of them. 'Why don't you call the police, if you're worried something might have happened to her?'

'I expect they're inundated with information right now. And I'd like to get my facts straight before we go to the authorities.' The colour had returned to Diana's cheeks. 'The Barretts still live locally. I was thinking you and I could pay them a visit.'

Izzy heaved a sigh. This seemed to be quite a leap of the imagination, even by Diana's standards. 'You know, it really isn't up to us...'

She met Diana's eye again and saw that the old lady was

quite determined. Diana was paying the Barretts a visit, with or without her. Besides, it probably wasn't this girl. Diana had said as much herself.

'Fine,' Izzy said. 'Let's go and see them.'

She wondered what she was getting herself in to. Was Diana overthinking things, drawing a connection between two things that weren't related? Or was she on to something?

3

Izzy rolled over, nuzzling into Jake, the solidness of his body making her whole. She watched the rise and fall of his chest, admiring those thick eyelashes, two black butterflies on his cheeks. In the thin morning light, her diamond ring glinted.

It was still early, too early to rise. She would wake him soon. But not yet.

What did he dream about, she wondered? Was this enough, or did he want more? Was she enough?

He adored Amy's kids and had assured Izzy that the co-parenting arrangement she had with their father, Mike, satisfied any yearning for fatherhood he might once have harboured. But would he come to regret that decision one day? He had no link to them, after all. They weren't his blood relatives. He didn't experience the same pang of recognition Izzy felt whenever she saw her sister in the glitter of Hannah's eye, the upturn of Lucas's smile, or Betsy's sassy sulk. He could turn and walk away from all of this at any time.

Not like Izzy.

'Are you just going to lie there and watch me, or can a man get a coffee around here?'

She grinned. 'I thought you were sleeping.'

'I was, until I sensed you boring into my soul with the death stare.' He opened one eye, ogling her.

Izzy giggled. 'Let's have five more minutes.'

She rolled over, and he followed, curving his body around hers. Outside, a pair of blackbirds serenaded one another.

Izzy had imagined mornings just like this when they had first viewed the house. It was hard to believe their forever home had become the subject of her darkest nightmares.

She had told him over dinner last night that Diana had a wild theory about who the girl might be. She dressed up the story with humour, recounting how Diana told the reporters on the doorstep where to go, Princess Anne-style. Jake had laughed, and Izzy made it sound like accompanying the old dear on a visit to the Barretts was a mercy mission. Doing everyone a favour by keeping Diana Wheeler and her wild imagination in check. She guiltily remembered making a joke about Diana's failing memory.

Izzy didn't want to tell Jake that she'd lain awake for a couple of hours after he fell asleep, wondering about the girl buried under their conservatory.

How much of her remained here in this place? Her flesh? Her bones? Her soul? Izzy wondered if she would ever be able to sleep soundly in this house again.

They went down to the kitchen together, Izzy – as she always did – pointedly ignoring the bare floorboards in the hall. The flooring would be finished as one of the final stages of the renovation, and that still felt impossibly far away.

'So, you're going to see them today?'

'Who?' She feigned confusion, as if there wasn't only one thing on her agenda for the day. As if she hadn't lain awake half the night thinking about it.

'The Bennetts. The foster parents you were telling me about.'

'Right, yes. Barretts. And yes, I told Diana I'm free this morning. I can't imagine she has anything better to do. They don't live too far from here, apparently, so we can walk over.'

She had, in fact, looked up their address on Google Maps yesterday afternoon. The Barretts lived on Clyde Street, the row of houses whose gardens backed onto theirs. If the body under their conservatory did turn out to be the girl they fostered, she had been close to home.

Jake planted a goodbye kiss on her forehead, and the silence of all that went unsaid hung between them.

Izzy had inherited Diana from Amy. That was the easiest way to think of it. *Her inheritance.*

Amy, it had transpired, had cultivated a friendship of sorts with their secondary school English teacher. Diana had reached out to Izzy in the wake of her sister's death, and somehow, at some point, they had fallen into the routine of having tea together once a week. Izzy was fond of the older lady, and maintaining her friendship with Diana felt like another link to Amy. But Diana was getting on, and her mind certainly wasn't as sharp as it had once been.

Izzy needed to keep herself busy, to stop her mind from roaming over the fragments of a story which could be just that – fragments. Figments of her elderly friend's imagination.

She dove into the Fletcher proposal, sketching out a concept for the luxury retreat they hope to create. She was steadily building a reputation as the go-to interior designer around here, and this would be an impressive accomplishment to add to her growing portfolio.

It was a remodel, completely gutting the existing interior of an old farmhouse at Amble and replacing it with a modern and luxurious open-plan concept. She would finalise the design, then detail a brutal and ambitious project schedule that would transform the space over several weeks.

For some reason, it was easier to do this for other people. When it came to her own renovation, Izzy struggled to see where to begin. Struggled to breathe, sometimes.

She sat back in her chair, stretching her neck and taking a deep lungful of air, envisioning the calm she needed. Just as her mother had taught her.

A knock at the door interrupted her meditation.

Diana had clearly dressed up for the occasion, her pistachio-coloured suit and matching hat making Izzy second-guess her own blue linen summer dress.

'Should I get changed...?' Izzy wondered out loud.

'Nonsense, my dear. It's only a social call.' Diana looped an arm through hers and they set off for the short walk to the Barretts' address.

It was already warm, even at this hour. The beach would be packed with day trippers, hoards bussed in, only to be bussed out again by nightfall. The reporters had finally abandoned their vigil on her doorstep and for the first time in almost a week, Izzy felt a weight had been lifted from her shoulders.

'Now, dear,' said Diana as she rang the bell at number forty-two. 'I suggest you let me take the lead.'

Maeve Barrett answered the door in an apron. It seemed

to take a moment for her to recognise her caller, a second until it registered. Her eyebrows raised in surprise.

'Diana, how are you?' There was the slightest hint of an Irish accent, diluted by years spent living over the water.

'Indeed, it's been far too long. I wanted to introduce you to my friend Izzy. She just moved back to the village.'

Maeve smiled at Izzy. 'Of course. You're Anne and Edward's daughter.'

'Izzy is getting to know her neighbours, and I thought it might be nice for the pair of you to get acquainted.'

Maeve reddened and ushered them in. 'I'm ever so sorry, but we weren't expecting visitors.' A vacuum cleaner lay abandoned, mid-task, in the middle of the hallway. 'Come this way, please.'

They stepped around it and followed Maeve into the living room.

'Make yourselves comfortable; I'll fetch us a pot of tea.'

Izzy helped Diana ease herself down to a brown crushed velvet settee and gave the room a cursory glance. She imagined what she would do with the place if it was up to her. Tear up the wall-to-wall carpet for starters. The original floorboards were probably under there, somewhere. And rip out that electric fireplace. Obviously, the three-piece-suite would have to go.

Her eyes came to rest on a crucifix hanging on the wall closest to the door. That would *definitely* be out.

On the sideboard and mantelpiece, photos fought for prime position. Izzy recognised the younger iterations of Maeve. She had been pretty, once upon a time. Dark curly hair and freckles. It was hard to guess her age now. Mid-sixties, perhaps? Auntie Sue would know.

In many of the photos, Maeve was pictured beside a tall

man, sandy windswept blond hair and light eyes creased in a perpetual smile. The husband, Izzy presumed.

The rest of the photos were devoted to the kids. Scores of them – she would have struggled to count. Gapped-teeth smiles, too-short shorts, badly cut fringes. Izzy wondered which of them might be the girl Diana remembered.

Maeve reappeared, burdened by a tea tray. Izzy helped her to set it down on the low table in the centre of the room. The apron was gone, and she had taken out the red plastic hair clip she had been wearing when she'd answered the door.

'How is your family?' Maeve kept her eyes down, immersed in the task of arranging the teacups. 'I haven't seen Sue in ages. Not since before...' She hesitated, starting over; the cheerfulness gone now. 'I'm so sorry about what happened to Amy. A terrible business. Truly awful.'

Izzy winced. It was two years since Amy had died, but she already knew that the spectre of condolence would follow her around for the rest of her life. A dark cloud trailing her, no matter how sunny life was. As long as she stayed in Seahouses, she would always be *that poor dead woman's sister.*

'They're great. The kids are happy at school. My mother is well.'

My mother is well. Whatever that meant.

Maeve hesitated. A beat. 'I volunteer at the hospital. Have done for years. Amy would often give me a lift in, save me waiting for the bus. And she always made time to chat.'

She glanced up, her eyes shining wet, and something in Izzy's stomach knotted. When Maeve spoke again, her voice was quiet. 'She was ever so proud of you, you know. Forever telling me about her big sister in Hong Kong.'

A tear pricked at Izzy's eye, a familiar stinging heat, and she willed it to pass.

'And I understand it was your garden where they found the... Well, you know.'

Izzy nodded but said nothing.

Diana seemed to sense her disquiet and changed tack. 'Lovely photos.' She nodded at the display. 'I was telling Izzy that you and Eric have fostered a lot of children.'

'Good heavens, yes. We've been blessed to welcome so many into our home over the years.'

'Izzy and her fiancé are considering fostering.' Diana added two sugars to her tea, stirring slowly, avoiding Izzy's glare. 'Now that they have that big house. I thought you would be well-placed to offer her advice.'

Izzy's heart lurched at the audacity of the lie, and it took all her effort to keep her features neutral. She swallowed against the knot in her throat.

Maeve beamed. 'I'm so thrilled to hear that.' She placed a hand on Izzy's, squeezing her fingers. 'It can be jolly hard work, but it's the most rewarding job you'll ever do.'

Diana took a sip of tea. 'Say, Maeve; I had one of your girls in my English class. Do you remember? A brilliant pupil. Wrote an essay that I still remember to this day. It's odd, the things that stay with you.' She made the pretence of recalling the details. 'If memory serves, she ran away.'

Maeve sighed. 'Unfortunately, a lot of foster kids *run away*.' She mimed inverted commas with her fingers. 'There's a certain level of drama when it comes to troubled teens. But they always come back.'

Diana shook her head. 'This one didn't.'

Maeve pursed her lips, nodding slowly. 'There was one girl who took off around the time she turned eighteen. Just upped and left, then sent us a postcard from London two weeks later.'

'Yes.' Diana was nodding. 'That's the one. What was her name?'

Maeve inclined her head, her eyes fixed on something in the garden. A tiny gold cross hung around her neck, glinting in the light.

'Kelly. She might have been good at her books, but she could be quite a handful, that one, if I remember rightly. A true rebel spirit.' Maeve chuckled to herself. 'But there's nothing anyone can do once they reach that age. Social services don't want to know. I think we still have her things up in the loft, just in case she ever comes back for them.'

'What happened to her?' The words came out before Izzy had a chance to think them through.

Maeve sighed, a sad, sorry heave of her chest. 'Messed up home life. You never know what they've been through, the things they've seen before they're brought to you. It can be difficult to get them settled. We did our best by all of them, but Kelly was quite headstrong. There were rows about staying out too late, that sort of thing. There was even a boyfriend, not that Eric and I approved of anything like that.' Maeve glanced at the crucifix on the wall, as if Jesus might be listening. She lowered her voice. 'Apparently, they'd had a falling out. Then one day she just packed her bags and left.'

Diana sipped at her tea. 'I seem to remember Kelly having lots of friends at St Helen's. Did she keep in touch with any of them?'

'Oh, certainly, she was popular enough.' From the way Maeve said 'popular', Izzy sensed she didn't think it was a positive attribute. 'A couple of girls from the village, one in particular. I forget the name. And a few more at school. I've no idea if she kept in touch with any of them.' Maeve brushed a crease from her skirt. 'It was a pity, but I was thankful to receive that postcard. I like to think she's settled down somewhere, and that she's happy. No doubt has a family of her own by now.'

'We can only hope.' Diana sighed. 'You mentioned you held on to some of her belongings?'

'Of course we did.' Maeve's eyes widened. 'I couldn't have her turning up for her stuff and tell her we'd chucked it out! Our loft is full of the children's belongings, most of it long-forgotten, I'm sure. But I don't like to take chances.'

Izzy thought how sad that would be: the weight of other people's forgotten possessions bearing down on you day after day. Waiting, with no cut-off point, for them to come and retrieve them, knowing they probably never would.

'You know, dear,' Diana said. 'Some days, I fear my mind isn't what is used to be.'

Maeve flashed her a sympathetic smile.

'What I would give to read that brilliant essay once more. Oil the old cogs, as it were.' Diana tapped her head. 'I suppose it may be among the items in your loft. Would it be a huge ask for you to let me read it?'

'Well...' Maeve raised an eyebrow, surprised by this request. When she spoke again, her words were tentative. 'You would have to give me a day or two, because Eric will need to get the stepladder—'

'Splendid.' Diana polished off the rest of her tea, setting the saucer down so forcefully that Izzy jumped. 'We'll pop back at the weekend.'

4

Then

I ALWAYS THOUGHT I WOULD LOVE LIVING BY THE SEA. WHEN they first told me where I was going – they're always *telling* you, never *asking* – I thought *yep, that'll do me.* How bad can it be, having the beach on your doorstep?

It's cold up here, though. Colder than Newcastle. And I miss Dawn. I even miss Jackson, her stupid boyfriend. He was all right, I suppose.

The problem is that there's just nothing to do. Nothing but hanging out. So that's how we fill the days. At the beach when the weather's nice, and at the arcade when it's not. Fruit machines, penny-nudge. *Hanging out.* Filling the hours, the days. Killing time. We spend a lot of time at the arcade.

Well, we normally do. But not for me this week. I'm grounded again.

I missed my curfew on Saturday. I'm not sure why it makes any difference that I'm home by nine o'clock, especially when everyone else stays out until way later than that.

For god's sake, I'm seventeen. Sam's parents ask her to be home by ten, but there are no consequences if she isn't.

There are rules at the Barretts', though. Maeve loves her rules. She says it's about establishing boundaries and having respect and self-discipline. Apparently, that's how you show you care about someone. It's kind of sweet, I suppose.

But I had a good reason for being late, this time: me and Bryan kissed. *Bryan and I,* I should say. I like his name. I like that there's an 'I' sound in Bryan, even if it's spelled with a 'y'. His mouth tastes of strawberries, like bubblegum, and his lips are soft. I wonder what my mouth tastes like.

We were in the arcade, the usual crowd, and I knew I was on borrowed time. If someone sees a big group of us – and someone nearly always sees – they might tell one of the parents. That's the problem around here. Everyone knows everyone. It's why we can't go to the pub, like my friends back home do. It's why we just *hang out* instead. Most of the parents don't mind if someone tells on us, but the Barretts don't like to get those kinds of phone calls, or have people come up to them at church or when they're out shopping.

It's not like we're doing anything wrong. But people don't like to see groups of teenagers. Our presence alone is offensive – they assume we're up to no good. But we're just *being*. Suspended in that grey area that exists once you're no longer a child but not yet an adult. We can't help who we are.

I knew I was on borrowed time, but I also knew Bryan was going to kiss me. I could just feel it: the electricity in the air, you know? Like watching a lightning storm over the sea. So, I stuck around for longer than I should have, even though it would make me late. Even though I knew I'd be grounded.

Elaine had brought a camera with her – one of those

new disposable ones. We all squeezed together for a group shot and Bryan pulled me to him with both arms, one hand around my shoulder and the other on my hip. So close that I could feel the warmth of his breath on my neck. He didn't move away after the flash had gone. Instead, he turned me towards him, angling me so that we were face-to-face, our lips only a kiss apart.

He's tall. I love how I only come up to his shoulder, how he has to dip his face towards mine, how I have to stretch up to reach him. How his broad shoulders and his height make me feel smaller, precious. Protected.

I replay it over and over in my mind, my fingers tingling and my stomach twisting at the memory of him. I'm going to ask Elaine for the photo when she gets the film developed.

The books I read are full of first kisses, stolen moments. Two lost souls finding one another in the universe. No one knows I read that kind of book. On library day, I bury them under my textbooks, just in case Sam sees them on the bus home.

It's not like he's the first boy I've kissed. And I'm not just talking about kissing for dares or spin-the-bottle. I mean, obviously, I've had boyfriends before. But Bryan is... Bryan. He's different. I think he genuinely likes me, like, respects me and all that. Not that it was particularly romantic; not with the others standing around watching us.

So that's why I was late. And now I'm grounded for a week. I'm to come straight home from school and stay in my room, only allowed downstairs for tea, which we eat together *as a family* at the table at 7 p.m. sharp. The Barretts love their schedule.

But when I think about Bryan and that kiss, I know it's worth it. Sam agrees.

He's so dreamy. That's how they would describe him if

this was a book or a film. Sam calls him a *total dream-fest.* We're not proper girlfriend and boyfriend. Not officially, not yet. And I can hardly call it a date, seeing as everyone else was there. But they do that, these new kids who've accepted me into their circle. We hang out in a group and people pair off. Then they become boyfriend and girlfriend. Then it's just the two of them.

Eric says Maeve's got a right to be worried about me being out late. We all know about stranger danger. 'It's not safe', he says, 'for young women, out there.' I had to resist rolling my eyes at that one.

There was that girl on the news. They found her body months after she went missing. Eric changed the channel, but we all saw. Maeve had tears in her eyes. The poor lass was only thirteen. But that was down near London, somewhere. Nothing like that happens around here.

Weirdly, I sort of don't mind being grounded. *Sort of.* It shows someone cares about me, at least. It's like a scratchy blanket – it irritates you, but you know you need it. And you know you'll miss it when it's gone, when it's just you out there in the world.

There was a bizarre delight in saying the words to Sam: *I'm grounded.* What I'm really saying: *someone gives a shit about me.* It feels like a long time since I've had that.

Not true: Dawn gives a shit. She just has a funny way of showing it.

She might come up here in a couple of weeks' time, just for the day. Jackson will be working on a site somewhere further along the coast, and Dawn says she'll see if she can cadge a lift in the van, take me out for an ice cream and a proper catch-up. Somehow, though, I already suspect this won't happen.

At least I know the Barretts mean well, with their rules.

Even if Sam makes fun of them. No swearing, no profanities, no taking the lord's name in vain. No friends over without asking permission at least a day before, no snacks if you don't finish tea. We each have chores, and everyone has to keep their room tidy.

They don't know how much it means to me to have a room. A space, all to myself, even if it is the smallest bedroom in the house.

Maeve actually apologised for that, back when I first got here. As if it was a step down from my usual deluxe penthouse at The Ritz.

And of course, I'm allowed out for school. Obviously.

It's kind of nice to be back, but I won't admit that, either. Year thirteen. Time to make it all count.

The summer holidays seemed to stretch on and on forever. At least I managed to get a job at Johnson's. I don't even know why they call it that – the owner is Mr Beresford. Maybe Beresford's is too much of a mouthful for a butcher's shop. I'm not sure I'll ever get over the smell of raw meat, or finding random smudges of animal blood on my clothes at the end of a shift, or having to put up with his son Kyle, but the money was all right.

The best part was serving the customers. Often you see the same faces and get to know their orders. Not just locals but people on holiday, who disappear once their week in a cottage or caravan is up.

I played a little game where I'd make up nicknames for them. Like the Colonel, who had white hair and a goatee and looked like he'd walked straight off the KFC logo. And Sunflower Lady, whose dyed straw-blonde hair was all wrong for her mahogany face, or Mad Hatter, a man with wild eyes and a seemingly massive collection of fedoras. It helped to pass the time.

Beresford's was only seasonal work though – this village, up here by the sea, swells with tourists in summer. It's just us, now that the holidays are over, and I can already feel the claustrophobia creeping in.

Anyway, it'll all be over soon. We've got our mocks, and then the real deal. A Levels. And after that, I can go home; back to my actual home. I wonder what will happen with Bryan, then? In that other life, After Exams?

I don't talk about that with Sam anymore – I can see how much it hurts her feelings. I don't talk about it with anyone. But it's the thing that rests on the tip of my tongue all day. The first thing I think of when I wake up, and the last thing that goes through my mind before I fall asleep at night.

The future.

Everyone's making out that our entire lives hang on a set of grades.

How can I tell them what I already know? That it doesn't matter how hard you try in school, how good your coursework is or how well you manage to remember the details of *Macbeth* or the French Revolution or geometric constructions by the time that exam paper is in front of you? That life in the real world is hard and being good at school can't prepare you for that, for any of it? Mam was clever. It didn't help her.

Besides, I know I'll do well. I keep that quiet, too. No one likes a swot.

Sam is so stressed out about failing. Can't she see that she already has everything she needs? That whatever grades she gets, she'll always have a mam and dad who step in and save the day? It's not like she's on her own. Not like me.

I've been here before, you know. Seahouses. I can't remember when. Mam brought me, so I know it must have been *before* before.

I didn't realise, not at first. But we were walking along the beach after mass, one Sunday back in those first weeks after I arrived, when Maeve and Eric were still trying to get me to come to church and I was too polite or too shy or too scared they'd kick me out if I said no.

It was the shape of the sky. That's the best way I can describe it. The shape of infinity. Knowing that I was just a grain of sand in a universe that stretches on beyond comprehension. I'd experienced nothing like it before.

Then I remembered that I had.

The memories are torn, tattered and frayed from all that's happened since. But I remember my hands were sticky with melting ice cream. I remember Mam helping me build a sandcastle; the wind blowing her hair into her eyes. And I remember looking up at that sky and understanding, then, that it never ends. None of it ever ends.

5

Now

THE LITTLE GATE WAS SQUEAKING AGAIN; DIANA WOULD NEED to oil the hinges. Maintenance. Keeping everything in motion. That's all it was at this point. Preservation, in one form or another. Keep the parts moving, even as the whole crumbles around them.

Not that her cottage was falling down. Far from it. This place had stood solid for more than a hundred years and would be here for at least a hundred more. Diana's days, on the other hand, were more closely numbered.

She eased herself into Lionel's chair, catching her breath after the walk from the car. Once upon a time, she used to drive all the way to Edinburgh and Newcastle. These days, she barely trusted herself to get to Alnwick and back.

Her father had thought driving to be *unladylike*. A skill that only farm girls learned. It was Lionel who had taught her, in the end.

She closed her eyes and began her daily recitation: her age, her date of birth, her parents' and her daughters' names. Her grandchildren's names. The dates at which she had worked at St Helen's. Then on to the trickier stuff: the second-most-recent American president, the nine countries whose name starts with a P, and the number of the mobile phone her daughter Jennifer had insisted she learn by heart.

All in order.

Perhaps she was worrying about nothing. Didn't everyone walk into a room, from time to time, only to forget what they had gone in to retrieve? Couldn't one be reasonably expected to have a loosening grip on first names after forty years of teaching in an all-girls school? She was particularly bad with women's first names, which probably proved her point.

And yet... she knew it was something.

She thought back to Granny Agnew, who hadn't known who any of them were by the end. The woman could sit at the piano and lose herself in Chopin or Brahms or Bach, but hadn't recognised her own daughter and granddaughter when they came to visit.

Anything but that. Diana prayed that her body would give out before her mind.

That morning, she'd opened the window to air the place out. She remembered that. That was a good sign.

The thick stone walls that helped to keep the cottage warm in winter prevented the place from overheating on warm days, but still, the fresh air was a welcome respite. It tickled her cheek, and Diana closed her eyes. From the back garden came the sound of bird song, and farther away, the echo of the retreating tide.

The Barretts had several girls at St Helen's over the years. Diana pictured the pair at parents' evening, many moons ago, dressed up in their Sunday best. Maeve sporting pearls and clutching a tiny leather handbag, Eric in a brown tweed suit and tie, his moustache combed and waxed.

Teachers made parents nervous, Diana knew that. Even if they weren't the actual parents.

But what was it about Maeve that she found so off-putting? Her godliness? Her goodness? The woman was just so damned *worthy*.

Or was it that Diana felt judged?

She hadn't lived a sinful life. Far from it. But there was something about people who made those kinds of sacrifices, who quietly sidelined their own happiness without complaining, that made everyone else feel... inadequate? Insufficient? Diana struggled to put her finger on it.

She could be imagining it, but the past occasionally came to her more clearly these days. Although Diana occasionally forgot to buy bananas, or what day it was, or the names of that delightful young couple who had bought the cottage next door, she could remember Kelly Reynolds.

A wonderful woman. For Kelly had been a woman. She may have been only seventeen, the last time Diana saw her, but her soul had been wise, old beyond her years. Kelly was what many would term *mature for her age*. Empathetic, with a keen wit, Diana remembered. What Maeve remembered as a rebel spirit, Diana would have called 'a free mind'.

She had tasked her English Literature class with an essay on *Tess of the d'Urbervilles. What is the significance of the presentation of omens in the story, and how do they serve to predict Tess's fate?* While many of the girls had correctly identified the author's symbols of foreshadowing, Kelly had been critical, labelling Hardy's approach as *overkill* and *heavy-handed.* Diana had enjoyed reading that riposte.

She knew Kelly had torn through their reading lists. Diana had even spotted her in Alnwick library, alone after school, taking out a stack of books. She'd kept her distance, respecting Kelly's privacy. No teenager wants to bump into their teacher outside the classroom.

And yet, Diana was burdened by regret. Should she have attempted to befriend Kelly, in some way? Might the girl have come to her if she was experiencing problems? Could Diana have done more?

Kelly had friends at St Helen's. She wasn't the most popular girl in the sixth form, certainly not a ringleader. Diana secretly despised those girls who held court, who enjoyed having others trail in their wake, doing their bidding. No, Kelly had been more circumspect. Nevertheless, the girl had had friends. Of that, Diana was certain. Good friends; one in particular. What happened to them? How had this young woman vanished, and nobody had wondered where she'd gone?

Diana dragged a chair from the dining table towards the bookcase, its feet leaving two brush streaks across the rug. The lovely couple next door had offered to help with anything around the house. 'Anything you need, anything at all, just knock!' that young man had told her, too earnest to disguise his enthusiasm for being helpful. Diana wouldn't bother them with this. Today it would be asking for help to reach the higher shelves; tomorrow it would be assistance with bathing and cooking. It was a slippery slope, Diana knew, and one on which she would not embark.

She steadied herself against the wall and noticed her hand was lightly trembling. A fall at this age would not be good news.

Stretched to her full height, and with her hand still firmly on the wall for balance, Diana reached up to the second-highest shelf and retrieved the item she was looking for.

St Helen's had presented her with four ring-bound photo albums as a retirement gift. Diana would have preferred vouchers, but she had kept this to herself, of course, and graciously accepted their offering. Only now, all these years later, she felt genuine gratitude. Curating forty years' worth of photographs must have taken quite an effort, after all.

The decade was printed on the front cover in embossed gold. No expense spared for the school's longest-serving teacher. Diana brushed a film of dust off the upper page edges and flicked past the first couple of years.

It was remarkable, she thought, how rapidly the fashions evolved, changing as quickly as the seasons. The early 2000s was an era marked by over-plucked eyebrows, poker-straight hair, and that awful lotion the girls used to affect the look of a suntan.

And then there she was. Diana's vision misted the instant she spotted Kelly, buried at the back of a group shot. Diana had worried that she might miss her, that her eyes might glide over the girl's photo, and she would not know her.

She needn't have worried. Diana brushed away a tear.

It was a school trip. But where? She didn't recognise the background, the gloomy interior of a castle. There were several places in Northumberland that looked like this. The gaggle of girls were squeezing themselves around a handsome young man – any excuse to be in proximity to the teacher the staff had jokingly labelled the *school heartthrob*. Which wasn't a difficult status to attain when you were practically the only male among some six-hundred women.

What was his name? It would be in this album, or her old class diaries, somewhere. *Or up here,* Diana thought, pressing a finger to her temple. And what class? History?

The students were bundled up in coats and scarves. Autumn term, if Diana had to guess.

She squinted at the faces, trying to recall the names.

Carly. Anna. Elisabeth. Ghosts of the women they had grown to become. All except for one, perhaps. Diana prayed her hunch was wrong.

She focused on the girl next to Kelly, arms looped casually over one another's shoulders despite the bulk of their winter coats. Samantha. Or Sam, as everyone called her. It was coming back to her so clearly now.

Bernadette Fearon, the headteacher, had assigned Sam to look after Kelly on her first day. Standard procedure for girls joining mid-term. They'd quickly become inseparable.

Samantha Mearns, that was her name. Although it had probably changed, now.

Diana's brow furrowed as she gazed out the window, the cogs of her mind clunking into gear. Sam's family lived in Seahouses, and she was fairly certain she had seen Sam in the village not too long ago. It wouldn't take much to find an address. A couple of questions to the right people.

She dabbed a cotton handkerchief to her eyes as she waited for Izzy to pick up.

'My dear girl.' She heard the crack in her voice and bit the inside of her cheek, hard, forcing herself to pull together. 'I've remembered something – Kelly had a friend. A best friend. Still lives locally, and I'd like to pay her a visit. Are you free tomorrow?'

She heard the whisper of a sigh at the other end of the line and knew what Izzy was thinking. *Dotty old Diana.* Still, she crossed her fingers. She couldn't face seeing Samantha on her own.

'Of course,' Izzy replied.

'Splendid. I'll pick you up at one.'

Diana placed the phone back in the cradle, her mind racing, the questions already burning.

What had become of Samantha Mearns? And what had gone through her mind when Kelly suddenly vanished? Had she ever questioned what happened to her old friend?

And again, Diana tormented herself by asking: *could I have done more?*

'Who was that?' The corner of Jake's lip was stained orange, a smear of ragu. Izzy wiped at it with her thumb.

'Looks delicious,' she mumbled, her gaze fixed on his mouth.

'Are you avoiding my question?' he laughed, his tone mock serious.

'Just Diana. She's remembered more about the girl she told me about. Kelly. Apparently, there was a best friend. Or I should say *there is a best friend.* Some woman who lives in Seahouses. She wants to call on her, see what she can remember.'

Jake frowned, lost in thought, as he stirred the bubbling sauce. Enough for five – the kids were coming for dinner tomorrow.

Izzy loved this about him. New recipes, everything made from scratch and prepared the day before so that he wouldn't be tied up in the kitchen when they were here. Help with homework, a shortlist of films that ticked all their boxes. The care and attention he put into every interaction they had with the children. If it was left up to her, they'd be eating frozen pizza or beans on toast from their laps in front of the TV, arguing over what to watch.

Diana was upset. Izzy had heard it in her voice and found it impossible to say no to her folly, despite the enormity of tasks on her to-do list. Perhaps there was still time to get out of it, to convince Diana that there would be a full police investigation, and it was up to the authorities to get in touch with Kelly's friends and family. Besides, it might not even be her.

'We should tell the police,' Jake said, as if reading her thoughts. Or not reading them. Reading the opposite. Telling her what she *should* be thinking. 'If this girl was reported missing, she'll be on the database, but a name could give them a leg-up. Sounds to me like the poor thing might have fallen through the cracks.'

Fallen through the cracks. Izzy pictured a concrete patio, fragmented by a sledgehammer. Dust clouding the air.

He stopped stirring and paused, his head cocked at an angle. Thinking this through. 'It's seriously weird that there wasn't a bigger investigation at the time.'

'The foster parents got a postcard. I told you that.'

He nodded. 'True. Yes, true.'

'From London.'

This detail seemed important. No one had fallen through the cracks. There were no cracks. Not in a place like Seahouses. A child couldn't go missing from here without an alarm being raised.

But Izzy thought back to the weeks after Mum left, when she and Amy were alone at home, two boats cast out at sea. Adrift on a perilous tide. Where had everyone been back then?

Izzy should have known better than anyone that the cracks – even a hairline fracture, a cut no bigger than a wisp – can swallow a girl.

'Well, I'm going to let DI Bell know, just in case.' Jake was already tapping out an email on his phone. 'What did you say the surname was?'

'Reynolds. Kelly Reynolds.'

Izzy turned the name over in her mouth, in her mind, wishing she had never heard it.

Night was falling now, the sky becoming velvety dark. Along the street, lights appeared in their neighbours' homes. She stared out into the gloom, wishing she could turn the clock back by a week to that day before their forever home became a crime scene. Or perhaps by two weeks; she would insist that they left the patio foundation as it was. Build around it, or something. How she wished she could tell her former self to do just that. *Leave well alone. Don't go digging.*

Or to three months ago, before they bought this house. She would tell Jake that yes, it has four bedrooms and fair enough, there weren't many properties in the area that had three reception rooms. So what if it had a large garden and was only five minutes from the sea? There were other houses. Other homes. It didn't have to be this one.

Or perhaps it was a sign? The universe telling her that this home of theirs, her future in Seahouses, was never meant to be?

The police might want to tear the place down. Izzy was sure they did that sometimes. Where the most heinous crimes had been committed, they ripped entire streets up.

A light flickered on in the house across the street. Jake had insisted they introduced themselves to all the neighbours the day they had moved in. Izzy would have preferred to crawl under a rock and stay there. But she loved that about him, too; always seeing the best in people. She didn't want to taint his view of the world by telling him what they were really like.

She wondered again how come no one had been suspicious when a hole – *a grave* – appeared in the back garden.

How long ago had it happened? Were the same people living around them now?

How did an entire village fail to notice when a teenage girl vanished?

She thought again about those cracks. Perhaps they were larger than she'd realised.

6

Diana hadn't slept well – Izzy could see it in the shadows under her eyes, the colour of storm clouds gathering at sea. They drove along in silence, each woman lost in her thoughts.

It was another bright day, the weather forecasters' promise holding true. The blue sky was interrupted by only a smattering of clouds, the breeze chasing them along at a hurried pace. Great weather for a run. She would get this over and done with – *get Diana over and done with* – and jog along her regular route to Bamburgh Castle and back. Clear her head and replenish her energy levels before collecting Betsy from school.

She pulled up at the address Diana had given her and killed the engine. An unfamiliar road. Izzy rarely came to this side of the village. She rarely had reason to.

The Green was an estate built in the 1970s to accommodate the demand for more affordable housing. Even back then, locals were being priced out by city dwellers who snapped up properties for weekend homes and holiday lets. It was most unfortunate, Izzy's father used to say, when young people were forced to leave the place where they had grown up. Izzy had known better than to voice her dream of getting as far away from Seahouses as she could.

He had petitioned the council on the issue. Letters, phone calls, public meetings. Edward Morton was the local GP but hadn't considered that the county council's housing policy might fall outside his remit. As far as he was concerned, everything that happened in this village fell under his remit.

It was hard to think about her father without thinking about all that came *after.* And it was hard to drive around The Green without thinking of Rachel, Amy's best friend. Or at least, the woman who *used to be* her best friend.

So many bad memories. So much lost. For Izzy, some days it felt as if every corner of Seahouses held some sadness, some sorrow. Why had she ever agreed to stay here?

It struck her, in that moment, that Amy would have been so much better at all this. *Had been so much better at this.* Past tense. At dealing with Diana. At dealing with loss.

Dad and Amy were cut from the same cloth. And Izzy was... different. Not cut out for this.

'Well, dear.' Diana interrupted her reverie. 'We can't sit out here all day.'

It hadn't been difficult to find Samantha Mearns. Or Samantha Shaw, as she was now. Diana had only had to call one particularly well-informed friend to get the address.

There were laws, these days, about things like that. *Data privacy,* or some such nonsense. But double-checking an old acquaintance's contact details against the electoral register could hardly be considered a crime, Diana reasoned. It was simply a matter of efficiency.

The girl had done all right for herself, it seemed. At least Samantha could afford to live in the village – Diana knew of many others who couldn't. The house was modest, a modern semi-detached with a porch and neat garden.

Diana's recollection of Samantha was of a fairly average girl, academically speaking. Certainly nowhere near as bright as Kelly, although, sadly, few were. But sweet enough – kind and even-tempered. The family had been in Seahouses for generations, as far as Diana knew. She shifted her weight from foot to foot as they waited for an answer at the door.

It took Samantha a moment to recognise her former teacher. Diana registered the initial confusion flashing over her eyes; a sight that had become familiar to her over the years. Then Samantha's expression brightened, and she broke into a bewildered smile.

'Mrs Wheeler... How are you?' She caught herself, and opened the door wider. 'Please, please. Come on in.'

Diana exchanged a glance with Izzy and followed Samantha inside. 'It's wonderful to see you, my dear girl. I must say you look ever so well.'

It was true – Samantha's mousy hair was now blonde, and she had a healthy, natural-looking tan. The extra pounds she'd carried as a teenager – *puppy fat*, they'd have called it back then – were no longer there.

Samantha smiled appreciatively at Diana; clearly, this was a woman well-accustomed to receiving compliments. Her gaze shifted nervously to Izzy.

'And you're Amy's sister. We met once, a few years ago, when you were over for a visit.' Her smile was sad now.

Bittersweet. 'She was a good person, your Amy. I was so sorry about... to hear what happened to her.'

Izzy nodded glumly, and an awkward silence descended.

Diana couldn't bear to think about dear old Amy right now. Not on top of everything else.

Samantha led them into an open plan kitchen-dining room. The space was newly refurbished, sleek marble countertops and shining black floor tiles. A wooden sign indicated 'This way to the beach,' its arrow ironically pointing the wrong way. Framed photos were hung in a cluster on the wall: two cherubic children, a portrait of the extended family posing in front of a Christmas tree, Samantha with her arms around a tall, muscular man with a shock of pale, curly hair. The perfect life immortalized in print.

Apart from a set of children's bowls stacked on the drying rack, everything was immaculate. The kitchen overlooked a large back garden and from here, Diana could see a summer house and a swing set.

'Izzy just moved back to the village, a house on Victoria Street. It was her place where they found the body last week...' Diana paused to allow her words to sink in, closely monitoring Samantha's reaction.

The story had made front page news for seven consecutive days, giving anyone potentially connected to the victim plenty of time to stew.

If four decades in an all-girls school had taught Diana one thing, it was the tells. Everyone had one; very few were aware of it. Thanks to a career in which she spent a considerable amount of time and effort discerning falsehoods from honesty, Diana knew exactly what to look for. Samantha was easy to read.

Samantha exhaled, a long whoosh of air. 'God, of course,' she said to Izzy. 'Must be horrendous for you.'

Good. So far, so good. Diana tried a different approach. 'What was the name of that girl you were friends with at school?'

Samantha tilted her head to an angle, lines appearing between her eyebrows. 'I had a lot of friends at St Helen's, as I recall.' There it was: the worry. 'Why? They're all right, aren't they? I mean, none of them are...'

Diana kept her eyes fixed on Samantha's. 'Your *best* friend. Kelly, was it?'

'Kelly?' A shadow fell across Samantha's face. Just a flicker, a dark thought forming. 'Kelly left before the end of our final year. Remember? She went back to Newcastle.'

Diana said nothing.

'No... That can't be *her*.' Samantha's tone was insistent. 'She went home. Anyway, they haven't said who it was. What makes you think it might be Kelly?'

Diana sighed, a sad sigh. 'She only lived a street away. And she's the only person I can think of who disappeared from around here.'

'Just call it a working theory at this stage.' Izzy added.

Samantha nodded. 'OK,' she said, slowly. 'So, it's probably *not* her. Because Kelly didn't *disappear*. She ran away.'

Diana leaned forward; her hands clasped together on the table. 'My dear, I'm afraid my memory isn't what it used to be. I'm trying ever so hard, but I recall very little detail about Kelly. I was hoping you could help fill in the blanks.'

'God, I haven't thought about her in years. She was... I don't know. Nice. Just a normal girl. She only lived here for a year or so. We were kind of close for a while, and then she left.' Samantha shrugged. 'I'm not sure what else I can tell you.'

'She lived with a foster family, as I recall?'

'Yes. The Barretts. Eric and Maeve. They're still here. I

run into them from time to time. Nice couple, no kids of their own. Although I think Kelly found them a bit... I don't know. Goofy. Quaint. She found Seahouses quaint, to be honest. She used to say it was too small, too quiet, and she couldn't wait to go back to Newcastle.' Samantha's voice cracked. She turned her face away from them just as her eyes misted with tears. 'Her life... it wasn't easy, you know? Her mum – Kelly's real mum – died when she was little and there was an issue with the family. They lost custody, I guess. They went to court over it; I remember her telling me that.'

Diana considered this, her lips pursing in concentration. 'And was anything bothering her? At the time she ran away?'

Samantha touched her nose. *There it was. That* was the tell.

She hesitated before speaking again. 'Kelly and I weren't actually friendly at the end.' Samantha looked at them both, gauging their reaction. She waved a hand to dismiss it, long fingers stroking the air, as if *weren't actually friendly* wasn't a big deal.

'We'd had a stupid falling out over some boy a few months before. Just a typical teenage girl thing. I don't know. Too many hormones or whatever.' She took a sip of water, her hand trembling ever so slightly. 'We would have made up eventually, I'm sure. But we never got the chance because she left.'

'And this boy,' said Diana. 'What can you tell us about him?'

'Honestly,' Samantha sighed. 'It was nothing. We both fancied the same boy. One of us went out with him, then the other. It was stupid. Seriously, nothing. I can't even remember what happened. But I know it wasn't *that* which was upsetting her.'

Izzy's eyes widened. 'So she was upset about something?'

'I mean...' Samantha was getting flustered, her cheeks reddening.

There was, Diana was certain, some mistruth to this story.

'She went quiet, I guess, for a while? Like *really quiet*. Withdrawn, like she had a lot on her mind. That would have been around the time she ran away. But I just assumed she was homesick. Everyone did. She always talked about going to Newcastle, going back to her family. When she left, it made perfect sense. And the Barretts didn't seem too worried. I think they even heard from her afterwards.' Samantha paused, remembering this detail. 'Yes. They had a letter from her. Maeve told my mum.'

'And you?' Izzy asked. 'Did you ever hear from her?'

Samantha glance down to her hands, which were folded on the table. 'I didn't expect her to keep in touch.'

Diana sighed. 'Well, let's hope this unfortunate soul doesn't turn out to be her.'

'I'm sure it's not...' Samantha paused, seemingly searching for the words. 'Look... It wasn't my fault or anything. The fall out. We were teenagers. We had an argument, and we were sulking. Kids do it all the time.' She scoffed. 'Mine can't go five minutes without World War Three breaking out.' She waited for them to laugh; they didn't.

Samantha was anxious for them to leave – Diana could see it in her posture, the clench of her jaw. 'If you think of anything, anything at all which might help the police in their enquiries—'

'The police? Why would the police want to speak to me?' She seemed genuinely baffled.

'My dear, if it does turn out to be Kelly, the police will want to speak to her acquaintances, you and I included. It's standard procedure.'

'Jesus.' Samantha dabbed at an eye. Her mascara had smudged; she would no doubt fix herself up before her husband came home. This was a woman, Diana realised, who put a great effort into keeping up appearances.

'Anyway, it's only a theory at this stage,' said Izzy, clearly equally eager for this discussion to conclude. 'We'd better get going.'

Samantha didn't protest. She rose from her seat.

Diana remembered a time when she had towered over this girl. Now Samantha stood more than a head taller. Once upon a time, not so terribly long ago, these girls had cowered at her raised voice. A single word from her would have caused them to fall into line, backs straight, feet together like soldiers.

She imagined what Samantha thought of her now. Possibly surprised to see her still around. And quite possibly thinking she had pulled the wool over Diana's eyes. On that, she couldn't have been further from the truth.

Izzy tied her laces and stretched. She'd seen a YouTube video on the best warm-ups for running, the motions that set the joints and muscles in position, readied the body for exertion.

She had Amy to thank for getting her into it. Another thing she'd inherited following her sister's death. She'd even taken Amy's old running shoes, wearing them out in the end. Two holes appearing where her big toes wore through the fabric. They were in one of the boxes in the loft, along with all the other things of Amy's that she had no use for but couldn't bear to part with.

The tide was out, the beach an expanse of golden sand, the rocky protrusion of the Farne Islands perching on the horizon. The day was cloudless, the sky so clear that she could make out the birds, soaring and swooping specks against the blue sky.

She picked up her pace at the top of St Aidan's, the long strait that ran to the foot of Bamburgh Castle. Finding her cadence, listening to her breathing. Feeling her body come alive. Clearing her mind.

Diana wasn't letting this one go. Izzy had gently suggested, as she dropped the old lady back at home after their morning excursion, that they wait for developments in the police investigation. Diana had scoffed at that.

There was something about Sam Mearns that made Izzy feel awkward. Or perhaps it was just the whole situation. *The meddling.* Diana's belief that she had some right to interrogate a woman just because she taught her Shakespeare once upon a time. It might not even be this Kelly.

She told Diana what Jake said – that it would take a week or two to check the dental records. Once the police had formally identified the body, then they would ask questions of the people who had known her. There was no need for Diana and Izzy to go digging.

But Diana ignored her. As always, Diana had her own ideas.

'We could visit the daughter? The woman you bought your house from?'

Izzy could see what she was doing. Making this about *her*. Making Izzy feel that she had a stake in all of this. But she had found herself agreeing. They had the woman's name and contact details from the sale. Anyway, what harm could it do? It would get Diana off her back.

And, if Izzy was being honest with herself, her curiosity was piqued. Who was the family that lived in their house before them? And what, if anything, did they know about the dead girl buried in their back garden?

7

'Hey you.' Jake stepped up behind Izzy and kneaded her shoulders, easing away some of the tension with his fingers.

She stopped chopping tomatoes, straightening her back and relishing his massage. 'Hey yourself.'

He hesitated a beat, and she heard it in the silence. Something he wanted to tell her but was figuring out where to start.

'I got a call from a friend in the pathologist's office this afternoon.' His voice dropped to a whisper. In the room next door, she heard the kids laughing.

'And...?'

'They're estimating she had been there for twenty years, give or take a margin.'

Izzy took a deep breath. 'That would tally with the time Kelly disappeared. At least, based on what Diana remembers.' She turned to face him. 'And the cause of death?'

Jake shook his head. 'That'll take a little longer. But the evidence is pretty well-preserved for a body...' He didn't need to say the rest.

'The salt. Whoever buried her mummified her,' she mumbled.

A pang of dizziness hit Izzy, just then; her head spinning so fast that she had to grip the edge of the countertop, steadying herself. Centring herself.

'Try not to think about it.' Jake leaned in, kissing her neck. 'For tonight, at least. Focus on the children.'

He was good at this, she realised. Compartmentalising. Spinning plates.

Jake somehow managed to simultaneously deal with several complex legal cases, all the challenges of lock-down, and the stress of the move – not to mention that their property had become a crime scene a week ago. And yet, whenever he was with Izzy, he had this knack of devoting his undivided attention to whatever was both-ering her.

'Ewww, kissing. That's gross.' They hadn't heard Betsy slip into the kitchen.

Izzy's youngest niece was going through a phase where intimacy between adults seemed to revile her. And even though they kept the PDAs to a minimum in front of the kids, Izzy hoped this particular phase would be short-lived.

Jake grinned at Betsy. 'Consider me suitably repri-manded. I shall leave your aunt in peace.'

Betsy sidled up to Izzy, looping an arm around her aunt's waist. 'Will you read me a story?'

'Not just yet, lovely. Before bed.' Izzy clocked the down-turn in Betsy's mouth and knew the sigh was coming before she heard it. 'We'll eat first, and then have some TV time.'

Normally, this would placate Betsy. But her youngest niece hovered at her side, shadowing Izzy around the small space. Izzy hoped it wasn't a precursor to another night-mare. Betsy had suffered from more than one sleepless night lately, and the problem seemed to be worse whenever she stayed over at Izzy's.

There was an entire strategy for dealing with clinginess. Izzy tried to remember what it said in the child psychology book, but nothing came.

'Need any help?' Lucas sauntered into the kitchen, drawn by the voices and cooking smells.

Izzy ruffled his hair. 'Nope. Table's set. We're just waiting for the lasagne to warm up.'

His shoulders sank, and Izzy saw that she had misstepped. Lucas might not wake in the night with bad dreams, but he hadn't been himself since the body was found. Wasn't there something about giving kids tasks to make them feel appreciated? Creating structure and routine to help them feel safe?

She rubbed the back of her hand against her eye. Over two years since Amy was killed and here she was, still fumbling around in the dark when it came to parenting. Besides, none of the books or podcasts had prepared her for the unique horror of their current situation.

'Oh no!' She clapped a hand to her forehead. 'I forgot the salad dressing. Could you help me?'

Lucas was a smart kid. He regarded her studiously. At thirteen, it was hard to fool him with these childish games, and Izzy had no doubt he'd seen right through her ruse.

'There was one in your recipe book. The one with the mustard. My absolute favourite.'

Massaging his ego – another tactic. Izzy busied herself at the larder, bringing out the olive oil and white wine vinegar and handing them to Lucas, who shrugged and got to work.

In truth, their Wednesday night dinners were a highlight of Izzy's week. It was exhausting, entertaining the three of them, but she started to miss them the moment they were gone. The house suddenly felt bereft without them. Empty. Void. A house this size needed people to fill it.

As Jake chatted to the kids about school, homework, and upcoming trips, Izzy let her mind wander. She tried to picture the family who had lived here before, sitting around a table in this same room, having these same conversations. There was the daughter, but what about other kids? Izzy wasn't sure how long the Choudhurys had owned the place. Perhaps there had been someone else living here twenty years ago?

She needed to find out.

By the following morning, the spark of curiosity in Izzy's stomach was aflame. That little fire burned in her, hungry for answers. She hoped Neena Choudhury might hold the key.

Diana was waiting for her at the gate of her cottage in Beadnell, resplendent in a brown suit and fedora, a partridge feather adorning its brim. Izzy tried to mask her grin. Trust Diana to dress for the occasion.

She had Neena's address from the paperwork from the house sale. Apart from plugging it into her sat nav, there had been no forward planning. They couldn't risk calling ahead – the police visit at the weekend would no doubt have spooked Neena. After conferring with Jake, Izzy had decided the best strategy was to turn up on Neena's doorstep and simply hope for the best.

It was surprising that Jake had agreed to this. Well, perhaps *agreed* wasn't quite accurate. He had, in fact, initially tried to talk her out of it. Suggesting, in words that echoed her own to Diana just hours before, that they wait for the police enquiry to progress. But he had sensed her curiosity was too powerful a force to contend with. It was their home, after all. They had a connection to the previous owners, whether they liked it or not.

She helped Diana into the car, surprised at the strength of the old lady's grip on her arm. Her mind flitted back to her days at St Helen's. Those years when she had hung on Diana's every word.

They had been putting together a production of *Romeo and Juliet.* An interesting choice for a girls' school. Izzy played the nurse – a huge role for a year eight to land. It was Diana, of course, behind the casting.

For an entire term, they rehearsed twice a week. At one point, just two weeks before opening night, Izzy developed a terrifying stage fright. It blind-sided her, left her feeling light-headed, her mouth cotton dry. Her confidence vanished and the lines she had spent months learning evaporated from her memory. When she closed her eyes, trying to visualise her part in the scene – just as Diana had taught them to do – she saw only thousands of faces staring blankly at her. Expectant. Waiting for her to utter the words that wouldn't come, no matter how hard she fought against her panic.

Diana had shrugged it off, dismissing it as part of the job. Something that would test Izzy's mettle, prove she was a true actor. She had gripped Izzy's arm and gone through an entire rehearsal performance at her side, a mirror of her actions, a mouthpiece for her lines until at last, as if by magic, the fog receded and the nurse's words came back to her.

As they waited at a red light, Izzy stole a glance at her passenger. A once-expertly coiffed blow dry was now a wispy chignon of white, a cloud that framed her face like a halo. A face etched with lines of laughter, and now, worry.

No. This wasn't just about satisfying her own curiosity.

She pulled onto the A1, the sea finally disappearing from her rear view mirror, the purr of the car's engine steadying her nerves and steeling her resolve.

Neena lived just outside Edinburgh in a smart port district called Leith. Guided by the robotic voice of the navigation system, Izzy snaked the Mini through the town centre and out into an enclave of Georgian terraces.

'We're here.' She spoke slightly louder than was necessary, conscious that Diana had been dozing during the drive.

Izzy glanced up at the house. The sandstone around the bay windows had blackened, but the front door was new. Number twenty-six was a mirror image of its neighbour; a pattern replicated the entire length of the street without a single exception. Behind a freshly painted iron railing, the little garden was empty apart from two wheelie bins and a rhododendron bush in full bloom. The downstairs blinds were drawn, no signs of life.

'I hope you weren't planning to wait outside all day,' Diana mumbled as she unclipped her seatbelt. Izzy rushed around the car to help her.

The doorbell was old-fashioned, a brass button that sounded like a fire alarm at the lightest touch. It made Izzy jump. She snapped her finger away and took a deep breath. Why was she so nervous?

'She might not even be home.'

'Indeed,' Diana purred. 'But then again...'

The sound of footsteps echoed from within.

Neena Choudhury was an attractive woman. Even without a scrap of make-up and her hair tied in a messy up-do, Izzy imagined she routinely turned heads.

'Can I help you?' Neena blinked at them from behind

large designer glasses, puzzled by the odd couple on her doorstep.

'I'm Diana Wheeler. How do you do?' Izzy watched as Diana went to offer a handshake before catching herself, dropping it back to her side, as if remembering at the last moment that strangers rarely touched these days. 'And this is my friend Izzy. Isabelle Morton. From Seahouses.'

Neena's eyes widened as she registered the connection. 'Oh my god! You're the one that bought the house.' She glanced up and down the street, furtively. 'You'd better come in.'

They followed Neena through to a front room where she gestured for them to sit on an expansive white sofa. Izzy surveyed the room with an admiring glance, unable to fight her pangs of envy as she took in the marble fireplace, ceiling cornices, and art déco coffee table.

Neena loosened her bun and re-tied it, anxiously fidgeting with the scrunchie. 'Honestly, my head's been all over the place – goodness knows what you've been going through.'

On the mantelpiece, Izzy clocked a family portrait taken in the room that she recognised as the open-plan living space of her house. A younger version of Neena beamed out from a group of four. Izzy couldn't help but notice the woman's resemblance to her mother.

Diana nodded. 'It's terribly sad. But why don't you tell us what you know?'

Neena shrugged. 'Most of it's from the news. I heard it on the radio on Friday morning – a body found in Seahouses, of all places. I thought that was bad enough. Then the police came on Saturday and told me it was our old place.'

She was crying now, silver tears streaking her cheeks.

Izzy wished she had a tissue to offer her. 'Did you grow up in Seahouses?'

Neena shook her head. 'We lived in Suffolk, most of my childhood. Bury St Edmunds. Mum and Dad moved up to Northumberland after his retirement. I went to boarding school for sixth form, but we spent the school holidays there, me and my brother Abby. Lovely place,' she added, quietly.

That would explain why neither Izzy nor Diana knew her.

'When was this?'

'Dad retired in 1994, 1995, maybe? Like I told the police.' Neena blew her nose on a tissue. 'Poor Mum. I'm almost glad that they're not around to see this. The police were asking all sorts.'

'Like what?' Izzy instantly regretted the urgency in her tone.

Neena regarded her cautiously, her eyes narrowing. '*Horrible* things. About Dad. Whether he might have hurt anyone. Whether anyone could have been holding a grudge against him. If he might have had an affair or something.' She bit back tears. 'Ridiculous stuff, really. My dad was the gentlest man you could meet.' Neena gave a half-smile, buoyed by the memory of her father. 'He literally wouldn't hurt a fly. Seriously. He would catch them in a jam jar and release them outside.' She allowed herself a sad chuckle at this.

Diana folded her hands in her lap. 'I'm so sorry to ask this. But does the name Kelly Reynolds mean anything to you?'

Neena shook her head. 'I don't think so. Why?' She hesitated, and when she spoke again, her voice dropped to little more than a whisper 'So, they know who it was?'

Diana shook her head. 'Let's just say I have the most dreadful feeling. You see, Kelly was someone I once knew. I taught her English. She disappeared when she was seventeen, back in 2003.'

Neena considered this. 'That's ten years younger than me. How would I have known her?'

'She lived in Seahouses on Clyde Street, the row of houses behind yours, with a foster family. The Barretts?'

'Right.' Neena spoke slowly. Remembering something. 'Religious couple? Yeah. I know who you're on about.'

Izzy's heart galloped.

'So, there was this girl,' Neena continued. 'Judith. The Barretts were her foster parents. I met her that first summer holiday after Mum and Dad moved up there. Seahouses bored me silly – there's not much for teenagers to do – so it was nice to have a friend, even if she was a couple of years younger. She took me surfing and we hung around the arcade. Nice girl.' She shrugged. 'Eventually she moved out and I went off to uni. I guess we sort of lost touch. Nobody was using email, back then.'

'But Kelly doesn't ring any bells?' Izzy leaned forward in her chair.

Neena frowned, concentrating, then shook her head. 'There were a couple of younger kids when Judith lived there, but I don't remember a Kelly. By 2003 I'd made junior partner at a law firm in London. I mean, I went up to see my parents for the odd weekend. But I didn't hang out with any of the locals. Just spent time with my folks, and my brother if he was around.'

'My dear girl.' Diana leaned forward and took Neena's hand in hers. 'Is there any possible link you can think of? Any connection?'

'Between my elderly parents and some random teenage

girl living down the street?' Neena was doing her best to hide her frustration.

'I'm so sorry to ask.'

'And I'm sorry to tell you it's a terrible, tragic coincidence. It has to be.'

Neena's gaze flitted from Diana to Izzy. A hardened, determined look. 'I'm telling you, categorically. I know my parents. *Knew* my parents. And I know they had nothing to do with this.'

8

Izzy tossed and twisted, the nightmare following her whichever way she turned. Unable to escape it. Unable to wake up. A shadow following her. Grasping at her conscious, pulling her towards the depths.

A girl. Buried in salt.

Izzy got a glimpse of her face – eyes white with terror, the wind buffeting her hair, her mouth warped in a scream. But there was no sound.

And so much salt. All around her, now. Izzy could taste it on her lips, feel it on her eyelashes, stinging her cheeks. It should have been sand beneath her feet; instead, it was salt that crunched between her toes. The beach was no longer golden but silver, a crystalline expanse, glinting under the reflection of the stars.

The girl was wading into the sea, her back to Izzy. Already, the water was at the girl's thighs, her white cotton dress billowing in the current.

Izzy ran after her, chasing her into the surf, the inky blackness instantly reaching her waist. She screamed above the wind, her lungs aching with the effort. Crying out for the girl to come back.

She had to reach her, to save her, but no matter how deep Izzy went, the girl remained just beyond her grasp.

The waves were rising higher now, threatening to suck them both under. White horses charging at the beach, a cavalry crashing around them. The tide pulling, urgent. Urging them. Deeper.

Izzy stretched out a hand again into the tarry unknown, pleading. Begging. The girl turned again; her face contorted in horror. A howl of fear and pain and terror. But still, when she screamed, no sound came.

And then there was something familiar about her... Her hair the same brown-blonde as Izzy's had once been. Blue-green eyes streaked with flashes of gold.

'Amy?' Izzy called out in disbelief. 'Amy!' she cried, fighting for precious air.

The wind whipped at the surf and blew clouds over the stars, plunging the beach into a darkness even more terrifying and bleak than before.

There was a thunderous roar, a wave surging, the swell stretching higher. The last thing Izzy saw before it came crashing down was her sister's face, Amy's eyes silently pleading with her through the darkness, before the sea swallowed them both.

Izzy sat up, panting, searching for breath, breaking the surface of her nightmare. She clutched the duvet with a trembling hand.

'Izzy. Izzy. Are you all right?' It was Jake, but he sounded so far away.

Breathe. Big gulps of air. *Not drowning.*

'It's all right, love...'

She felt his hand on her back, grounding her. An

anchor. It took her a moment to realise her lungs were no longer on fire. No longer full of salt.

The bedroom window was open, just a slice. From here, she could hear the sea, the waves lapping a gentle lullaby.

Not drowning. Not buried in salt.

Jake folded her towards him, and she inhaled his familiar scent, her heart rate slowly returning to normal. He stroked her hair, his words slurred with drowsiness. 'It was just a bad dream. Go back to sleep.'

Izzy closed her eyes, forcing herself to relax, listening as the pulse in her ears steadied. But whenever the mist of sleep descended, she felt the familiar dark pull of the tide, and saw only the face of her sister.

It was mid-morning by the time she woke again. She had finally drifted off just as the thin dawn light started to break over the horizon and, even then, slumber had come in fits and starts. Now, the sun shone brightly, peeking through the gaps in their blinds.

From the back garden below, she heard voices – Jake and a woman. She flipped the pillow over, pressing her cheek against the cool side, straining to listen. Auntie Sue? No, it wasn't her. This voice was deeper, with a raspier edge.

DI Bell.

Izzy dressed quickly, throwing on the summer dress she had worn yesterday and pulling her hair into a low knot. There would be time for a shower later.

She brushed her teeth and rushed down the stairs and out into the garden. 'Morning.'

'Isabelle. I hope I didn't disturb you?' Pam Bell flashed a sympathetic smile. Genuine sympathy? Izzy found it hard to tell. 'I heard you had a bad night's sleep.'

Jake flushed, clearly wondering whether he had overshared. Izzy laid a hand on his shoulder to reassure him.

'I've been having awful nightmares. I can't help it; I keep thinking about whoever it might have been.' She purposefully kept her eyes on DI Bell and avoided glancing at the freshly turned soil where the conservatory foundation once stood.

The inspector nodded. 'Well, I can help you with that – we've had a positive identification on the name you provided.'

Something in Izzy's stomach shifted. The name *she* provided?

'We fast-tracked a check against Kelly Reynolds's dental records. I came over to thank you for the information.'

Izzy sat down, her hand trembling on the wooden chair, her mouth dry. Jake had made a coffee for DI Bell, a little espresso in one of the fancy cups. It seemed so incongruous in the hand of the seasoned detective sitting just feet away from the place where they'd excavated the victim.

DI Bell took a sip. 'I've just been over to inform the family.'

'The foster family, you mean?'

She hesitated. A beat. 'Yes. Distraught, as you can imagine. There are biological relatives too. But that'll be handled by our colleagues in Tyneside.'

Handled. As if informing a grieving family was an item to be ticked off a list.

'And what now?' Izzy heard a crack in her voice and hoped DI Bell didn't notice.

'Now there'll be an investigation. The investigation that should have happened at the time, but that's a discussion for another day.' The corners of DI Bell's mouth turned down in disapproval.

Izzy couldn't help but think back to a time when she had urged DI Bell to look more closely at Amy's case, to look for the answers they might have missed at first glance. How DI Bell had failed to take her seriously – how everyone had failed to take her seriously – until it was almost too late.

'Do you know how she died yet? And the salt? What does that have to do with anything?'

Jake caught Izzy's eye, flashing her a warning look. 'I'm sure it's all just conjecture at this stage. The autopsy won't be concluded for a couple of weeks, at least.' He turned to DI Bell. 'I expect the investigation will focus on Kelly's contacts, for the moment?'

DI Bell nodded without taking her eyes off Izzy. 'Indeed. We'll know more once the boys in the lab are finished. But in the meantime, if you do learn of anything else, I'd thank you for keeping us informed.'

Izzy thought again of her words. *The name you provided.*

How had she managed to get twisted up in this?

'There's something about that woman.' Izzy sighed once DI Bell had gone. 'I don't know. I can't put my finger on it.'

The cup the detective had been drinking from sat discarded on the table in front of her, its brim crusted in a tidal mark of coffee and a smudge of pink lipstick.

'Pam?' Jake shrugged. 'Don't mind her. Besides, she's one of the good ones.'

Izzy wondered again how close her fiancé was to the detective who had failed to identify her sister's killer. She swallowed the knot of bile in her throat.

Jake sat back, closing his eyes.

'Besides, she didn't have to come over to thank you for

your information. She could have claimed it as her own policing.'

Izzy resisted the temptation to remind him that it was Diana's information, not hers.

'She probably realised that you would hear sooner or later. That grapevine is so small, it could fit in a plant pot.'

'About that...' Jake took a sip of coffee. 'My mate at the pathologist's let slip that the postmortem is delayed. There's quite a backlog, according to Daniel.'

Izzy frowned. 'Can't they fast-track that too?'

He shrugged. 'Different department, different budget code.'

'But they must know something? I thought you said it was well preserved?' She quickly caught herself. 'The evidence, I mean.'

'Daniel is doing his best. But they have other cases on the slate, too.'

'What can be more important than solving the murder of a teenage girl?' She couldn't hide the outrage from her voice.

Jake sat up, looking at her now. 'A *historic* murder. That means there's a slim chance of ever finding who was responsible, and a slimmer chance that they're still around.'

'So what? The police just don't care? She didn't matter in the grand scheme of things? Is that what you're saying?'

'No, no. Nothing like that.' Jake held up two hands in mock surrender. A warning not to shoot the messenger. 'It's just that the chances of getting justice...' He started again. 'The police have to prioritise resources, right? It's all about results. You know that.'

She thought again about DI Bell. How old was she, Izzy wondered? Nearing retirement. She had hinted there'd be a proper investigation, but surely, the last thing she wanted was a complex case landing on her desk at this stage of her career. Far easier to package it up as unsolved and leave it for the next person to figure out. Could they do that? Brush over the evidence? Not dig deep enough? Leave secrets buried where they had lain?

Izzy took a deep breath. It was warm again. The kind of weather people in Seahouses prayed for. A few gardens away, someone started a lawnmower, the splutter of an engine giving way to the drone of the blades.

'But the salt? I thought that would have preserved some of the evidence?' She didn't understand why this couldn't be a cut-and-dry investigation. Surely, as autopsies went, preserved evidence was a winning ticket?

'The soft tissue would be preserved. Yes. Possibly.' Jake shook his head. 'At best, they might be able to work out the cause of death, but the chances of finding DNA on the body? I don't know, honestly.'

'I just don't get it. Why would you kill someone and then bury them in a way that preserves everything?'

Jake seemed to consider this. 'Presumably, whoever buried her didn't understand that the salt could have that effect.'

'Or perhaps whoever buried her wasn't the same person that killed her? She might have been buried by someone who actually wanted the murderer to get caught?'

She chewed this over. Could someone have been deliberately preserving the evidence, hoping it would be found one day?

'Either way, this isn't going to help your nightmares.'

Izzy sighed.

'Look, Izzy.' Jake leaned forward and took her hand in his. 'They're doing everything they can. We have to be patient. I know it's awful, the disruption and everything.'

He waved a hand in the vague direction of the former conservatory, and her heart sank. Did Jake really think it was the *inconvenience* that was unsettling her?

'I just want to know what happened to her.' Izzy's voice was small now, and she fought off the urge to cry. How silly. Crying for some girl who had died twenty years ago, just because she had been buried in their garden?

Jake stroked her hand, his thumb tracing a line along the curve of her wrist. 'Maybe because it's got you thinking about your sister? About what happened to her?'

'This isn't about Amy.' She pinched the bridge of her nose between her thumb and forefinger, hoping the pressure would stem the tears that now threatened to fall. 'Don't you see? It's this place. *Seahouses.* Full of snoops and curtain twitchers, yet a girl can go missing and end up dead and buried just yards from her front door, and nobody notices for twenty years?'

She was properly crying now, unable to hold back any longer. Hot, angry, hateful tears seared her cheek. She watched as one landed on Jake's hand, clenched in her own.

But perhaps this was about Amy?

Or perhaps this was about her, too? Two teenage girls a lifetime ago. Two girls that a village allowed to drown in grief, refusing to throw them a life raft. A pair of innocents who had fallen through cracks that shouldn't exist in the first place.

9

Then

How quickly things can change. It's like the tide. It can turn on you in an instant and before you know it, you're stranded on a rock, surrounded by water. Watching as it creeps higher and higher around you, the panic saturating your bones, with no way of getting back to dry land.

Sam's not speaking to me. I guess it's official now. Now that the whole bloody school knows.

I swear I didn't know she liked him. Not like *that*, anyway. I'd have let her have him. Of course, I would have. Does she really think I'd put some lad before her? My best friend?

At least, I thought we were best friends. Stupid me, again. I suppose some of this is still new to me. Well. It seems I'm being forced to learn the hard way.

I rake over our conversations about him, dredging over the memory of everything she ever uttered on the subject of Bryan. She said he was good looking, but that's not the same as fancying someone, is it? We all say Mr Tait is good looking, although that's probably because he's St Helen's' only male teacher under forty. Definitely not the same thing as loving someone.

How could she be so stupid? Does she seriously think she's *in love* with some lad who barely notices her? Does she even know what love means? *Do any of us?*

I know Mam loved me, and Nanna. And I know Dawn did. *Does.* Love is doing anything to hold on to the person, being ready to sacrifice everything – anything – to save them.

Did Dawn do that? I park that question for later.

I've got lots of time to think about stuff like this, now. On the bus home from school, I sit alone at the front with the other girls who've got no mates. Barbara with cross-eyes whose mam works at Tesco and who all the other girls snigger about behind her back, saying she's got bad breath. Stacey, who has dandruff and nobody wants to sit or stand next to her or even *talk to her* in case it's contagious.

It's definitely not. I know this. Even so, I don't sit next to her. Dandruff isn't contagious, but being a loser is.

That's what they call them, the girls who sit in the middle of the bus. And the girls at the back of the bus label them the same way. Or similar. Maybe not as bad. For some to be winners, others have to be losers. It's the way of the world.

It was from a film, a few years ago. That word. *Loser.* I'm sure nobody said it before then, no one in England, at least. Now it's an entire caste, a layer at the bottom of the food chain.

And now, I'm in it.

I can't believe how fast I've fallen, or that I can chart my fall from grace in a matter of feet – the length of a bus. There's loads of that in the books I read. *A fall from grace.*

Like girls are on a pedestal, but it's precarious, and there's always some bastard waiting for you to lose your balance and come toppling down.

It makes me feel bad for how I looked down my nose at Kyle Beresford. Fair enough, he's got acne even though he is a fully-grown man, and has a weird habit of standing a little too close when he's talking to you. Or maybe he just did that with me?

He'll lose interest now. Bryan, I mean. He likes me because I'm pretty but also because I'm popular, because I know how to have a laugh, because I'm always at the centre of the crowd.

Was. I was popular.

If I could only just get through to Sam, I could make her see sense, make her understand. I would gladly let her have him. To hell with my pride.

Well, maybe not quite. Because it hurts, doesn't it? To have someone not only turn on you, but turn the others against you, too? The ones who were meant to be your mates?

They rounded on me quickly enough. Which just proves that they weren't my mates, not really. Everyone I knew before, my *real* friends, the people I grew up with, they're miles away. These girls, I almost get the feeling they've been waiting for something like this. Waiting for me to trip up.

Bryan says it's daft, that Sam's being an idiot. That she'll come around. But he gets this look on his face whenever he says that. It's the dimples. That's what gives him away. It's how I know he's secretly enjoying this, on some level at least.

Not me and Sam falling out. No, not that. I mean having two girls – best friends – fall out over him. He is enjoying it, being in the middle. The two of us vying for his affections.

That's also in the books I read. I'm enjoying them a lot less these days, I must say.

The thought leaves a bitter taste in my mouth, but I can't help picturing those dimples, the sparkle in his eye, the way he's walking differently. How he holds his shoulders back and stands just a little taller.

I press my nails into my palms so hard that they leave little white halfmoons on my flesh. If I wasn't on the bus, I would scream.

It came out of nowhere. We were all larking around, the whole gang – including me and Bryan. We had been down to the dunes *for a walk*. That's code for whatever couples do, down there. The boy asks the girl if she wants to go *for a walk* and then we head down to the dunes, find a secluded spot where no dog walker is going to stumble upon us and where we're sheltered from the worst of the wind. There's kissing, hands under clothes, layers are peeled off, cold sand against bare skin. Sand everywhere.

We had been *for a walk*, me and Bryan – *Bryan and I* – and had rejoined the others back at the arcade. And something had shifted. The air smelled different, like it does before a storm. I knew it right away. It was the way the other girls avoided my eyes.

The bottle of White Lightning that we'd been passing around earlier was almost empty. Maybe it was the drink that set her off. Who knows?

Suddenly Sam was all teary, but when I tried to ask her what was wrong, she clamped her mouth closed tight and turned to look in the opposite direction. I tried again, desperately trying to coax a response from her, almost in tears myself. This time, she pushed me away. A hard, rough shove to my shoulders that made me stumble backwards.

The others fussed around her, telling me to leave her alone, as if *I had done something wrong.*

That's the craziest thing in this whole situation. As if it's me that's done something wrong. Not her. Not him.

She wouldn't come to the phone the following morning. Her mum said she was out for the day with her gran, but I heard it in the sigh of her voice that she was under strict instructions to lie.

I met up with Bryan that evening. He can't call the house, so we have a system. If he wants to meet up, he lets the house phone ring once, then hangs up. If he can't meet, or there's a change of plan, he lets it ring twice. I usually wait a while, to let the idea settle that it was probably someone dialling a wrong number, and then I make an excuse to leave the house and call him back from the phone box at the end of the road. It'll be much easier when I get my own mobile. Dawn has promised me one for Christmas.

Bryan's dad answered. I always call him Mr Shaw. It's polite, and Nanna taught me that manners get you everywhere. You can have nothing, but you'll always have your manners. And Mr Shaw is a nice guy. He gives us lifts home, never questioning us on the evenings we're particularly giggly and reek of cider. He knows the Barretts, and I'm sure he is aware of their views on boyfriends, but he's looked the other way more than once to give me and Bryan the space we crave.

And I crave Bryan right now. I need the solidness of him, the way my hand looks small in his, the race of his heartbeat against mine. When he suggested we meet up, I leaped.

I knew he had no better plan than *going for a walk* – it's all he wants to do these days, but god knows why. He hasn't got the guts to go through with *it.*

We've come close once or twice. It's not me that shies

away, getting scared at the last minute, as if *it* is something so sacred that we need to be afraid. I'd rather just get it over and done with.

I never tell him any of this.

Besides, he's working his way up to *it*. On Thursday he unclipped my bra, his hands roaming across my naked breasts, and explored further down, a furtive expedition beneath my underwear. Perhaps we are getting close to actually going through with it. Who knows? With Bryan, it's hard to tell.

We walked back down Main Street, holding hands. No chance of being spotted by the Barretts – they spend Saturday nights at home, no exceptions. Sunday's a busy day for them, after all.

And that's when we saw them. Sam, the twins, Elaine, and, in the spot that I should have occupied, Gemma Nolan.

They saw us too; I felt the heat of their gazes tracking us, staring us down. *Their disdain.*

I gripped Bryan's hand tighter, equal parts defiance and terror that he might, for some reason, choose this moment to let go.

With the weight of Sam's envy on my back, I walked along, keeping my head held high. The traffic light was red at the crossing. I turned to face him as we waited, permitting myself a glance towards them. Just a peek over his shoulder to confirm they were still watching us. And then I leaned towards him, parting my lips, and pulled him in for a deep kiss.

Let them watch. I don't care.

It riled Sam, though. Good. The last thing I saw as the light turned green was her scowling at me, her grey eyes now bitter with envy.

Did it make me feel better? No. Not really. What would

make this better would be to have my friend speaking to me again. For all of this not to have happened. To go back to the way things were.

Apparently, I should have known, according to Elaine. I should have understood the code words, the not-said-words, reading between the lines and picking up on the invisible cues. Well, I didn't. And Sam didn't even give me a chance.

But was that enough to cut me out? To convince them all to turn against me? What did Sam say to make them hate me?

Who knows what stupid story she might have told them? Who knows what lies they whisper when I walk by them between classes, when we queue up in the lunch line, while we're waiting for the bus? What rumours has Sam spread about the girl in care, the girl from the rough part of Newcastle?

It shouldn't hurt as much as it does.

We didn't go through with it, me and Bryan. Give him a little more time, perhaps. It's not like I'm going anywhere. Not yet, at least.

Every day, I count down the time until I can get out of here. Thirty-one weeks and six days.

Sometimes I visualise it like sand falling through the egg timer from Nanna's kitchen. I kept it, for some reason, after she died. Dawn said I could take whatever I wanted from the house, but there were so many things to choose from. I was torn between wanting to take it all and wanting to never see any of it again, still unable to comprehend why we couldn't just live there, the pair of us, together. I spotted the egg timer and stuffed it into my schoolbag.

It's on the desk in my bedroom now. A reminder of Mam making eggs for breakfast on the good mornings when she would come home. Always perfectly soft in the middle, with runny centres that trickled down the spoon like liquid sunshine.

Sometimes it feels as if the sand is gliding through, the little stack at the bottom growing, the days slipping away, disappearing, grain by grain. And then, at other times, it feels as if it has stopped. As if this – foster care, Seahouses – might stretch on forever. Sand falling, but time stands still.

I know I can make it. I just have to wait.

I don't know if I can wait. I don't know if I'll make it.

I thought I had nothing to start with.

Now I know how *nothing* truly feels.

10

Now

IZZY WATCHED AS THE WOOD PIGEON FLITTERED BACK TO THE branch, disappearing once more between the leaves. That same spot. She must have a nest in there.

She – because Izzy had decided, at some point, that only a female bird was capable of such commitment – had completed more than a dozen runs in the past half hour. Returning to that same spot, again and again.

Her dad would have known if it was, in fact, a female bird. *A twitcher,* Mum used to tease him. On their walks after Sunday lunch, he would excitedly point out the egrets and kittiwakes, fulmars and terns. And further inland, larks and sparrows, wagtails and dunnocks. Thrushes and wrens. *Look over there, girls. By the stream. A dipper.*

The echo of his voice came to her, whispering names that now meant nothing to Izzy without him there to guide her. Without him at her side, his arm outstretched, showing her precisely where to look.

Amy used to say their dad was one in a million. But now

she was gone, too. Sometimes Izzy struggled to remember the exact position of the freckle on her sister's left cheek or precisely how her perfume smelled on her skin; the way she used to look up to the left – or was it the right? – when trying to remember something.

At least Izzy had the kids. And, once in a while, one of them would do something – typically the most insignificant gesture, the way one of them smiled or laughed or cried or got angry – that made her feel like Amy wasn't so terribly far away after all.

The pigeon was singing; a round and throaty whistle. To its mate? Izzy had no idea. It took flight again, flitting across the other gardens to some unseen point.

How she envied that bird. How she wished she could spread her wings and take off, soaring above the village, riding the tidal breeze. Just seeing where it would take her. No particular destination in mind. Perhaps she would go to Hong Kong? Circle the city, looking down on her old haunts, trying to spot the remnants of a life she'd been forced to discard. A good life, whatever that meant.

Would she return to Seahouses? To Jake and the children and the life she was building, here? Was there enough to pull her back, like the wood pigeon to its nest?

Jake had made mince and dumplings for dinner tonight. One of Amy's recipes from the book that Lucas had curated in her memory. An homage to her weird twists on classic dishes, combinations of foods that definitely should not be eaten together, but somehow worked. One of their ways of keeping her memory alive, of paying tribute to the woman who meant everything to each of them, once upon a time.

The house was still now that Jake had left for work. Without his presence, without the children, it was just an empty shell – a frame of bricks and mortar. Silent, with only

Izzy's mind to keep her company. Her memories, her dreams, her doubts.

She thought back to the detective's visit that morning. She shouldn't be so hard on DI Bell. Mistakes happen. It's difficult to see something when it's right under your nose.

And now? Was Kelly's killer staring them in the face?

She closed her eyes and leaned back, feeling the soothing warmth of the sun on her eyelids. Insects hummed in the potted plants at the edge of the decking. From here, the sea sounded so far away. And, from much closer, the coos of the pigeon as she returned once more to her nest, a soft refrain that danced on the breeze.

From deep within the silence of the house, she heard a knock at the front door. She rubbed her eyes. She had showered after DI Bell's visit but hadn't been able to muster the energy or effort to put on make-up. Maeve Barrett probably wouldn't mind. In fact, she might appreciate it.

Izzy knew she should invite Diana inside, go through the protocol that good manners dictated. Offer her tea and a seat and a natter. But she ached with a weariness, a grey mist of fatigue that made even getting up to answer the door feel like a herculean effort.

Thankfully, Diana seemed impatient to go. Either that, or she sensed Izzy's reluctance to turn this into a social visit.

'We should get a move on, dear. I don't want to keep Maeve waiting.'

The truth was, Diana worried the net might be closing. The Barretts would have heard from the police, by now, that the remains were indeed Kelly. The box of her possessions might have already been handed over as evidence, and Diana was kicking herself for not retrieving it sooner. The key to a successful investigation was to stay one step ahead. She despised the feeling of being on the back foot.

But mostly, she felt exhausted. Drained. In her heart, and against all instinct, she had dared to hope that it wasn't Kelly. She had pleaded with the almighty, and the universe, and any spirits that might be listening, to let it be someone else.

Did that make her a bad person, she wondered? Wishing ill on some stranger to save herself the pain?

After receiving a telephone call from Jake that morning – who must have known Izzy would have neither the strength nor inclination to inform her herself – Diana had wanted nothing more than to crawl back to bed and weep. To mourn Kelly – that dear, bright, amusing young woman – but also to wallow in the guilt that she could, indeed she should, have done more.

Facing the Barretts felt like penance, yes, but Diana wanted more than that. *Needed more than that.* A guilty conscience loved a kindred spirit. She should have done more, of course, but what had the Barretts done when Kelly vanished? An urgent longing, a yearning, burned within her – a craving to see their regret for herself, if only to provide a salve to her own.

She looped her arm through Izzy's, for physical support as much as a sense of solidarity, and they made the short walk to Clyde Street.

Maeve was a mess. She looked diminished, somehow – frailer – and Izzy instantly regretted this expedition. *Talk about stupid timing.*

She was about to tell Maeve that they would call back another time, that they would leave her in peace. That they had made a mistake. Forget the box of Kelly's things – it could wait. How stupid of them to intrude like this, to barge in on a family's private grief. Izzy, of all people, should know how that felt. But before she could give voice to this, while she was still searching for the words that might be remotely appropriate, Diana piped up.

'Maeve, my dear. We heard the terrible news. We're here to offer our condolences.'

And, before Izzy could say anything – let alone protest – she was following Diana over the threshold.

She couldn't imagine this house full of children. It was nothing like Amy's place, which was always warm, the smell of something baking, just the right amount of mess. Even their old house – the home in which Izzy and Amy had grown up – had been in a constant state of disorder, despite their mother's efforts. The evidence of their father's many and varied interests had lain scattered about the house, every corner cluttered with the girls' debris: books and toys, and later, tennis racquets and wetsuits and school bags.

The Barretts' place was cosy, but it had a fusty quality, despite the obvious attempts of its occupants to create a welcoming home. Izzy could see that Maeve had vacuumed that morning. On a side table, a bottle of furniture polish and a yellow dusting cloth sat discarded, abandoned, mid-task. DI Bell's visit had presumably interrupted her housework.

Eric Barrett was recognisable from the photos Izzy had seen on her first visit. Still a head taller than his wife, his sandy hair now streaked with grey, and the same neat moustache. He stood to greet them, attempting a smile. But his eyes were rimmed with red, his face etched with anguish, and Izzy experienced another pang of guilt for encroaching on their heartache.

She helped Diana lower herself to the sofa. The clock on the mantelpiece ticked loudly, echoing in the silence.

At last, Eric spoke. 'It's very thoughtful of you to visit. The police came by this morning. We were hoping...' His voice cracked, and he pressed a hand to his throat as he cleared it. 'Kelly was a great kid. Maeve and I... We've been praying it wasn't her. At least now we know for certain, I suppose.'

Maeve took a handkerchief from her sleeve and dabbed at her eyes. 'We should have done more. We should have pressed social services back then. But how were we to know? When we got that postcard, I assumed...' Her eyes brimmed, and she stopped, her gaze drifting towards her feet.

'I'm so sorry for your loss.' Izzy felt the inadequacy of her words. Kelly might not have been their biological daughter, but the Barretts had clearly been fond of her. And, no doubt, felt responsible.

Maeve glanced up at them through her tears. 'I just keep hoping that she didn't suffer, you know?'

'My dear.' Diana leaned forward in her seat. 'You mentioned you'd kept a box of Kelly's things?'

To Izzy's surprise, Maeve nodded. 'Eric brought it down from the loft yesterday. I haven't had the heart to go through it, I'm afraid. I'm not sure that I could bear to, just now.'

'I would so love the chance to read her work again, one last time. And it might help you. With the grief,' Diana added.

Izzy suppressed an urge to roll her eyes. She adored Diana, but the woman could be quite insensitive.

'I suppose you're right.' Maeve heaved a wearied sigh and nodded to Eric.

He stood, and with slumped shoulders, trudged out of the room, before returning moments later with a battered cardboard box. One word – *Kelly* – had been written on the top in a black marker pen. Eric placed it on the coffee table and withdrew a penknife from his pocket, slicing across the packing tape.

Maeve eyed the box. 'I'd always imagined she might come back for this one day.'

Eric folded back the lid and pulled out an envelope of photographs. 'There's not a lot in here. Some pictures.' He handed them to Diana. 'A few books. Kelly loved to read.' His voice was small, strained. 'And some CDs.'

He turned one of them over, a faint smile dancing on his lips as he remembered. 'Beyoncé. Probably a collector's item by now.' The smile vanished as quickly as it had appeared.

Diana opened the envelope of photos and flicked through them until she saw something she recognised: a copy of the print she had found in her retirement album. 'I remember this trip. I have the same photograph at home.'

She now recognised it as Warkworth Castle. Autumn term, a visit they repeated every year for the sixth formers. The girls were huddled around one of the school's only male teachers. *Kenneth Tait.* That was his name. A delightful young man, barely out of training. God knows how he'd coped with the onslaught of teenage crushes fuelled purely by angst and oestrogen – talk about a baptism of fire. Somehow, he had managed to retain his authority, even out of school premises on trips like this.

And dear Kelly, there at the back, with Samantha's arm wrapped around her shoulder. She looked... Diana studied the girl's expression, searching for meaning. *Content.*

Diana realised that she had been staring at this particular photograph for slightly too long. She passed it to Izzy.

Maeve pulled an old-fashioned egg timer out of Kelly's box. 'She had this with her when she arrived. Goodness knows where it came from.' She placed it on the table with a shrug. 'Oh my.' Maeve's breath caught in her throat. She pressed a hooked finger to her lips as if pushing back against the urge to cry. 'The postcard from London. I'd forgotten that I kept it with Kelly's things.'

'Can I read it?' Diana asked, her hand already outstretched.

Maeve shrugged, her eyes glistening, and handed it to her.

'Dear Maeve and Eric,' Diana read aloud. *'Thank you for having me. I'm sorry that I ran away, but this is for the best. I'm safe and you need not worry. Kelly.'*

The ticking of the clock filled the silence in the room. From the street outside came the sound of children laughing as they played.

Evidence, Izzy thought.

'The police will need to see that.' She glared at Diana, hoping that she had only imagined the old lady glancing at her handbag, a half-thought of taking it away with her.

Izzy picked up the photos again. Kelly on the beach and at school with various friends, often standing alongside the girl who had grown up to become Sam Shaw.

The brutal injustice struck her again, and her heart ached for the seventeen-year-old who would forever remain that way. The girl who never had the chance to go to university or travel the world or get married and have children of her own. Whose life had been cruelly cut short and whose disappearance had gone ignored, the girl forgotten in a shallow grave filled with salt.

There was a group photo; Izzy recognised the backdrop of the arcades as they had been back then. She'd spent enough evenings hanging around there herself as a teenager. Laughing with friends and flirting with boys, especially the holidaymakers that filled the village every summer.

She spotted Kelly at the front, wrapped in the arms of a gangly boy who had not yet grown the bulk to fill out his wiry frame. A crown of pale curls, almost milky white. Everyone was looking at the camera, beaming smiles, but the tall boy was gazing at Kelly. Distracted.

A knot tightened in Izzy's stomach. 'This boy. His face is familiar.'

She held out the photograph to Maeve, who peered at it through half-moon reading glasses and nodded.

'That was the one I was telling you about. The boyfriend. At least, Eric and I suspected as much. He still lives locally.'

Izzy exchanged a glance with Diana, a frown forming on the face of her former teacher. 'What's his name?' Her mouth was dry.

'Bryan. Bryan Shaw.'

11

'BRYAN *SHAW*? AS IN SAMANTHA'S HUSBAND?' IZZY TRADED another glance with Diana, whose expression was a mirror of her own surprise.

Maeve shrugged. 'Yes. Didn't you realise?'

Izzy pressed a finger to her temple. Her ears were buzzing. 'Let me get this straight: Bryan Shaw was Kelly's boyfriend, and he ended up marrying her best friend?'

'Well...' Maeve frowned. 'That makes it sound worse than it was. They were only teenagers, back then. He and Kelly had a falling out, like I told you. It's one of the reasons we discourage such carrying-on. It only distracts them from schoolwork and what-not.'

Funny that Sam never mentioned it... Izzy's mind was racing. Why would Sam have concealed this important piece of information?

'Like I told you before, Kelly could be a bit of a tearaway. Who knows, perhaps Sam saw him first? I never wanted to get involved in the details.' Maeve shuddered. 'It always seemed to me that Kelly had made quite a sorry little mess for herself.'

Eric's face creased into a frown. 'You don't suppose that it had anything to do with... what happened to her, do you? Because Bryan is a decent sort. Very decent.'

'Kelly was depressed before she disappeared.' Diana's voice was soft, but Izzy heard the determination beneath her words. 'I remember now. I'm trying to understand why and work out whether it could be connected to what happened to her.'

Maeve gazed out of the window, fixated on some unseen point beyond their house, her eyes vacant. 'I spent a lot of time thinking back to those months. Wondering, asking myself if I had missed something.'

'We did everything we could for her.' Eric took his wife's hand, folding it between his. 'You're not to blame yourself.'

A silver tear rolled down Maeve's cheek.

Eric turned to Diana and Izzy, his eyes sheening. 'I'm sorry, but this is awfully hard for us.'

Izzy took their cue to leave and helped Diana up. The unease gnawed at her, a disquiet spreading from her stomach and down her limbs. Why had Sam not said anything about Bryan?

Eric stood to see them out, but Maeve remained in her seat, still staring out of the window, transfixed. Her eyes hollow and her expression vacant.

'Thank you, dear.' Diana's voice was little more than a whisper. She patted Eric's arm. 'I'll let you know if we hear any news.'

'Thank you.' He attempted a brave smile, the threat of tears at his eyes once more.

. . .

At a safe distance from the house, the door closed behind them, Diana sighed. 'Well, my dear girl. This is all highly irregular.'

Izzy frowned. 'Odd that Sam didn't think to mention that she married the boy who broke Kelly's heart.'

'Indeed. Although that sort of thing happens all the time in villages. I wasn't the first girl in Seahouses that Lionel courted. Samantha is probably embarrassed, that's all. And what about that postcard?'

'Well, Kelly couldn't have written it.'

'Precisely. We can assume it was sent to the Barretts by whoever killed her, which means that Kelly's attacker knew her.'

'The killer was covering their tracks, making sure no one looked too hard.'

'They did a good job of forging her handwriting.' Diana was thinking out loud. 'This wasn't a senseless or random attack. Kelly knew her murderer, and her killer knew how to cover up for their crime.'

Diana's thoughts were still a jumble at this stage. A fog at dawn, obscuring the view. But sunlight was breaking through the cloud; a pale, silvery light. Shapes and colours were being slowly illuminated, a picture emerging.

Kelly's killer had been level-headed enough to dispose of the body in a way that ensured it wouldn't be discovered. They had been calm enough in the days that followed to take additional precautionary steps, without forgetting the little details. But they would have slipped up somewhere along the way. Humans were incapable of perfection, and Diana had learned long ago that nothing was flawless. The challenge was to find the flaw.

'I suggest we call on Samantha Shaw again. See what she has to say for herself.'

. . .

The way Diana said it left Izzy feeling like she had little choice in the matter.

What she really wanted was to go home, to run a nice hot bath and lie back for twenty minutes, ignoring the hideous three-piece bathroom set and the beige tiles and just soak, feeling her anxiety dissipate with the steam. Enjoy the peace and quiet before Jake came home from work, swiftly followed by the arrival of Betsy with Auntie Sue and Emily, and then Hannah and Lucas.

But she was also troubled by the fact that Sam had omitted this one important detail from her story. She remembered her dismissing it, even changing the subject, when Izzy had asked about the boy they had fallen out over. She wanted to ask Sam again, to her face, and see her reaction.

Izzy suggested it would be quicker to drive to The Green and let the implication hang there in the space between her and Diana. As if this were way down on her list of priorities right now, far below her interior design business, her nieces and nephew, her own home renovation. Her soon-to-be husband. As if, despite the volume and complexity of the tasks piling up on her plate, she had not spent every hour of the past week thinking about Kelly Reynolds.

She drove back through the village, ignoring the temptation to become melancholy as they passed the pub and the arcade where she and Amy had spent their teenage years. Izzy had learned, over the past two years, to pack her grief away in a little box. Always within reach but tucked away in a safe place. Now, she focused on Samantha Mearns. Sam Shaw. What was she hiding?

. . .

Sam answered the door red-faced and glistening, dressed in yoga gear, her blonde hair tied up in a tight ponytail that betrayed her mousy roots. Her eyes grew wide as she took stock of Izzy and Diana, the smile quickly vanishing from her face.

'Come on in.' Her tone was resigned as she waved them inside.

In the front room, a sound system played a Britney Spears track. Sam switched it off and kicked her exercise mat to one side. 'I wasn't expecting visitors.'

Izzy could have sworn she sounded annoyed at the interruption to her workout.

'It's not good news, I'm afraid. You had better sit down.' Diana gestured to the sofa opposite her.

Sam's jaw clenched, and Izzy noticed a vein throbbing at her temple.

'It is Kelly. The girl they found.' Izzy couldn't bring herself to say *we*, the girl *we* found.

Sam's eyes grew wide, then glistened. She pressed a fist to her mouth, a kiss to her knuckles. Shaking her head but saying nothing.

Diana took a deep breath. 'They confirmed her identity from her dental records. There will be a postmortem to establish the cause of death.'

Sam's tears fell now, silently. She brushed them away with a manicured finger.

'All this time...' she whispered. She cleared her throat. 'All this time, and she was right here.'

Diana had seen a lot in her decades of teaching and recognised genuine distress. Something in her troublesome knee clicked awkwardly as she stood but she masked her discomfort. She joined Sam, taking a seat beside her on the wide cream sofa.

'It's a shock, I know. We should think about holding a memorial service for her, give us an outlet for our grief. Izzy will help; she has experience of organising events. But first, my dear. Is there anything else you want to tell us?'

'About Bryan, perhaps?' Izzy chimed in.

Diana swore under her breath. She understood that Izzy was annoyed at Samantha's omission, but she also understood that these things were often more complicated than they initially seemed. Besides. She was quite sure that they would make better progress with Sam if Izzy let her do the talking, rather than firing accusations at the girl. Sometimes, saying nothing at all was the best way to draw out the truth.

Samantha met Izzy's eyes with a defiant glare.

'*My* Bryan? You're not suggesting he had anything to do with this, are you?'

Diana jumped in before Izzy could make matters worse. 'Why didn't you say mention it earlier?'

'Why should I? That had nothing to do with what happened to her.' Samantha sniffed. 'What *might* have happened to her. They broke up. He dumped her for me.' She shuffled in her seat. 'It's not the best feeling in the world, believe me.'

'Something was troubling Kelly before she left. She became quiet. Withdrawn. You even said so yourself. Was it because of Bryan, perhaps? Because the two of you got together?'

Samantha pressed her lips together into a tight line, fresh tears streaking her face. 'All that happened months before.' She wiped her cheek with the back of her hand. 'I can't remember when, exactly. Around Halloween, I think.'

She glanced at Izzy, then Diana. 'She was well over it by the time she ran away. Well over Bryan.'

Diana pulled out a packet of tissues from her purse and offered one to Samantha. 'So what was bothering her in those last months, if it wasn't seeing the two of you get together?'

'I don't know!' Samantha wailed. 'I told you before, we weren't speaking.' She looked away, scanning the framed photographs on the mantelpiece.

Diana followed her gaze. 'Please, dear. Do try to remember. We were a family at St Helen's, even if we weren't always friends.'

Samantha took a deep breath. 'There were rumours. About Kelly.' She clutched the tissue in her hand, gripping it so tightly that her knuckles turned white. 'That she had a boyfriend. An older man,' she added, her voice quiet.

Sam thought back to that term. How generous she had felt, befriending Kelly. Her mum had told her about the new girl living with the Barretts. *She's had a tough time.* Sam had rolled her eyes. When Mrs Ferron asked her to watch out for Kelly at school, Sam had thought only of the extra brownie points it might earn her come the end of term.

Kelly was from a rough part of Newcastle. Sam had gleaned that much from the whispered discussion between her parents, and that she was in foster care meant there was no real family to look after her. Sam had imagined she would be scruffy, skinny, sweary, and stupid. It had been a surprise – a pleasant surprise – that first morning, when she'd called on Kelly to walk with her to the bus stop, to find that she was none of those things.

Kelly with her smart words and sassy mouth, who could

stop teachers mid-rant with a wisdom that seemed to surpass theirs. Even Mr Tait, who everyone decided was the absolute definition of hotness. Kelly was more grown up than anyone else in their group, and they were drawn to her like a magnet. Moths to a flame. Kelly with her clear skin and soft, golden hair.

Sam had triumphantly claimed Kelly as *her best friend,* instantly demoting Gemma Nolan to second fiddle. She hung on Kelly's every word – they all did. Kelly knew so much about the world – the real world, out there, beyond Seahouses – and talked confidently about going to university. No wonder Bryan had fancied her the moment he laid eyes on her.

Bryan, who was growing taller and broader by the day, morphing from the skinny lad Sam had known her whole life into some kind of dreamy surf god. That summer, Sam had woken one morning to realise he was no longer the goofy boy she knew from primary school but a bona fide hottie, with legit muscles and boyband hair. But by then, it was already too late.

If she thought about it hard enough, Sam could remember the precise moment she realised Bryan had a thing for Kelly. The moment her heart had broken in two.

Sam had taken a long, hard look at herself in the mirror. At her spots and puffy midriff, the paunch that her mother promised would melt away as she grew taller.

She made some changes – skipping breakfast, actually taking part in cross country instead of crying off with feigned period pain, and spending her pocket money on an expensive anti-acne face wash. She begged her mum to let her get highlights, taking her from a non-descript mousy brown to sun-kissed blonde.

But none of it had the desired effect.

So, she had turned on Kelly, putting into action a plan that would guarantee Bryan would soon see Kelly in an entirely different light.

She winced as she recalled the fall-out. How quick the other girls had been to believe her. How eager they had been to see Kelly's imagined dark streak.

But things got out of hand. The entire group ostracised Kelly. Bryan, of course – her kind and generous Bryan – had been the last to jump ship. By then, Kelly had no one else.

And then the rumours had grown lives of their own, morphing into shadows that no longer bore any semblance to the truth. That Kelly was a thief, a lesbian, that she had a criminal record. That she was a slag – Sam shuddered at the word. *Sleeping with an older guy. Sex with a married man. A slut.*

Sam couldn't call them off, not without losing face. She couldn't tell them she had fallen out with Kelly because Kelly had fallen for the boy she loved, and by then Sam was with Bryan. Actually *with him*: proper boyfriend and girlfriend. Official. Everything she'd ever wanted.

Almost.

She knew that she just had to keep quiet – to live with the lie she had told – and let Kelly get on with her life while she, Sam, got on with hers. She had done it for twenty years and was not about to tell the truth now.

In the still of her beautiful kitchen, the heart of her beautiful home, Sam could see that Diana was troubled by her words; it was there in the crease of the old lady's brow, her down-turned mouth.

'An older man?' Diana was incredulous. 'Who?'

Sam watched her exchange a glance with Izzy and registered the doubt in the other woman's face.

'Like I said. It was only a rumour. We weren't friends by then, so I've no way of even knowing if it was true or not.'

She suddenly wanted them out of the house, far away from the perfect family and home she had worked so hard to create, so hard to preserve.

She was saved by an alarm on her phone. A reminder to shower, giving herself enough time to blow-dry and curl her hair, fetch the kids from school and get dinner in the oven so that Bryan could come home to a clean, tidy, orderly house and a polished, slim, untroubled wife.

'I'm sorry,' she said, 'but I must be getting on. I'm sorry about what happened to Kelly. I truly am. But it's nothing to do with me. With us.'

Sam saw them out, smiling sweetly but inside, urging them to hurry. Wanting them gone. She would hoover the living room this afternoon, wipe away any trace of their visit.

She watched as Izzy helped Diana into her car, tenderly guiding the old lady by the elbow, warning her to mind her head as she climbed up into the seat. As Sam watched, she wondered; did they believe her?

12

Sam closed the door behind them with barely a polite goodbye. Diana did so hate when these young people forgot their manners.

If the girl hadn't been in such a hurry, she might have seen the police car that swung into the street just seconds later. Diana watched from the passenger seat as the car approached.

Izzy paused at the driver's door, holding a hand up to screen her eyes against the sun as the lady inspector parked in the space behind them. Diana wound her window down, just an inch, to better hear the conversation.

'Isabelle. Fancy seeing you here?' The detective intoned her words as if it was a question.

'We were just calling on Samantha Shaw. She was friends with Kelly. We wanted to tell her that the body has been identified. Her husband was Kelly's boyfriend, back when they were in school, and we just thought—'

Izzy was gabbling, and Diana resisted the urge to roll her eyes. After all, there was no need to be nervous.

'I'd rather you left that up to us, if you don't mind.' The

detective's stony glare was enough to silence Izzy, and Diana wished that her young friend might grow a backbone one of these days.

The detective peered into the car.

'Good afternoon, inspector.' Diana flashed a smile at the lady detective, but got a frown in response.

It was understandable, she supposed. She knew that the likes of this woman had little appreciation for people like her, particularly when their incompetence was exposed.

'Diana. Good to see you. Forgive me for asking, but you wouldn't have been questioning a potential witness in a murder enquiry, would you?'

'A potential witness?' Diana feigned incredulity. 'Heavens, I hadn't considered that. No, I'm simply thinking that some of the old St Helen's girls may wish to organise a memorial service for dear Kelly. Just exploring the idea at this stage.'

The inspector held her gaze. 'Happy to hear that. Because this is serious, ladies. We might only get one chance to get it right.' A beat. Waiting to make sure Diana got the message, no doubt. 'And I'd appreciate it if you would stay away from people involved in the case.'

'Understood, inspector,' Diana said. 'Loud and clear.'

She resisted the temptation to remind the detective that this was a tight-knit community, and presumably, the list of potential suspects was still quite large at this stage. It was unreasonable to expect them to avoid their neighbours until this dreadful business was concluded, and goodness knows how long the official investigation might take.

Besides, the blasted woman's name momentarily escaped her, and Diana struggled to recall if this particular detective had been involved in that *other* incident. Best behaviour was her safest bet, for now.

'I saw Maeve and Eric Barrett earlier.' Izzy spoke quickly, not allowing space for the woman to interrupt. 'They mentioned Kelly sent a postcard after she disappeared. They kept it in a box of her things.'

The detective clenched her jaw. Dear Izzy had a lot to learn about dealing with the police, Diana mused. The secret, she had learned, was to say as little as possible, and give them absolutely nothing until you were certain they had already discovered it for themselves.

'Thank you. We're aware of that and are looking into it.' The detective opened the car door for Izzy, a signal that they should leave and an attempted reminder to the women of precisely who was in charge here. 'And please, ladies. Let's leave the police work to the police.'

Izzy climbed into the car and placed a palm on her chest, as if to slow her heart, which was no doubt racing.

They made the brief journey back to Beadnell in silence. Diana watched as the coast swept by, resting her hands in her lap, deep in thought.

Her memories of that year were blurred, fragments that didn't fit together. Names and faces of forty years' worth of girls blending into one tangled mess. She tried to isolate her mental image of Kelly Reynolds, willing the pieces to solidify.

It was twenty years ago, she reminded herself. Understandable that the picture wasn't clear. But how badly she wanted to remember. How desperately she wished her mind was as sharp as it had once been.

Izzy parked in the lane at the front of her cottage and helped Diana down. It was a silly car. Absolutely no need for a vehicle of such size unless one lived on a farm, although Diana understood that this type of model was very in vogue these days.

She bid farewell to her friend and took a moment to appreciate the view of her cottage. The old climbing rose was in full bloom, each flower a feathery cloud of pale pink silk. Every year, Diana wondered if she would live long enough to see it blossom again.

The memory of Lionel came to her, as he often did. This place had been a huge step up from their first home in Seahouses, which they had quickly outgrown after the arrival of their daughter Jennifer. They needed something bigger and had fallen in love at first sight of this cottage. A garage, three bedrooms, and enough space for a proper dining table.

She pictured a younger version of herself watching from the kitchen window as Lionel played with the girls in their modest front garden, helping them to catalogue shells collected from the beach. Her lovely Lionel, barbecuing sausages in summer, sweeping away snow after a rare fall one Christmas, planting bulbs of hyacinths and tulips and alliums in the cold autumn ground and watching them flower in spring. Devotedly tending to his rose, season after season.

The windowsills would have to be repainted soon; the pale and flaking paint was evidence of a constant losing battle against the salt in the air. Diana tried to remember the last time it had been done, but came up with nothing. A blank space.

She refused to let it bother her. Instead, she took a deep breath and closed her eyes, listening to the rhythmic chant of the sea and the hum of insects that danced between the flowers.

The cool of her kitchen was a welcome respite from the warmth of the day. Diana slipped off her shoes and walked stocking-footed across the flagstone floor towards the sink.

She filled a glass with water and sipped slowly, willing her mind to clear. Making space for the memories.

Kelly. She focused on the girl now. Her long blonde hair, hanging in a neat plait down her back. The tip of a pencil resting on her lip, a frown of concentration. *Macbeth*. Upper Sixth English Literature. The girls reading the parts in turn. Dissecting, analysing, reading between the words on the page. Fine-tuning their critical thinking. Kelly had been head and shoulders above the others.

And then that last term. Kelly's grades slipping. Several detentions for missing deadlines. Or was her mind playing tricks on her? Diana had been preoccupied by events at home, at the time. Her own daughters, in their thirties by then. Grown women themselves, with all the problems that brought. Lionel's health. The cancer that had eventually forced him to take early retirement from the newspaper. She had been distracted; it was no wonder that she struggled to remember what happened with Kelly.

There were records at the school. Registers of attendance. Would they go back that far? It was all on computer, now. Digitally enshrined for eternity. Or did they delete these things? So much time had passed.

Her old writing desk was now upstairs in the spare bedroom, the room that had once been Sandra's. A beautiful mahogany piece, a wedding gift from Lionel. It was still unusual, back then, for a married woman to keep her profession, and he had been exceptionally proud. The gift symbolised his faith in her, in his commitment to her career.

Now, something was pulling her towards it. Diana followed without questioning the instinct that guided her.

She opened the desk, pulling down the hinged top. The stale air from within hit her. Musty; the smell of old wood and paper and ink. It sparked a thought and Diana froze, giving it the space to form. She held her breath and tried to still her mind. Allowing it to come back to her.

A vision of herself sitting here, marking books. Filling out reports. She traced a finger along the leather lining of the desktop, pushing herself to *think*.

There were boxes in the garage. Why hadn't she remembered them sooner? Old diaries, lesson plans, folders of coursework. Paperwork and books that Diana couldn't bear to see go to waste.

Or had they been thrown away? Had Sandra, in her crusade to clear out anything among her mother's possessions that she considered junk, got rid of them? When had Diana last seen them?

She hurried, taking the steep stairs as quickly as she dared.

The boxes were still there. A dozen moving cartons, paperwork organised by year. A broad smile spread across Diana's face.

It took her no time at all to locate the correct box. She brushed off a film of dust and dragged it along the floor of the garage, unwilling to risk attempting to carry it. The last thing she needed was to put her back out again.

In the adjoining kitchen, she pulled up a chair and extracted a handful of folders from the box. Diana read the first page, mumbling the words to herself out loud.

It was not what she was looking for.

She riffled through the rest of the contents, the words blurring on the pages in front of her, her hand trembling with the sense that she was getting close.

And there it was. The girls' performance reports.

She traced a finger down the list of names until she landed on Kelly Reynolds. The paper shook in her hand, a leaf trembling in a breeze.

Kelly had scored As for her first year coursework. No surprise. And, just as Diana remembered, an impressively high grade in the autumn term mock exams.

But the girl's marks began slipping. Diana shook her head. Kelly had fallen down to a D by the January mocks, and her last piece of coursework on *A Midsummer Night's Dream* had not been handed in.

And then it came to her, the mist finally lifting and the sun bursting through the clouds.

There had been a week that term when Kelly had not turned up. February. Frost on the playground. Whispers among the girls and in the staff room that she had *run away*. The school secretary had taken an anxious phone call from the Barretts, swiftly followed by another from social services.

But then Kelly had returned, and the Head of Year had asked them all not to fuss, and besides, Diana hadn't had the energy to pry. Not with everything that had been going on with Lionel. And soon, she had forgotten.

Kelly had run away once before.

How had she not remembered this sooner? Diana cursed herself.

And now, it fell into place. The girl had been depressed, quiet in class, eating lunch alone. Acting up, failing to hand in coursework, falling into regular detentions. Her hair unwashed, her face pale.

She had run away but, somehow, they managed to bring her back. Presumably that was why nobody asked too many questions after Kelly disappeared for a final time.

Diana could kick herself. Why hadn't she done anything? She had watched a bright and vivacious girl crumble before her eyes, colour fading away to grey. It was too easy to blame the distress of Lionel's diagnosis. She'd had a duty of care to those girls.

To Kelly.

She should have known. She should have done something, anything. Acted on her concern before it was too late.

Instead, she had let her down.

Had Diana given up on Kelly? Was that what had really happened all those years ago?

She should call Amy. *Izzy*.

Izzy.

Because Amy was no longer here, she reminded herself.

Diana wiped away the tears that wetted her cheeks now, tumbling from nowhere. She needed to concentrate.

Had it been boy trouble? No. Instinct told her that Kelly's problems had run deeper than the folly of adolescent love.

There had been a falling out with Samantha, yes. Diana could picture it now. Turning up to class late one afternoon and finding the others teasing Kelly, giggling behind their hands.

Girls could be acutely vicious.

But would Kelly have run away because she had been cast out of her friendship group? She seemed more mature than that. Certainly, she was far more adult than the other girls.

Samantha's words echoed in her mind. *An older man.*

Someone who had come into the life of a formidable yet vulnerable young woman and shaken her to her very core.

Diana heaved a weary sigh. This was all her fault. If only she had seen what was right in front of her.

She was properly crying now. Tears of regret, of sorrow, of guilt. They landed on the page in front of her, spots blotting the paper, turning it translucent.

The light outside was falling, the bright sunshine of a May afternoon seeping away, fading towards dusk. What time was it?

Diana glanced at her watch, her eyes widening in surprise.

Where had the hours gone?

How long had she been sitting here?

Fear gripped her, icy tentacles lacing around her heart as she realised with a certain dread that she had no recollection of the past few hours. She shivered, the skin of her arms prickling in goosebumps.

Granny Agnew. *It's happening.* It was happening all over again.

It was futile to resist the tears now, and she allowed her grief to flow, weeping openly. Letting it all out. Salty streams coursed down her face, running into her mouth, dripping from her chin. Mourning for the forgotten girl. For herself.

She closed her eyes and spoke the words aloud. 'I'm so sorry, Kelly. I'm so truly sorry.'

13

Izzy had slept through the night for the first time in a week; a long, dreamless sleep. She woke to the smell of coffee and the sight of Jake grinning, his head propped up on his arm.

'Guess what?' he whispered.

'You made coffee?'

He edged closer to her, his face no more than a kiss away. 'The kids are still asleep.'

Izzy turned into the pillow. 'Don't come so close when I haven't brushed my teeth!' she moaned, her words muffled against the cotton.

'Oh, come on...' Jake pressed the length of his body against hers. 'You know that's the last thing on my mind.'

He flipped her over and rolled on top, the weight and warmth of him a comforting reassurance, and interlaced his fingers with hers as he planted a trail of kisses along her collarbone.

They made love quietly, urgently, just as they had in the early days of their relationship when Izzy's grief had been all-consuming. Her love for Jake – her desire to make one good thing come out of a terrible situation – had forced her to create a space in her heart. To pack her sorrow away, stored in a little box for later.

Afterwards, they lay there, satiated. Izzy rested her head against his chest, listening to the drumbeat of his heart. A percussion just for her. Outside, the birds sang in the trees. She couldn't hear the wood pigeon.

It was Jake who moved first.

'Stay,' she urged him. 'What's the rush?'

He flashed her a perfect smile. 'The rush is three hungry delinquents who will eat us out of house and home unless there are catering provisions.' He kissed her forehead. 'Full English for five, coming right up.'

Izzy watched him leave and turned over onto her side. This felt like something. *This was something.* It might not have been the life she had dreamed of, or the life she had expected. But different didn't necessarily mean bad. Did it?

She made her way downstairs, where the smell of bacon greeted her at the kitchen door. Lucas, still in his *Harry Potter* pyjamas, was being expertly mentored by Jake in the art of the perfect fry-up.

Izzy resisted the temptation to remind them to be cautious. Lucas was far more at home in the kitchen than she was.

The girls were in the living room. She took a seat next to Hannah, who was frowning at her phone. Izzy caught a glimpse of a Salt Girl article on the *Daily Mail* app before Hannah shut the screen.

'What's the plan for today, then?' Hannah asked brightly, as Jake and Lucas carried through trays piled high with grilled bacon, sausage, scrambled eggs, and mushrooms.

'Well, you lot are off to your clubs this morning.' Izzy spooned baked beans onto Betsy's plate. 'And I have to run a quick errand.' She looked up now and caught Jake's eye.

'I can drive them, no worries.' His voice was level. 'Are you working?'

Izzy wished she had told him last night about Samantha Shaw; about the fact that Sam had failed to mention her husband had been Kelly's boyfriend first. *That she had not only got together with her best friend's ex-boyfriend but married him.* But the kids had been there, and they had agreed not to discuss the investigation in front of them. And she would have told him this morning, but...

'Just visiting a friend,' she mumbled, hoping he would know better than to ask more.

She saw them off, football kits and ballet outfits freshly laundered, shoelaces tied, snacks packed. Jake waved to her as they piled into the Range Rover.

'Be good,' he mouthed.

Izzy leaned back against the closed door and took a deep breath, absorbing the tranquillity that fell in the silence of the house.

Diana had called yesterday evening, blabbering on about remembering how Kelly had run away once before and she couldn't believe she had forgotten.

She hadn't been making a lot of sense, saying over and over that it was all her fault, that she should have seen what was staring her in the face all those years ago. To placate her old friend, Izzy had agreed to make a further call on Sam Shaw.

She showered, washing away the traces of Jake, and blow-dried her hair. Once upon a time, her Saturdays had been a blank canvas – sleeping off a hangover, then yoga classes and brunches, shopping trips, lunch dates, facials, before getting ready for another night out. The newest restaurant, a speakeasy, some rooftop bar – Hong Kong always had a hot-spot, the latest place to see and be seen.

She longed to take Jake for a visit, to let him experience the bright lights and colours and taste the flavours of her life before. To show him who she used to be. But the more time that passed, the more that person was morphing into a stranger, even to her.

Not a stranger, perhaps, but someone else. A different Izzy. A woman who was almost unrecognisable next to the woman she had been forced to become.

She glanced at her watch. Precisely two hours until the children and Jake came crashing back through the door. Their Saturday afternoon plans consisted of a long walk, the promise of an ice cream from Coxons on the way home, and movie night in front of their new flatscreen TV. She dressed, her mind roving over the perilous landscape that was her past, her present, her future, and set off on her errand.

Diana was ready by the time Izzy arrived, already waiting at the gate. Punctuality, Diana liked to think, was common courtesy.

'Lateness is a choice,' as Lionel used to say.

Izzy helped her into the car. At least the Mini was easy to get in and out of – nothing like that blasted truck. *Chelsea tractors,* the newspapers called them, although Diana did not think Izzy would find this amusing.

They meandered along the coast road, Izzy navigating the turns as the car twisted towards Seahouses. The sea was an infinity of navy, broken sporadically by gentle waves which crashed down in curls of white foam. Beautiful weather for an afternoon on the beach, if one was so inclined.

They pulled up outside Samantha's house. A white van was parked in the drive with bold blue letters proclaiming its owner to be *Shaw's Services. Family business since 1976.*

Diana had seen it around the village, of course, but took a mental note of the details, now. She batted away Izzy's offer of assistance in getting out of the car, leaving her friend to anxiously watch.

She instantly recognised the tall blond man who answered the door.

Bryan Shaw hadn't changed much. He had filled out his frame, but the pale hair that Diana had seen in Kelly's photographs was the same, only shorter. Fine lines webbed at the corners of his eyes, the evidence of a lifetime spent smiling. His fitted t-shirt clung to his modestly slim and perfectly proportioned body.

'Bryan, I presume?' Diana stepped up. 'Is your wife home?'

A look of puzzlement flashed over his features. His face was tanned, Diana noticed, from days spent working outdoors, earning a living the honest way through sweat and toil.

'She's out,' he mumbled. 'Can I help you?'

'I hope so, dear.' Diana was already squeezing past him into the house. 'Let's have tea while we wait.'

In the plush living room where they had sat just twenty-four hours earlier, Diana and Izzy made themselves comfortable while Bryan busied himself in the kitchen, no doubt firing off a panicked text message to Samantha.

'Now, dear,' Diana said, her voice low. 'I suggest you let me take the lead.'

Izzy looked as if she was about to argue with her, but

before she could say anything, Bryan reappeared, burdened by a tray of refreshments.

'How is Samantha coping?' Diana didn't look at Bryan, but instead, issued a curt nod to Izzy to pour the tea. Bryan had prepared a pot with a small jug of milk on one side.

'She's fine...'

'The poor dear. I heard she had a terrible shock yesterday...'

Bryan's features stilled, his jaw squaring. 'Yes. The police visited. They told us about Kelly.'

Diana could have imagined it, but there was a quiver in his voice when he said her name. *Kelly.*

'I imagine it is rather upsetting for you, too.' Diana gazed out of the window. 'I used to teach her, you know. Used to teach both of them.'

Bryan said nothing.

'We're organising a memorial service for Kelly. The thing is,' Diana continued, 'my memory is not what it used to be. I've been trying to recall the time before Kelly left, but I may have a few blanks. She ran away once before. But of course, you'll remember better than I do.'

Bryan ran a hand over his chin, his fingers raking over day-old stubble. 'She used to talk about it all the time. Running away, I mean.'

Diana let the silence hang there. Waiting for Bryan to say more.

'God, we were so young back then. I must have been what, seventeen?' He looked down at his shoes. 'She was my first girlfriend. It was all fairly innocent.'

Diana nodded, wondering what constituted *innocent* in this day and age. 'Do you remember why the two of you broke up?'

Bryan shifted in his seat. 'She was a nice girl. But she

changed. Started to get depressed. It was hard for her, being here. Her friends – Sam...' He trailed off, remembering. 'There was some stupid row. I was never certain what caused it. But they all stopped speaking to each other.'

Diana spoke softly. 'Was that what got her down?'

'I don't know.' He sighed. 'We stayed together for a while, but... One day, it ended.'

Diana tried another tack. 'You said she often talked of running away.'

'Yeah. Her family – she had an auntie or something – was down in Newcastle. Dawn, her name was. Kelly went on and on about her. She used to talk about going to live back there, going to Newcastle Uni and living with Dawn. How different things would be once she was home.' He took a sip of tea, his eyes avoiding theirs. 'Sometimes, we used to talk about going together.'

'But you didn't want to?'

'It was just talk, as far as I was concerned. I never wanted to leave Seahouses.'

'And then you got together with Sam?'

Bryan blushed again. 'It just... sort of happened, I guess. Me and Sam. We've known each other our whole lives. Me and Kelly broke up, and then, there she was.'

Diana pushed again. 'Do you remember when Kelly ran away? That first time?'

Bryan thought carefully before answering. 'Yes. Someone from social services – her caseworker or something – came to see me at home. Asking loads of questions. About what she'd said, anyone she had mentioned. Where she might be. I told them the truth. But we had been broken up for a few months by then. How was I supposed to know?'

'And when she disappeared for good?'

Byran shrugged. 'They came again. Brought the police,

too, that time. But what else could I tell them? I just assumed the same as everyone else. That she'd had enough and gone home. It's funny. I've thought about her, from time to time, over the years. Wondering how she was getting on.'

'And you never thought to check?' Diana instantly regretted her steely tone. It wouldn't help, not here, not now.

'I just... Well...' He searched for the words. 'It's Sam. It's always been a sensitive topic. She doesn't like to talk about her.'

Diana understood. To be the love of your life's second choice must be hard to reconcile. 'Those final months before Kelly left. What do you think was bothering her?'

Bryan huffed. 'Not me, that's for sure.' Diana could have been imagining it, but he seemed almost hurt by this fact. 'I heard she was seeing someone else, but I don't know. None of us were really speaking to her, by the end.'

His eyes glistened now, and Diana realised there was a gap in the story.

'How did things end, exactly? Between you and Kelly?'

Bryan hesitated a beat before answering. 'I told everyone it was mutual. That we drifted apart. But the truth? She broke up with me. Kind of caught me off-guard. Told me it was for the best.' He set his cup down, anxiously licking his top lip. 'I don't think my wife likes that version of the story, mind you.'

No, Diana thought. *I bet she doesn't.*

'I hope they find him.' Bryan's eyes steeled on hers. 'I hope they get whoever did this to her. Kelly was a special girl, and she didn't deserve this. Any of it.'

14

Then

It was overcast all day today. *All bloody day.* The sky was a thick blanket of cloud when I woke up this morning, and even now, there's no end in sight. No end to any of it.

I went to the arcade this afternoon, just for something to do. See who was knocking around. Looking for something, someone, *anything* to kill the time.

I wish I hadn't bothered.

Sam was there with Bryan. Honestly, you should see them. It's totally gross. Not the kissing. As if I care about the kissing. No, I don't mean that. I mean the way she melts around him, moulding herself to fit his shape. Not a physical thing. Like, on an intellectual level. Laughing at his jokes, even though half of them aren't funny and he knows it. Telling him what he wants to hear. Being the girl she imagines he wants, instead of just being herself. It's puke-inducing. Completely cringeworthy. As if she hasn't got an independent thought in that stupid head of hers. As if he can't see straight through the act.

And I know Bryan doesn't like it. I can tell by the way he winces at that fake laugh. The way how, when he kisses her – because she's constantly trying to neck on with him, especially when there's an audience – he keeps his eyes open. Looking over her shoulder. Waiting for something better to come along.

Just waiting, though. Not actively seeking.

Not like when he was with me. When we would head down to the dunes, just the two of us, rolling about in the sand. Only interested in each other. When he only had eyes for me.

He loves that I'm clever. *Used to love it.* Perhaps he still does? He would get me to recite Shakespeare to him. I once delivered my favourite scene of *A Midsummer Night's Dream*, down there in our spot among the dunes.

The course of true love never did run smooth.

It's ironic. Two guys going after the same girl, just like me and Sam – two girls going after the same guy.

Further irony: Bryan probably didn't understand what the play was about. I never told him. Just said the lines he wanted to hear. Perhaps I'm not much better than Sam after all.

I can't complain that he got together with her. After all, it was me that called time on it. Told him we should just be friends. Whatever we had, it had run its course. Well, almost. It would have ended eventually. Better to do it now and save myself the pain of the inevitable. Rip the plaster clean off.

Bryan didn't even fight it. That's the worst part.

Poor Bryan. He's weak, that's his problem. Doesn't dare criticise or even think for himself. Doesn't dare to imagine a life beyond this shitty village.

Critical thinking. Mrs Wheeler is always banging on

about it. It's about not taking things at face value, looking deeper. Questioning, challenging, even questioning yourself. It's the difference between an A and a B in English Lit, according to her. The difference between getting into Newcastle and failure, for me. There are other universities, but that doesn't feature in my plan. There's only one place I want to be, one way to make this work. Everything depends on me getting in.

I had my offer letter this week. I told Mrs Wheeler, of course, and Mr Tait. Who else cares? I need an A and two Bs, but I can do it. I can feel it in my bones. I lie awake at night, staring at the ceiling, imagining myself running over the finishing line. And soon, all of this will be ancient history.

I ate lunch with Barbara yesterday. Barbara Martin. That's how desperate I am. I ignored the glares and side-glances of the other girls – I've almost become used to them – and carried my tray over to the corner table where Barbara sits alone.

She's OK, I suppose. She was surprised to have company, and maybe I caught her unawares, because she had absolutely no craic. Zero.

Turns out it's true about her having bad breath. Poor lass. Although who am I to feel sorry for anyone these days?

On my way home from the arcade, on Main Street, I passed Kyle Beresford. He still has awful skin and still has that awful habit of staring. Still has dark stains on his jeans from long days spent working in his dad's butcher's shop. Our eyes met, and he went bright red. And I realise – *I enjoy this.* Perhaps I need Barbaras and Kyles to remind myself that I'm not that the bottom of the pile. Not yet, at least.

I won't think about them, any of them. I'll stay focused on the end, on my goal. *University*. Dawn says it's impressive.

Nanna and Mam would be so proud. She can't wait to have me home for good. Just the two of us. Well, three if you count Jackson. If he's still around by then.

I'm going to get a job when I get back. A proper job, in one of those bars on the Quayside. According to Dawn, there are loads of them now, a new one opening every week. Cocktail lounges and late-night dance bars and fusion restaurants, whatever that means. They're always looking for staff. Jackson has a friend who knows a guy that manages a place, and he reckons I'll have no trouble finding work.

I can picture myself somewhere like that. Somewhere swanky, with a neon sign and a DJ and a guest list, and people queuing down the street to get in. Mixing cocktails behind a bar, my hair and make-up done, wearing my best outfit and a pair of high heels. A world away from Seahouses.

I can see it already. *Feel it*, like it's just around the corner. Within touching distance. *My new life.* I'll go to lectures during the day, come home and do my work, then head out to my job in the evening. I'll have so many friends that I won't know what to do with myself, while Sam and Bryan and all of that lot will still be stuck in this place.

I'm so close.

I was thinking about this as I walked, the thoughts sour on my tongue. Wanting to put as much distance between myself and *them* as possible. Trying to focus on the future, rather than the past. Rather than *now*.

I ambled home, taking the long way around. Why not? I wasn't in any hurry. And that's when I met him.

N.

He asked me how I was doing, and I realised with a jolt of sadness that he was the first person to ask me that all day and truly mean it. I guess he saw the sadness. It's hard to hide, some days.

N suggested I join him for a walk on the beach. Apparently, I looked pale, and the fresh air would do me good, he said. Growing bodies and minds need vitamin D. Was I sure I was getting enough? He was heading that way himself. Did I want to tag along? Keep him company? Just a short walk.

It wasn't like I had any better offers.

The tide was out. I love the beach like that – impossibly broad, the sand glistening with salt, glinting under the pale winter sun hidden behind the clouds. It reminds me of the time I came here with Mam, a time so long ago that I can barely remember it. *The shape of the sky*. That's what infinity looks like. I wonder if she's looking down on me.

N asks a lot of questions. He's easy to talk to, for a grownup. And he listens. Actually really listens. Hears the space between what I say. Understands all that I can't give voice to. *Reads between the lines on the page.*

I found myself explaining what had happened – with Bryan and Sam, and the way those girls collectively turned against me. And you know what? He laughed. He said that in a few years, I'd see the funny side of it, too.

N says it's because I'm so much more mature than other girls my age, and they simply can't handle it. No wonder, he says, that they're all so jealous. He reckons I'm probably much prettier than all of them, too, and clearly so much smarter. I should feel sorry for them if anything.

A small part of me hopes he might be right. *Wants* him to be right.

And Bryan? N thinks that soon enough, I won't even remember Bryan Shaw. That there's an entire world out there of better-looking, funnier, more charming guys. And one day I'll meet a man who's worthy of me.

Worthy of me. I hadn't thought of it like that before. Was Bryan not worthy of me? Is that why he failed the test?

I started to cry a little. At first, I blamed it on the wind, but soon it became impossible to pretend. 'Come on,' N said. 'There's no need to be like that.'

He hugged me, and it felt so good to have someone – anyone – actually care about me. I mean *really* care about me. To have someone see me and realise that, yes, I am hurting. I do matter.

I'm not invisible.

I felt better after that. Better than I have done in ages. By the time we started walking back, I could have sworn I had a smile on my face.

Once we got to the top of the dune path, N suggest I went on ahead. People might think it was odd, he said, seeing the two of us alone together. The last thing I needed was even more people talking about me behind my back.

He's right about that.

We said goodbye and promised to do it again some other time. He says if I ever feel down, I know where to turn.

Who to turn to.

I fold the phrase over in my mind. It's as if I was lost, and someone just gave me a compass.

I'm not completely alone. There's at least one person out there who cares.

15

Now

The silence echoed in the house after they left. A thing in and of itself; it crept into every corner, consuming the space that the arguments and laughter and chatter had occupied just hours earlier.

Izzy sank back into the sofa, feeling the groan of the ugly old leather, and let the quiet wash over her. She closed her eyes, listening carefully to the sounds beyond; the drone of a passing aircraft. A dog barking. The hum of the fridge. She exhaled: a long, slow, steady sigh.

She always needed an hour of downtime once the kids had gone back to Mike. *Time to decompress,* Jake said. As if the house, when they were here, was a pressure cooker. Or maybe it was just Izzy? With her constant fretting for everything to be just right and her certain knowledge that she was getting it wrong.

Parenting seemed to be a constant trial-and-error experiment, and in the early days, she'd had more than her fair share of mishaps. And now this. Just when she thought she had cracked it, the girl under the garden had sent her hurtling back to square one.

She'd noticed how Lucas couldn't bear to sit alone in the living room, so close to the scar of the old conservatory. He didn't need to voice his anxiety over what had been buried out there, just metres away, for Izzy to understand the reason for his apprehension. Betsy followed Izzy and Jake around the house, never wanting to be far from either of them for long. Last night, Hannah had suggested that Izzy left the girls' bedroom door ajar, allowing a slice of light from the landing to spill across the floor. She'd claimed it was for Betsy; Izzy knew it was because Hannah didn't want to sleep in total darkness.

Snakes and ladders. You made progress, inch by inch, square by square, but one unlucky roll of the dice could see you careening head-first back towards zero. So far, Izzy had no strategy to help them get through this. There was nothing she could say or do to shield them from the horror that had taken place right here, in the home where she had promised them they'd be happy.

At least Auntie Sue got it. She frequently reminded Izzy of those first few months after she had come home from Aberdeen, the three of them fumbling their way through the darkness of Izzy's mother's disappearance, forging a path based on nothing but instinct. Feeling the way, arms stretched out to one another across the heavy black night.

Upstairs, footprints traced a path over the landing. Jake knew to give her the space she needed, and Izzy loved him for that, as much as she loved him for a million other seemingly insignificant things. What more could her father have wanted for her than to find a man who knew what she needed before she even knew it herself?

She sighed, folding her hands on her chest, feeling her

heartbeat beneath her fingertips.

Kelly.

Izzy pictured the gangly blonde girl standing at the front of a group photo, wrapped comfortably in the embrace of a handsome boy, surrounded by her friends. Hard to reconcile with the image she pushed away, now, of an old football buried beneath their conservatory. The picture that haunted her nightmares.

It was odd, thought Izzy, how people's perspectives differ. How Bryan and Sam had lived through the same experience, but each emerged from it with a different version of events. She could see both sides, of course. The jealous best friend. The boy who was caught piggy-in-the-middle.

And Kelly? Where had all that left her?

What had prompted her to break up with Bryan? He'd suggested it came out of the blue. Was it that she began planning to run away as early as that October, and was worried he would try to stop her? Hold her back? A desperate bid to slash all ties to Seahouses before she fled?

'Hello, sleeping beauty.'

Izzy was roused by Jake's voice. She rubbed her eyes. When had she nodded off? He took a seat beside her.

'You looked so gorgeous that I couldn't bear to wake you. But I'm starting to get peckish. How do you fancy going for a curry over in Alnwick?'

She shrugged. 'I could do.' She hesitated, her brow knotting in a frown. He had that look on his face, a glint in his eye. Her lovely Jake, who she could read like a book. 'Just the two of us?'

'Actually, I invited Daniel. My mate at the pathologist's

office.'

Izzy nodded. *Jake's friend on the inside.* Might he be able to tell them more about Kelly? Suddenly, she was ravenous.

The day felt young as they set off in the Range Rover, the sun still perched high in the cloudless sky. Day trippers milled around the top of Harbour Bank, with Coxton's doing a roaring trade in ice cream and clusters of drinkers spilling out of The Ship, eager not to miss out on the last few hours of good weather.

Jake chatted as they pulled onto the trunk road, talking around anything except for the one topic on Izzy's mind. She did her best to stay tuned to the one-sided conversation. The firm was dealing with a complicated inheritance case; the Duchess of Northumberland was involved, somehow, although Izzy had missed the finer point of precisely how and it was now too late to ask. A charitable donation. Some old dear bequeathing everything to a *garden*.

Outside, the greenery flashed by; glimpses of the coastline visible over the open fields that dipped towards the sea.

She couldn't help but remember Amy's will. The last wishes of her sister had turned Izzy's life upside-down and left more questions than answers. But if all that hadn't happened, she would never have met Jake. Wouldn't have grown close to the children. Life had a funny way of throwing you off-course, sometimes, only to show you the right direction.

They found a parking spot right outside Korma Kameleon on Fenkel Street, the shadow of the castle looming over the cobbled roads of the ancient market town. Jake reached over, resting his hand on her lap, palm up. Izzy gratefully accepted it.

'Remember, Daniel is not supposed to talk about the case.' Jake checked the rear view mirror, as if someone might be outside the car, listening in. He shrugged. 'But the man's the most dreadful gossip. Just be polite and subtle.'

'Got it,' Izzy squeezed his fingers. 'Subtle.'

They made their way into the restaurant, her hand nestling in Jake's. It had been a while since they had gone out to dinner. *Out* didn't include the pub, of course, or Auntie Sue's kitchen, or fish and chips on the bench at the top of the harbour, watching the fishing boats trail home at the end of the day. Nowhere in Seahouses counted as *out*.

Izzy had thrown on an old Burberry silk blouse and a pair of three-inch metallic green heels with a matching clutch bag. Her prized possession, once upon a time. It had been so long since she had worn proper shoes that they pinched across her toes and nipped at the heel. As she felt the weight of the other diners' curious stares, she wished she had listened to Jake's advice to keep it casual.

Daniel was younger than them. His rust-coloured hair showed no trace of grey, and his eyes bore only the hint of the lines that would one day become entrenched.

He smiled warmly, clearly pleased to finally meet the elusive Mrs-Ridley-to-be. 'Jake tells me you're from around here?'

Izzy shrugged, feeling a familiar flush in her cheeks that blossomed any time someone asked about her formative years. 'I'm from Seahouses. Went to St Helen's.'

She used to tell anyone who would listen that she had left Northumberland when she was eighteen; that her high-flying career had taken her from London to Zurich and then Hong Kong; that she had only moved back here under difficult circumstances.

But she said none of this now. Izzy had learned that the true story made people uncomfortable.

'Nice, nice.' Daniel nodded, ducking his head with each word as if he was listening to music. 'I'm from the Borders, myself. Been down here ten years already.'

'Daniel and I have crossed paths on a few cases,' said Jake, although Izzy already knew this.

'Yeah. Small world around here. Not too many of us working on this side of the law.'

Izzy resisted pointing out that there weren't too many people working on the *other* side of the law, either: crime rates in Northumberland were among the lowest in the country, and even those were largely concentrated in the towns towards the south of the county. She had googled it, back in the days when she was still searching for any excuse not to stay.

'Still. It was a shock to... well, you know. At your place.' Daniel crunched a poppadum between crooked teeth, dusting his lips in crumbs. 'We don't get many cases like *that*. Poor girl.'

'Yes,' said Izzy. 'Poor girl.' They were interrupted by the waiter. 'Sparkling water for me, please.'

The phrase didn't come naturally to her, but after Amy's death, Izzy had been forced to recognise that her drinking was getting out of hand. It had been like standing on the precipice, staring into a terrifying abyss, only to have someone yank her back by the collar before she had plummeted in head-first.

Jake and Daniel negotiated their order with the waiter while she sat back, picking at a cuticle. Impatient to learn what the pathologist might be willing to let slip.

The conversation meandered through social niceties, a bit of banter between the boys. Such-and-such judge and you-know-who said you-know-what before they somehow came back to the subject of the body found in the garden of Jake and Izzy's new house.

'Such appalling luck. I really feel for you, having to deal with all that.' Daniel shrugged. 'Although quite an interesting case, from a professional perspective, I must say. Never seen one buried in salt.'

One. Izzy squirmed, but pushed her unease aside. 'I can't get my head around it. Why on earth would someone do that? Surely it would preserve the evidence?'

They were interrupted again by the arrival of their food.

'It would have preserved the soft tissue, at first. If she'd been dug up weeks or even months after burial, we might have been able to establish a cause of death. As it happens...' Daniel eyed the steaming curry in front of him. 'Well. Twenty years is a long time to be buried in the ground.'

'My aunt's partner suggested the salt might have been an attempt at keeping animals from digging.' Izzy spooned rice and curry onto their plates, grateful to have a reason not to look Daniel in the eye.

'It could be.' Daniel seemed to consider this. 'It would reduce the smell from the decomposition until the conservatory was built over it. Perhaps the killer was being pragmatic, thinking about the short-term and not worrying too much about what proof might be preserved down the line.'

'So, not much you can tell from a body that old?' Jake sounded far too interested, far too enthused. *So much for subtle.*

Thankfully, Daniel seemed to miss it. 'We've done reasonably well. There was enough of a sample left to work with.'

Izzy's stomach lurched. Suddenly, her appetite deserted her.

'There's a fractured tibia.' Daniel took a mouthful from a fork piled high. 'The shin. A stable fracture.'

'What does that mean? She fell?' Jake's voice was a whisper.

Daniel shook his head. 'More likely, she was struck by a blunt object with force. That's what the report will say. Although that couldn't have killed her.'

Izzy pushed a forkful of curry around her plate, tracing a bright yellow line through a neat pile of clean white rice. 'I just can't understand why someone would murder a seventeen-year-old. Who would do such a thing?'

Daniel chewed pensively, waiting until he had swallowed before speaking again. 'The father, probably.'

Jake shook his head. 'She was in foster care. I don't even think there was a father on the scene.'

'Not *her* father.' Daniel lowered his voice to a whisper. From across the table, Izzy could smell his breath. Hot, onions. 'The baby.'

'What baby?' The words snagged in her throat. 'Whose baby?'

'Didn't you hear?' Daniel was sweating now. The restaurant was warm, but Izzy suspected it was more likely from the heat of his food. He wiped the sheen from his brow on a starched white napkin. 'Sorry, but I assumed you knew. The grapevine is remarkably small, in Alnwick,' he said again, leaning towards her and issuing a conspiratorial wink.

She stared at him. 'What baby?'

'The victim's.' Daniel glanced from Jake to Izzy, his smile rapidly fading as he took in their shock. 'The victim was pregnant when she died.'

16

IZZY SET HER STEAMING MUG OF COFFEE DOWN ON THE TABLE and opened her sketchbook.

That morning, there had been a fleeting moment in which she had been able to visualise the renovation the way she intended to see it. *Hoped to see it.*

The vision had vanished as quickly as it had come to her. All but one piece. She clung on to that, now. One piece was better than nothing.

Interior design was like that, she had found. The same way that an outfit needed an accessory to make it work, or a dish needed seasoning. There was always some vital ingredient that a space required to make everything fit, and typically, it was elusive. To her, at least. The harder she concentrated on trying to identify it, the further it retreated into the shadows of her mind.

The kitchen floor. She'd been thinking white – contemporary, clean, calming. And then it came to her: black and white. So simple.

She frantically sketched now, clinging on to the vision like remnants of a dream at dawn, afraid that if she so much as blinked it might disappear again. Black. White. Together, a pattern. Contrasts, yet complements.

A bit like her and Jake.

She paused, her pencil hovering over the sketch pad. Jake with his sunny outlook and her with her... What was it? Tempestuousness? No, nothing like that. *Fluctuations.* Yes. A temperament that was unpredictable – even to her.

Some mornings she woke with a feeling of lightness and found joy in the simplest of pleasures, and on others, there was an indescribable ache in her heart and a bleak sadness that things would never be right, no matter how hard she tried. That was Izzy. Up and down, with neither rhyme nor reason. Never knowing what state she might find herself in.

Jake liked order, routine, predictability, control, and it manifested in the consistency of his moods. Izzy preferred spontaneity. A last-minute weekend away. Picking a restaurant as they walked down the street. Spur of the moment purchases, not caring if she might regret them later. She seemed to – *used to* – thrive on chaos.

But that was her *before*. Who was she now? Now that she was jointly responsible for three children, had a mortgage and her own business, and a wedding to plan?

She turned over a new page and allowed her hand to guide the pencil, a blank space before her mind's eye. Not drawing anything in particular but feeling the grind of the lead against the paper, her hand unleashing curves and loops, spirals and random patterns.

She cautiously studied the finished doodle. At first, there was nothing, no resemblance or recognition – just a scribble, whorls and coils, loops and... Then she saw it. Waves. Swell.

With the page closer now, just inches from her nose, she saw it even more clearly. *The sea.*

Was that her? Wild, changeable, capricious. Deep. Irrepressible. Yet strong, steady, reliable. Was it possible to be all those things at the same time?

Izzy shrugged it off, imploring herself to focus. She took a sip of coffee, now lukewarm.

Monochrome tiles were a big improvement to the concept. She swapped out the gold chrome fittings and added shiny black accents and pops of colour of the walls. *Yes.* It was beginning to make sense now. As a concept, as a space... And yet, something was still missing. She just couldn't see what.

She should have carried on, buoyed by her focus, but a new thought entered her mind.

Since last night, she'd been replaying Daniel's words on repeat. *"The victim was pregnant when she died."*

It caught her off-guard, breaking her concentration.

She couldn't tell Diana, not just yet. Jake had stressed repeatedly on the drive home that it was not only confidential information but risked jeopardising the entire investigation if anyone was to find out. If it drove a suspect underground.

No. She couldn't tell a soul, for now.

Besides, it wasn't a silver bullet, not necessarily. There had been huge advancements, according to Daniel, in the extraction of DNA from old samples, but post-mortem paternity testing wasn't a sure thing. Just because there was a pregnancy didn't mean there was enough material to locate a father.

Material. Izzy had almost thrown up in her mouth.

Not one, but two lives lost. Just *material*, now. Cells and matter.

And the baby's father wasn't necessarily the man who killed Kelly, Izzy reminded herself. Although there was a good chance he might know what – or who – she had been so afraid of.

She felt a new pang of regret for Kelly. Keeping such a secret.

Izzy scratched the inside of her elbow as an idea began to form.

Kelly had been forced to hide her pregnancy from her foster parents, but what about her biological family? Bryan had mentioned an aunt in Newcastle. Izzy wracked her brain for a name. Donna? Danielle? No, something more poetic. She closed her eyes, but nothing came.

Absent-mindedly, she clicked into Facebook. Where to begin with a search like this? Reynolds would be too common a name. Izzy chewed on her lip, biting so hard that she tasted the tang of blood. She scrolled through her feed.

It had been months since she had logged in, and now she remembered why. Seeing her old friends, her old haunts, her old life continuing without her, was a punch to the gut. She took a deep breath.

Mathilde and Chiara, out for dinner with her friend Adam. She felt a pang of guilt. *Adam.* Thankfully, he was much better at keeping in touch than she was. She clicked his name, craving news of her friend. He had a new squeeze, a lean American guy called Tim with impossibly white teeth. She browsed Adam's recent posts, clicking over photos from a trip to Bali. Pictures of the two of them surfing, brunching, strolling along the beach to catch the sunrise.

Dawn.

Kelly's aunt.

She clicked the search icon.

There were dozens of women named Dawn Reynolds, but only three lived in the North East. She studied each of them closely. Two were younger than Kelly and the other was probably old enough to be her grandmother. Perhaps Kelly's aunt had moved out of the area? She widened her search to include the whole country.

Izzy guessed the aunt would be at least twenty years older than her niece, making her late fifties or older. More than two dozen women fit that description. Izzy scrutinised the thumbnails of their profile pictures, looking for any family resemblance. She sighed. Reynolds might not even be her last name. It was like searching for a needle in a haystack.

Perhaps she should send all of them a message? She chewed at a worn fingernail. And say what? She could pretend she worked as a researcher for a television show, looking into the stories of people who'd vanished. But Kelly's family – this aunt, Dawn – seemingly couldn't have cared less when her niece disappeared. Besides, the police had already informed Kelly's relatives, according to DI Bell.

Izzy recalled the detective's words. *Handled.* And she had mentioned Tyneside. That meant there was some family still living in the region. Izzy searched again, using only the first name, but that was no help at all.

Why hadn't the family come to them?

God forbid it, but if anything happened to Hannah or Betsy or Lucas, Izzy would want answers. She would at least want to know where they had been, to see the place with her own eyes. It was odd that the influx of rubberneckers after the news broke hadn't included any of the Reynolds family. Or perhaps it had? Perhaps Dawn Reynolds had already been here? In their street. On their doorstep.

She jumped at the sound of the front door opening.

'Through here,' she called out to Jake.

It had taken a couple of weeks after moving in just to get

used to the *size* of the place. Izzy had found that they could move from room to room and still not bump into each other. Some days she wondered if Jake was playing hide and seek, deliberately staying quiet so that he could jump out and surprise her, just to make her smile.

It felt like a world away from her one-bedroom apartment in Hong Kong. Calling it a *bedroom* was appropriate – the double bed had taken up the entire room, after all. Izzy had been able to reach all four walls without moving from her mattress.

She had laughed when the realtor had first showed her around, boasting that the kitchen was large for an apartment of that size. It was, but only because it was on the edge of an open-plan living space and encroached on territory that technically could also be classed as a dining area. But she had loved it. As small and cramped as it was, that apartment – that life, in that city on the other side of the world – had been everything she'd ever wanted.

Now, they had all this *space*. She and Jake, rattling around this big old house. The two of them were not enough to fill it.

He had bought a bag of salad from Tesco Express, and Izzy set about chopping cherry tomatoes, cucumber, and walnuts. Last night, Jake had put two grilled chicken breasts in the fridge, ready to be sliced.

'That looks lovely,' he said as Izzy set two plates on the table, as if he hadn't done half the work.

'Busy morning?'

He shrugged. 'I can't stop thinking about Kelly, to tell you the truth.'

He didn't say it, but Izzy heard a familiar echo in his words. *The poor girl.*

She pushed the salad around her plate. 'I wonder what

happened to the aunt. Kelly was close to her, according to Bryan Shaw.'

'Who knows?' Jake mumbled.

He could see in Izzy's eyes that she was thinking about their three. That's how he thought of them. *Their three.* Did Izzy think of them as *theirs*, or just hers?

Jake had never imagined becoming a father himself. It was just one of those things he couldn't wrap his head around, no matter how hard he tried. Besides, it wasn't like his own father had taken much pleasure in parenthood.

His old man had seen Jake as an inconvenience; at best, a test of his patience. Someone to mould into his own form only to consistently find him lacking. Nothing Jake could say or do ever earned more than a begrudging nod of approval from Bancroft Ridley.

Jake hadn't even wanted to go into law. That had been another of the old man's ploys. When Bancroft died of a heart attack on a grouse shoot, Jake had imagined he'd finally be free of his father's unreasonable demands. It came as a shock to learn that his inheritance was tied to the condition that he took over the family's stake in the practice.

His fate; signed, sealed, and notarised.

He still remembered the day Izzy walked into his office. She had been mesmerising. Beautiful, undoubtedly, but there was something more. Some unearthly quality that shone from within, despite her obvious distress. Jake had literally fallen head over heels; tripping over a ridge in the carpet where water damage had stretched the rug and landing at Izzy's feet. The fall had almost been worth the humiliation, just to see her smile.

It was her strength. It was almost magnetic, pulling him

towards her. Even at her weakest point, within touching distance of rock bottom, Izzy had been a force to contend with. The police had been at a loss over Amy's death and were ready to write it off as an accident. But Izzy had fought for her sister, trusting her instinct that the truth was more complicated and more horrible than any of them had imagined. And she had fought for him, too. Even when he had tried to push her away – at least, to give her the distance he thought she needed – she had clawed her way back. No one could tell Izzy what was good for her.

She would fight for those children, if it ever came to it. He could see how this new upset was troubling them, and he could see how desperately she wanted to shield them from the trauma. She would do anything to protect the kids. Jake almost envied them, having someone like their Auntie Izzy in their corner. A lioness.

If only Kelly had someone like that, too.

'There must be some way.' Izzy swirled a strand of hair around her index finger, a habit whenever she was distracted.

'Some way of what?'

'Of finding her. The aunt. Getting in touch.'

Jake sighed. He hated to see her like this: her thoughts consumed, her energy sapped. He could see the signs of an obsession forming and recognised a familiar determination in the crease of her brow. A resolve to find out what, who, how.

But more than that, Jake hated how *sad* the whole thing made her. He could see it now in the hollows below her eyes, the way the corners of her beautiful mouth were down-turned. The way she woke in the middle of the night, panting to catch her breath.

She pierced a tomato with her fork. 'Are you going back to the office this afternoon?'

He ground black pepper onto his salad – anything to avoid Izzy's gaze. Those beautiful sea-coloured eyes, shades of blue and green, flecked with gold.

'Actually, I thought I'd work from home. Lots of reading to catch up on.'

He glanced nervously at his briefcase. He couldn't tell Izzy, just yet, what nature of reading material was best caught up on outside the office, away from prying eyes. Not until he knew for certain that the answer he was looking for was in there. 'Why don't you go out for a run? Lovely day for it.'

She looked out into the garden, the light from the French doors illuminating her face in profile. Staring at the scar of earth where the conservatory had stood.

'Yeah. Maybe.' She gave an indifferent shrug.

'Go on. Nothing happening here that can't wait.'

Izzy sighed. 'You're right. As always.'

She stood, leaning over to kiss him, her lips warm on his. He eyed his briefcase again, wondering what answers lay within.

17

THERE HAD BEEN MORE CUTS TO PUBLIC SPENDING THIS YEAR.

For Northumbria Police, that meant all resources were directed to fighting serious crime and deploying officers in the urban areas in the south of the constabulary. Performance was measured not only by success, but how much it cost to achieve it. The villages and rural areas by the coast could go weeks without seeing a bobby on the beat. Most people didn't notice it, but Jake understood the consequences it could have for Kelly Reynolds.

He'd caught up with Cameron Smith on Friday. Just a quiet pint in the Red Lion. In their grammar school days, Cameron had taken pity on the skinny boy who was always picked last for rugby and was forced to sit at the front of their bus home to Corbridge. Jake had returned this favour of friendship by helping Cameron with his homework from time to time.

Their paths had crossed again after university when Cameron – then a digital forensics investigator with Northumbria Police – was assigned to a case of white collar fraud which Jake had defended. Jake had lost, but they'd gone for a beer together and stayed in touch afterwards. It was useful for someone in his position to have friends in the force, and Cameron saw the value of a pal on first-name terms with most of the barristers and judges on the county circuit.

The Red Lion had been packed with a Friday lunch crowd. Jake arrived five minutes late and was glad to see his old friend had already managed to bag a table.

Cameron had bemoaned his shrivelling budget, and the rumoured layoffs that would come later in the year. It wasn't the fault of the new Commissioner, he said with a shrug. Just the way things were, forcing them to chase results. Cases with smaller chances of success were being side-lined as detectives focused on the quick wins and bigger fish.

That's when Jake knew that the odds of finding Kelly's killer were diminishing. It was as if a stone had been dropped in a lake, plummeting straight to the bottom.

'Any news on your girl under the patio?' Cameron sipped his pint and eyed Jake over the rim of his glass.

'Not *my* girl and not a patio. She was under the conservatory.' He shuddered, a sudden chill catching him off-guard. 'Nothing yet from the lads in the lab?'

Cameron lowered his voice, glancing at the drinkers on the next table. 'They're working on it, but this is hardly the top priority. The likelihood of finding evidence on a twenty-year-old body buried in those conditions is slim to nowt. I wouldn't count on forensics.' He shrugged. 'It'll need some good old-fashioned detective work to crack this one. A *lot* of it.'

Yes, thought Jake. And even if they interviewed everyone who knew Kelly, presumably they would end up in the same circle in which Izzy now found herself. A trail whose conclusion led right back to the beginning.

He had walked back to his office from the pub deep in thought. Wondering how to move this forward. He slung his jacket over his shoulder, enjoying the warmth of the sun through the thin cotton of his shirt. Market Street was bustling with shoppers and the pubs were already busy, even though the clock above the town hall had not yet struck two o'clock.

Jake would be the last to suggest that the police weren't taking this seriously enough. No, it wasn't that – just that the mountain in front of them was almost insurmountable. Any fool could see it.

There had been press coverage; that always helped, although without new news on the case, the media reports had dried to a trickle. And it was hardly as if there was a grieving family braying on the Commissioner's door, demanding justice.

Jake was already worried the police would perform nothing more than a perfunctory investigation. Interview Kelly's contacts and pray for some success. If nothing came through, the case would be allowed to quietly gather dust until there was a fresh lead.

It wasn't good enough.

The injustice of it gnawed at him, a little fist in his side. If Kelly had been from a middle-class family and a good home... Well. There would have been an outcry when she had gone missing in the first place.

The whole system – the system he was part of – had let her down.

He would have to do some detective work of his own.

There was a vacant bench in a shaded corner of Market Place and Jake sat, glad to take the weight off his feet and trying to ignore the nagging feeling that he was missing the bloody obvious.

Izzy had been quite convinced that the previous owners weren't involved. But it had been their back garden, after all. He needed to look into the construction of the conservatory. It was too small to have required planning permission, but the Choudhurys would have needed a building regulation certificate. The council would have copies in the archive.

Always follow the paper trail.

He glanced at his watch and hoped that Mirna, the surly assistant in the council planning department, might be persuaded to fast-track this request. He fired off an email from his iPhone.

And what about Kelly? All they had was her name and age and the fact that she had been in foster care. There would be more documents somewhere. You just had to know where to look.

Jake had hurried back to his office that Friday afternoon with a spring in his step.

It had been a pleasant surprise when Mirna came through for him. Earlier that morning, a courier had delivered a string-tied manila folder to the offices of Moore, Moore & Ridley, the cover adorned with Mirna's distinctive handwriting. Presumably she had heard about the body under his new house and taken uncharacteristic pity on Jake.

The application and approval certificate were unlikely to tell them much, other than that the builders had stuck to code, but he would send Mirna flowers to thank her.

Jake was far more nervous about a second document that arrived an hour later by fax. He had shoved it into the manila envelope, his hand trembling, and locked the folder inside his briefcase. He hoped it was worth the risk.

From his home office, he listened. The house was quiet. Izzy would be gone for an hour, tops. Jake had to work fast.

He started with the building regs application. They were still using paper forms back then, although everything had moved online now. It had been filled by Rafa Choudhury, who provided the name and address of a builder and estimated dates for the work. The form had been filed in November 2002 – five months before Kelly went missing. The application had been approved, and a certificate concluded the work had been completed in early April.

Jake tried to fight against the sick feeling in his stomach and keep a clinical, focused approach, thinking this through logically.

If Rafa had planned the conservatory to cover up a burial site, that was one hell of a premeditation. Of course, it didn't mean he hadn't seized the opportunity when it eventually arose.

Jake read everything again, carefully, trying to quiet the voice in his head that told him he was missing something, but there was nothing out of the ordinary.

He took a deep breath as he retrieved the final document in his dossier.

On Friday afternoon, he had called Guy Hendrick, an old chum from law school. An intolerable bore at the best of times, and sadly, the only person that might be able to help Jake out.

'Ridders, long time no see!'

Jake cringed at hearing his old nickname. 'Long time indeed, old boy. How's things?' He could hear the plummy tones that crept back into his accent as if by instinct. The words felt foreign, wooden in his mouth.

'Same, same. A few more pounds on the scale and a few more grey hairs.' Guy guffawed at his own joke. 'Melanie's badgering me about going on some ghastly cruise with her parents, as if anyone in their right mind might consider that a relaxing holiday. And the girls are constantly on the fleece. What can I say, they learned the dark art from their mother! You did the right thing, Ridders, choosing the bachelor life. You're the envy of us all.'

'Actually, I met someone.' Jake's voice dipped. 'We're getting married.'

He would have liked to put a time frame on this, but so far, Izzy was dodging all conversations on that subject. Jake had imagined she would be thrilled to have a wedding to organise. Instead, she made only occasional mutterings about keeping things low-key. His heart sank each time, his worry that she might be having second thoughts bubbling to the surface. And what would happen now? Now that their dream home had turned into a nightmare?

'Splendid news, my friend. Please tell me there's a stag do in the works?'

'When there is, you'll be the first to know,' Jake lied, imagining he could think of few things more torturous than a night out with Guy Hendrick. He changed tack. 'I'm actually calling about a somewhat delicate matter.'

He heard the creak of wood as Guy sat up straighter in his chair.

'Fire away, old boy. You're familiar with my fondness for delicates.'

'I'm after some court records. A custody hearing involving a minor—'

'Come off it, Ridders.' Guy sounded serious now. 'You know I'm a straight shooter. No funny business, and with good reason.'

'No, no, nothing dodgy.' Jake wondered where to begin. 'That girl, the body they found. In Seahouses.'

'Yes...?'

He could hear Guy's breath in his ear. 'It was our house. The place I just bought with my fiancé.'

'Dear god.'

''Fraid so. The victim was in care. I want to know if there are any remaining relatives.'

'The police will find anyone and inform them. Jake, those files would be sealed, you know that. If there's a public interest case for them to be opened, then make it through the proper channels.'

Jake squeezed his eyes closed and pinched the bridge of his nose. 'I'd rather like to offer my personal condolences.'

A beat. Jake heard Guy shuffling something on his desk.

'Level up with me here, Ridley. What's really going on?'

Jake sighed. 'I'm just... *concerned* about the way the police are handling things, that's all.'

He didn't want to say any more. The less Guy knew, the better. *Those lines are becoming blurred again.*

'And this isn't for some other case you're working? Or the press?'

'I just want a name, nothing more. There would have been a custody order by the council, but who was looking after the girl before they took her into care? No details of the hearing, and I solemnly swear it will never get back to you.'

'You always were a piece of work, Ridders.'

With that, Guy had hung up, leaving Jake wondering if he might ever hear from him again.

He had almost given up hope by the time he'd received a text that morning from Guy, telling him to wait by the fax machine; a more secure, less traceable method of communication. Jake had stood there as the machine whirred to life, open-mouthed when he saw that it was forty-three pages long. He'd kicked the door closed so that his secretary wouldn't disturb him, counting the sheets of paper as the machine spat them out.

Guy had more than delivered – he'd sent the entire bloody file. There was a scrawled note on the first page: *destroy after reading.*

In the quiet of his home office, Jake skimmed through to the details of the parties. Newcastle City Council versus Dawn Reynolds. An address in Scotswood. He jotted it in his notepad.

There was a noise from downstairs.

Izzy.

He scooped the custody papers up with one hand, the other prising open a drawer. The desk had been his old man's and Jake didn't know why he was still holding on to it after all these years – two of the locks were broken and the drawers had a tendency to stick. There were footsteps coming up the stairs now. He shoved the papers into the open drawer and began the effort of closing the damned thing; the exertion causing his face to sheen. *Now where was the blasted key?*

Izzy walked into the room just as he locked the desk drawer and slipped the iron key into his pocket.

He turned to smile at her, convinced his face would give him away. He didn't see the page at his elbow, didn't have time to catch the single sheet as he accidentally brushed it from the desk.

They both watched as it rocked in a fall, ebbing a convoluted path to the ground, where it landed at Izzy's feet.

'What's this?' She bent to retrieve it. Jake's heart fluttered. He said nothing.

Izzy frowned, scanning the page. 'Building regulations? The conservatory?'

Jake licked his top lip and slowly exhaled. 'Yes, they're

public record. Just thought I'd request a copy, see if anything was amiss...'

She paled. 'Shaw's Services?'

'Yes, yes,' Jake was stuttering; the key burning against the cotton lining of his pocket. 'I imagine it's the building firm that put the conservatory up.'

'Shaw. As in Bryan Shaw? It's got to be. That's Kelly's ex-boyfriend.'

And then Jake saw what he had been missing.

18

'BRYAN SHAW?'

'Yes.' Izzy raked a hand through her hair, her eyes still on the page in her hands. 'The boy Kelly dated. She broke up with him and he started seeing her best friend. Married her, in fact.'

'And he has a builder's firm?'

'Yes. Shaw's Services.'

It was all falling into place now. Bryan had lied to them. And Sam?

Jake frowned; confusion etched on his brow. 'I thought he was her age? Wasn't he still at school when she disappeared? I can't imagine he would have been working for a building firm...'

'I don't know!' Izzy immediately regretted her outburst. She forced herself to soften. Concentrate. 'I'm still thinking this through.'

Jake cupped a hand beneath her elbow. 'Sorry. It's just that it doesn't make a lot of sense.'

They exchanged a glance, and Izzy saw the fear in Jake's beautiful brown eyes.

'Unless...' She pressed a hand to her mouth, pursing her lips against her knuckle. 'It's a family business. It says so, right there in big letters on his van. Back then, his father would have been running it.'

'So, what's the theory here? He found out his ex-girlfriend was pregnant by her new man, killed her in jealousy, and buried her at one of his father's building sites?'

Izzy swallowed, a knot of bile rising in her throat. 'I suppose his father might have helped him to get rid of the body.'

There was something else, though; she could feel it in the air, a static charge of energy. Impulse. Intuition. What else had Bryan lied about?

'Maybe they didn't break up.' She spoke the words slowly, carefully measuring each one, weighing up the ideas as they occurred to her. 'Maybe he was still seeing Kelly – or he'd gone back to her – and was two-timing her with Sam. Maybe he was the father.'

'Or he was seeing Sam behind Kelly's back,' Jake added.

'Whatever it was, he didn't want Kelly to be pregnant. And he didn't want anyone to find out.'

Izzy thought of Bryan Shaw, that muscular surfer's body and blonde hair that had been bleached by the sun. He'd seemed like such a nice guy. A family man. Honest, even kind, perhaps. She remembered how he had painted himself as the wronged party. How he had gone on to live a happy life with a wife and two adoring children in a neat three-bed semi, whereas Kelly...

God, she had been so stupid to believe him. She chewed at a nail, already bitten down to the quick.

'I need to call Diana.'

Diana picked up on the third ring, whispering a breathless hello.

'We've found something. About Bryan Shaw.' Izzy leaned back against the bare wall of her hallway and stared at the wooden floor. They would sand and re-varnish this floor, eventually, but that was a long way off and she wasn't sure how much more she could take of it until then.

There was a pause before Diana spoke again. 'Why don't you come over and tell me all about it?'

Izzy hadn't showered yet after her run; she could smell the salt of her sweat on her skin. She was supposed to see Auntie Sue and Emily. A planned afternoon out in Bamburgh for tea at the Copper Kettle, a treat they indulged in once a month.

'I'll be there in an hour,' she said, and put the phone down.

Diana tried to avoid looking at the clock in her kitchen. *A watched pot never boils.*

Instead, she paced about the house, trying to find a task with which to distract herself while waiting. The photographs on the mantelpiece were coated in a grey film. She took out the feather duster and ran it over each one in turn.

At an old picture of her and Lionel, she paused. One of her favourites. Oh, how young they had been. How impossibly long life had seemed from that vantagepoint. Diana envied the young lady in the photograph, her whole life stretched out in front of her. The many wonderful adventures that awaited.

It was taken at a party in London, some newspaper awards ceremony to which they had been thrilled just to be invited. The late sixties, Diana guessed. Everyone dressed up in their finest.

She had borrowed a pair of shoes from Betty Clarke, the perfect shade of rose to match the bridesmaid's dress she had dyed. Her hair was teased into a modest beehive – the hairstyle had been all the rage. She'd even done a practice session the week before with Betty, who was quite the expert in all things glamour. They had followed a step-by-step guide from *Mademoiselle* magazine.

Diana had been blessed with beautiful hair. Lionel always said so. Thick, brown, and naturally wavy. Even that felt like a distant memory.

It had been a terrible time after his diagnosis. Lionel was consumed by anxiety and guilt at the prospect of leaving her behind, and Diana had faced her darkest fear; that she might be forced to grow old without him.

She sighed, sinking into her husband's leather armchair. The best seat in the house, according to Lionel, who used to retire there after dinner with his pipe and the perfect view of the harbour. She watched the boats nudging one another, bobbing on the gentle sway of the waves.

After an eternity, there was a knock at the door. In her eagerness to get it, she rose just a little too quickly and was forced to pause for a moment until the dark clouds at the edge of her vision receded. Even standing up was an effort these days.

Izzy's hair was still damp, and she hadn't bothered with make-up. Diana hoped her friend was taking care of herself.

She set about making the tea, waiting for Izzy to offer to take over the chore. The poor girl clearly had a lot on her mind, and in Diana's experience, something hot and sugary was the best way to draw someone out.

'Do you need some help?' Izzy asked at long last.

Diana sank into a seat at the table. 'That would be splendid, dear.'

Oh, how she missed Amy. Delightful Amy Saunders, with her constant smile and can-do attitude. Diana sniffed back the urge to cry, which often befell her when she remembered her friend.

'Use the green cups, dear. The ones that match the pot.'

Amy had never needed direction.

Izzy set the tea on the table and cradled her cup in her hand, avoiding Diana's eyes. Diana slowly stirred in her sugar. She knew the virtue of patience.

'There was some news from the pathologist. It's not great, I'm afraid.'

Izzy was biting her lip, which gave Diana the sense that it was possibly the most dreadful news, and she did wish the woman would spit it out. Instead, she waited.

'Kelly was pregnant when she was killed.'

There was a whoosh of breath, and Diana wasn't sure if it came from Izzy or herself. She sensed, rather than felt, her pulse quicken.

Was that why Kelly had been so depressed? And then another question formed quickly after the first: who? Who had done that to her? Diana felt a stab of regret, once more, for having failed the girl.

Izzy looked her in the eye and spoke a little more slowly than strictly necessary, as if to labour the gravity of her point. 'But we mustn't tell anyone. Absolutely no one; and I mean it, Diana. If whoever did this finds out that there could be evidence linking him to Kelly, he might flee.'

Diana nodded slowly, still processing this terrible news. *Who had done that to her?* And had he killed Kelly? Logic dictated that the father of Kelly's unborn baby was the most likely suspect for her murder, but that wasn't the only possibility.

'And who was the father? This mystery older man,

perhaps?' She noticed Izzy flinch and knew that there was more to come.

'Jake checked the records from when the conservatory was built. It was Shaw's.'

'Ah. That, my dear, could be rather problematic.'

Izzy nodded. 'I'm wondering if Bryan was telling the truth about breaking up with her. And about... how close they were. It's too much of a coincidence.'

'I never put much store in coincidences.' Diana took a sip of tea, craving the sugar. She vaguely knew the Shaws; everyone in Seahouses did. And that meant that, technically, she had known Bryan Shaw all his life. Then again, how well did one really know one's neighbours? Someone out there had hurt Kelly.

'So you're assuming what, exactly? That Bryan was responsible for Kelly's condition and he killed her, then used one of the Shaw's construction projects to conceal her body?'

'Something like that...' Izzy mumbled. 'I'm even wondering if Bryan's father might have been involved. It would take a lot of effort to move someone alone.'

'What about the DNA? A simple test should prove who the father was. Are the police making headway?'

'It's not so straightforward, apparently. The pathologist is still working on extracting a sample. The body... Kelly...' Izzy seemed to be searching for the right words. 'Twenty years is a long time. They need a good sample to create a profile for a paternity test.'

'But once they have the profile, they can run tests on potential suspects, see if there's a match. They could test every man in the village.'

'They could test Bryan. Jake reckons the fact that he was her boyfriend and that his father built the conservatory would be enough to get a warrant. As for them testing everyone, that's unlikely, apparently. Not for a crime committed so long ago. They'll only test someone where there's a reasonable cause for suspicion.'

'Do they know yet?' Diana eyed her friend cautiously, an idea forming. 'Do the police know who built the conservatory?'

'No. Not yet. Unless they did the same search as Jake.' Izzy appeared to consider this for the first time. 'Which I'm sure they'll do, if they haven't already.'

'Well, dear. That means there's no need for us to inform them. As you say, they'll get there in their own time. And I'm quite certain that delightful lady detective wouldn't appreciate our help.'

'Surely, we should tell them? Just in case?'

Diana fingered the rim of her cup. Such a pretty set. A gift from Lionel after a trip to France. What would he counsel her to do in this situation? She longed to ask him. Lionel had always given the best advice.

Her heart sank again for Kelly. Such a tragic waste of life. And such terrible luck.

Because it came down to poor luck, sometimes. Diana was no fool – she knew what young people got up to these days. Kelly certainly wouldn't have been the only girl from St Helen's to find herself in trouble. And Diana could think of several young ladies who had evaded similar scandals through nothing short of sheer bloody good fortune.

But the father of Kelly's child may not have been the same person who killed her. Even if her ex-boyfriend's father had been the one to build the conservatory.

She needed time to think this though, but her instinct, she had learned, was powerful. It paid to heed it.

'What if Bryan wasn't the father? If the police go in there

with guns blazing and run DNA tests on him, everyone in the village will find out about the pregnancy. The real killer could flee.'

Izzy frowned but said nothing.

Diana pressed on. 'What we need, my dear, is to buy time. The heat is on now. People will start remembering and start talking. We must give the police the space to do their work. Meanwhile, we can give them some help behind the scenes.'

'Give them some help... how?'

Diana smiled for the first time since their discussion began. 'I've had a brilliant idea.'

19

Izzy wiped away the mist on the mirror and considered her reflection.

She'd taken advantage of the fair weather over the past couple of weeks and had the faintest hint of a tan. As much of a tan as one might hope to get in Northumberland, at least.

It had been more than two years since she'd had a proper holiday. She closed her eyes and allowed her mind to wander, her imagination and the heat of the bathroom transporting her somewhere hot, somewhere she could swim in the sea without getting hypothermia. Somewhere the sun would warm the sand until it was too hot to walk on. A hotel with waiter service by the pool and daily fruit plates in the room and a turndown service before bed. Where the concierge carried your luggage everywhere and the bartender knew how to make a wicked martini.

That felt like a parallel universe.

She sighed, opening her eyes to the reality in front of her. The threaded web of creases at the edges of her eyes was deeper than ever, and she struggled to even remember the last time she'd had Botox.

Back in Hong Kong, she'd had a standing appointment at the hairdressers. Now her roots were showing, mousy-brown tips betraying her true colour to the world. As much as she wanted to, Izzy found she barely cared.

She looked good for her age, though. Thank god for all those *preventative* treatments she'd done while she'd still had the chance. Her fortieth birthday had slid by at the beginning of lockdown, celebrated with a modest takeaway for two, a glass of champagne, and a consolatory FaceTime with the kids. Although she regretted not marking the milestone in style, she liked that most people might struggle to guess how old she was.

She massaged a serum into her skin, her fingertips raking in slow, circular movements across her cheeks, just as the assistant had demonstrated at the beauty counter in some far-away brightly-lit department store. The bottle was almost empty, and she would have to go online to order another. Nowhere around here sold it.

The picture came to her again. *Her wedding day.* She held the image, playing with various elements of the photograph in her mind's eye. No matter how many times she did this, something was always off. Never quite right. A church? Not St Cuthbert's. A registry office, perhaps. A long white dress? She squirmed at how ridiculous she looked, and even the Izzy of her vision blushed, uncomfortable beneath layers of silk and boning, lace and stares. Something shorter? More discreet, low-key. Tailored? A suit?

She mentally erased the veil, the bouquet of flowers, the snowfall of confetti dusting the ground at her feet. All that remained was her and Jake, standing hand-in-hand.

Was she over-thinking this whole thing?

Anyway, they had to finish the house first. The police had written to confirm that their garden was officially theirs again, and the builders were coming next week to begin work on the orangery. She should get Finn back over to make a start on the kitchen.

Things, things, things. Tasks. Important tasks. And yet, despite everything she needed to do, Izzy had agreed to *this.*

Diana's plan was madness, but somehow, Izzy had found herself saying yes. She was indulging a friend, a lonely old lady with too much time on her hands. At least, that's what she kept telling herself.

Again, Izzy thought of Bryan Shaw. As hard as she tried to keep an open mind, it all seemed to be far too much of a coincidence.

Bryan was a fit man. Had he been strong enough as a youth to carry Kelly to her shallow grave? Or had he lured her there? Called her to meet at the back of the gardens for crisis talks about the pregnancy? Waited for her, out there, in the darkness?

Did Bryan's father help him dispose of the body? And what about Sam? She had betrayed Kelly once. Had she committed the ultimate act of treachery against her friend?

Izzy brushed her teeth excessively hard; there was blood in the sink when she spat.

The heatwave was set to continue for another week, according to reports. She had to laugh at *heatwave* – the mercury was barely nudging twenty-nine degrees. There was even talk of a hosepipe ban if it went on much longer.

Incredible, Izzy thought, that a nation obsessed with the weather and with such a variable climate could be so ill-prepared for even the slightest fluctuations. Too hot or too cold, too windy, the wrong kind of leaves on the track... Something always seemed to go wrong.

For now, it meant that the hotels and B&Bs were fully booked, the good weather creating an impossible optimism among tourists eager for a staycation after the heartbreak of the previous season's lockdown. The owners of the local businesses were happy, at least.

She slipped on a pair of shorts and a white linen shirt, which she rolled up to the elbows. Diana had warned her to look inconspicuous. At least the weather helped in that regard, Izzy thought, as she dug out Jake's old baseball cap and rummaged in her handbag for her sunglasses.

There were already crowds milling around Harbour Bank. Izzy circumvented the queue that had formed outside Coxton's and headed up Main Street, stepping into the road to avoid the occasional knot of tourists who took up the entire width of the narrow pavement.

Her reconnaissance mission yesterday had not taken long. She had driven around the village, her eyes scanning the side streets for the distinctive van.

Bryan Shaw had been working down at Slate Hall, fixing the roofing of the riding school stables. Another casualty of the storm that had hastened the demise of their conservatory, no doubt.

She walked along South Lane, the breeze from the open fields carrying the scent of wildflowers, animals, the sea. Bryan was there again today, his van parked halfway down the single-lane road, dipped at an awkward angle on the grass verge.

Izzy hesitated, wondering what to do. The lane was empty; if he came back to the van, he would see her. She turned and headed back the way she had come from, resolving to wait for him on the main road.

A single-storey building stood directly opposite the entrance to the lane. She crossed the street and leaned against the far side, hidden from view of the road. The bricks were rough, scratching against her skin through the thin fabric of her shirt.

She wished she smoked or had some habit to indulge – anything that might make an onlooker less suspicious. She kept her head down, her gaze fixed on her trainers, trying to avoid potential eye contact with anyone who might chance a glance in her direction, conscious that she looked shifty. A butterfly danced by, carried by the gentle breeze. From behind the houses, a lawnmower droned.

Thankfully, it wasn't a long wait. She heard the sliding door of the van in the distance and panicked that Bryan could be travelling by road.

Not part of the plan.

She leaned out from behind the corner of her hiding place and watched the junction, her heart thundering in anticipation.

She need not have worried. Bryan emerged on foot at the top of the lane, his muscular arms tanned, squinting in the sunshine. He held a hand to his eyes, glancing left and right as if deciding which way to go before he turned down Main Street towards the centre of the village.

Izzy stepped out and walked back to the road with slow, measured steps. She felt stupid. That was the word for it. *Absurd.*

Diana had been surprisingly full of confident advice on how to follow someone without being spotted. *Stay on the opposite side of the street. Keep a safe distance. Blend in with the crowds. Never lose sight of the target.*

Izzy wanted to laugh now. Tonight, she would tell Jake

about her silly little adventure and they would have a good giggle over dinner.

Perhaps.

Or perhaps he wouldn't see the funny side of this at all.

There were few people about at this end of the village and at this time of day; certainly, no crowds to blend in with. In fact, there was nowhere to hide. Izzy's heart began to hammer again, sweat forming on her brow, under her arms, in the small of her back. Willing Bryan not to glance over his shoulder and if he did, not to recognise her.

He passed the primary school, and she followed, keeping her head down. Wondering where, exactly, he was going, and if this stupid plan had any logic to it whatsoever. *Why on earth had she agreed to do this?*

He was even broader than she had remembered from just a few days ago. Wide shoulders, powerful arms.

How had he done it? Had he taken a weapon? Or had he used his bare hands? Had he spared a thought for his unborn child as he had shovelled soil over its mother's corpse, hidden there in the dark?

Her mind flitted to Hannah, of all people. They'd had *the talk*, but perhaps it was time for a refresher. A gentle reminder of the perils of the world, how one little mistake can send everything crashing down. At least Hannah knew that if she ever found herself in any kind of difficult situation, her aunt would be there for her. Who had been there for Kelly?

Eventually they reached the centre of the village and she picked up her pace, shortening the gap between her and Bryan. Her eyes never once leaving him as he wound through the clusters of people.

He greeted the occasional passer-by with a wave, an inaudible greeting here and there, but didn't stop to chat.

She stayed close behind him; as close as she dared, an invisible thread holding her to him, pulling her forward.

Finally, he arrived at his destination.

The café was busy, and Bryan joined the back of a line. A customer came out; there was the tinkle of the bell above the door and the bright sound of chatter from within. Izzy pretended to read the chalkboard menu in the window, watching him. *Cheese savoury. Tuna melt. Kipper pate.*

She couldn't have eaten a thing, even if she'd wanted to.

It was Bryan's turn now. Her stomach lurched as he stepped up to the counter. Their entire stupid plan hinged on this order. Diana Wheeler and her bloody detective games...

They should have just gone to the police, told them the Shaws built the conservatory. Izzy could see that now. *But she was so close.* She held her nerve. Held on to that gossamer-thin thread.

She couldn't see his face, so she watched the woman serving him. A brunette, young. A girl more than a woman; most likely working a summer job. The girl smiled and offered a flirtatious giggle, her little hat perched on her head at a jaunty angle.

Izzy had read an article on DNA testing last night. A secret code buried within our bodies, unique to each of us. Almost impossible not to leave a trace of yourself behind. She had angled her phone away so that Jake wouldn't see what she was reading.

The server was taking cash from Bryan, handing him his change.

Izzy shuffled to one side, pushing her sunglasses higher up her nose. Praying that her disguise, if you could call it that, would work.

Bryan came out of the café, blinking in the bright

sunlight. A sandwich in one hand, wrapped in brown paper. And in the other, a cup of coffee. Izzy sighed with relief.

There was a crowd, now, milling at the top of Harbour Bank. A swarm of people, the sunshine drawing them out. Thick enough to lose him.

She stayed as close as she dared, never more than a few feet away. So close that she could reach out and touch him, if she wanted to. Following that unmistakeable crop of blond hair as he bobbed and weaved through the crowd towards the harbour.

There were no seats – Bryan seemed to have noticed this before she did. He paused for a moment, scanning the harbour, looking to see if there was an empty bench further down. Satisfied there were none, he turned to walk back the way he'd just come from, bringing him face to face with Izzy.

She held her breath; the air snagging in her throat.

But he looked right through her. He cast his eyes over Main Street, squinting against the sun.

He was weighing up his options, evidently keen to eat his lunch and enjoy his coffee before it got cold. Blood thundered in Izzy's ears as she exhaled, long and slow.

Bryan seemed to give up. He shrugged, plonking himself down on the low wall of a flowerbed outside The Ship.

Izzy followed the crowd, allowing herself to be washed along by the tide of people heading in the direction of the water's edge. Only once she had reached the bottom of the bank did she risk a glance back in Bryan's direction. He took the last bite from his sandwich and shoved the screwball of paper wrapping into the pocket of his jeans.

She tried not to panic. That wasn't what she was here for.

He stood, now, and took a sip of coffee. From the angle

of his head and the cup, Izzy could see that it was almost empty.

A man walked by with two dogs who strained at the lead, dragging their master along in their wake. She fell into step behind the man, her eyes still fixed on Bryan.

At the roundabout, Bryan hesitated, checking his watch. Two coaches were queued outside the entrance to the carpark, backing up the traffic down St Aiden's Road. He drained the rest of his coffee.

The rubbish bin was already full. Bryan thew a cursory glance around then wedged his cup into the opening.

Izzy waited a beat, her eyes never leaving the cup. She vaguely registered Bryan in the periphery of her vision as he crossed the road, heading back up Main Street in the direction of Slate Hall. She darted towards the bin, fingering the Ziplock freezer bag in the pocket of her shorts.

A squadron of wasps was patrolling. Already, Izzy could smell the remnants of discarded fish and chips, the stench of stale grease and the saccharine of curdled ice cream and beneath it all, a bitter reek. She quickly checked that nobody was watching her too closely and freed Bryan's cup from its place atop the mound of litter.

Her heart sounded a percussion as she slipped his discarded cup into the cellophane bag, a chorus in her chest that continued for the duration of the walk home.

20

The sick feeling was still there as Izzy let herself into the house, a knot that sat high in her throat.

From upstairs, from the makeshift office Jake had created in one of the bedrooms, she heard him talking on the phone. She ran the cold tap, filling a glass, and noticed that her hand was still shaking as she took a sip.

The anxiety was beginning to subside, and in its place, a feeling of relief. They had Bryan's DNA. Now it would be a simple case of testing whatever remained of him on the cup and matching it to the sample the pathologist had been able to recover from Kelly's remains. If the police could prove he was the father of Kelly's unborn child, that nudged him to the very top of the list of suspects. If not, at least it would rule him out.

Perhaps she should put the cup in the fridge. She would google it.

She made a coffee, her hand steady, now, and took it out to the garden. A bird chirped from the tree, but there was no sign of the pigeon. Izzy sipped, forcing herself to focus.

Bryan might well have been helping his dad out back

then. A summer job, weekends, school holidays, working for the family business. Entirely feasible that he'd been involved in the conservatory's construction. Quite possibly, he'd helped to dig the foundations that became Kelly's grave. Had he, in his panic, seen a way to get out of the mess he was in? The mess he had made?

From inside the house came the sound of footsteps descending the bare stairs. This house with all its secrets and shame, whispering to her.

Jake appeared at the back door. 'Thought I heard you come in.'

She attempted a smile. 'You were on a call. Didn't want to disturb you.' She hesitated, wondering where to start. 'I saw Bryan Shaw this morning.'

'Oh.' A beat, and Jake's face creased into a frown. 'I assume you didn't say anything to him. You know, what Daniel told us was in strictest confidence, and—'

Izzy waved a hand, dismissing his concern. 'Of course not. He didn't see me. But I took his coffee cup.'

'His what?'

'His coffee cup. His DNA, Jake. You could give it to Daniel, help him match to... you know.'

'You took a DNA sample from a suspect?'

She heard, now, how ridiculous it sounded. When she spoke again, her voice was small. 'The police will need it at some point. If word gets out that Kelly was pregnant when she died, Bryan might flee. Then they'd never be able to get a sample from him. I'm just... trying to help.'

Jake took a seat in the chair next to her; the wood, worn by the seasons, creaked against his weight. 'Darling, I'm afraid it doesn't work like that. The conditions for collecting DNA samples are extremely strict. It has to be done by a senior police officer, for starters. And unless someone is under arrest for a crime, it can only be given voluntarily.'

Izzy felt her shoulders sag. 'But won't they be able to use it? Just to check, one way or the other?'

'At best, it would be inadmissible as evidence.' Jake sighed. 'At worst, you could get in trouble for interfering with the investigation. That's the kind of thing that gets cases thrown out of court.'

So, it had been for nothing, after all. They were no further forward. Izzy would have to break it to Diana that her idea of providing help 'behind the scenes' was, in fact, of no use to anyone.

'There's something else, though.' Jake regarded her cautiously. 'About Kelly's family. You have to understand, the court records are sealed but...'

'You found out what happened?'

Izzy had wondered about the circumstances that had brought Kelly to Seahouses in the first place. What had gone wrong at home to make the council to take her into care? She took another sip of coffee. It was cool now. Bitter on her tongue.

'It was Kelly's aunt who fought for custody...' Jake scratched his ear; a tell that he was imparting sorry news. 'Kelly's mother's sister.'

The aunt in Newcastle that Bryan had told them about. Izzy's heart hammered in her chest at the familiarity of this. A dead sister, custody of a niece; she saw now where Jake's sadness stemmed from. She took a slow breath, steadying herself.

Jake continued. 'The court, however, deemed that the aunt was unable or unfit to look after her. They ordered that Kelly was taken into care.'

Unfit or unable. Caring for someone else's child was not

just a case of how much you loved them or how badly you wanted to help them; there was a stress-test. A measurement that didn't consider emotion. And Izzy? If she had been subjected to that same rigour, if she'd had to go before a judge and prove her capacity to look after Amy's kids, would she have passed?

She thought back to the early days after her sister's death. That raw, excruciating time, when her sorrow had driven her to despair, and she had numbed the pain with alcohol. How useless she had been. How selfish. How she had been ready to give up. And how, somehow – with the love of Jake and Auntie Sue, and her desire to finally do right by Amy – she had dragged herself back from the edge.

And now this. Would she ever be able to give Amy's kids the security and stability they needed?

'What happened to her?' Izzy wondered out loud. 'The aunt, I mean.'

What would have happened to me if I'd been in that situation?

Jake shrugged. 'All I have is a name and an address. At least, the address she was using at the time of the hearing.'

He retrieved a note from his pocket, a sheet torn from his jotter, and slid it across the table to Izzy.

Izzy bit her lip, studying Jake's scrawl.

The address was in Scotswood – not the nicest part of Newcastle, but not the worst. A working-class neighbourhood close to the city centre.

Not that Izzy had ever been there; not that she could recall, at least. Trips to Newcastle invariably involved shopping at the boutiques and department stores or evening performances at the Theatre Royal, perhaps lunch or dinner or even cocktails in one of the city's hundreds of bars. Not trawling around the residential areas or the suburbs; definitely not places like Scotswood.

And how could they even be sure she was still there? What were the odds that Dawn Reynolds had not moved in the two decades since Kelly's custody hearing? Izzy sighed, turning the problem over in her mind.

It wasn't much, but for now, this address was the only hope Izzy had.

21

Then

I've been out walking with N. Only it's not just walking.

We talk. Mostly, I talk, and N just listens. He's a good listener. They say that about people, and I used to think, how can someone be good at listening? All you have to do is sit there and say nothing. But now I can see, now, how hard some people find it. They want to offer advice, to tell you that you're wrong or you're right, instruct you to do this or do that. All I want is to be able to say everything, get it all off my chest, and not have someone judge or question or prod me.

Dawn isn't a good listener. Dawn is a bad listener. She's always too tired or too stressed. Too many other things going on. There never seems to be the time, the space, to just hear me out. But these days, I miss even that.

Sometimes, when we're out walking, N holds my hand. Not in a creepy way; it's comforting. And I realise that one of the crazy things about loneliness is missing a touch. *A human touch.* He only does it when no one is watching, though. We both know other people might find it weird if they saw us together. It's this unspoken thing between us. One of the many things we both feel, but never say. We don't have to say them to make them real.

Nobody would understand. I barely understand it myself. I just know this is different. *Completely* different.

I know it should feel wrong, and that I should feel bad, but I don't. Where that should be – that embarrassment, or shame, or pity or whatever – wherever that should exist, there's just an empty space. A hollow inside me. Does that make me a bad person?

The Barretts were at church on Sunday, of course, and I stayed home alone. I listened to some music, turning it up as loud as I dared. That entire house to myself and I should be able to enjoy it, but I can't. I'm flat these days. Grey, like the sky, stretching on and on for eternity. The only spot of colour in my existence is the time I spend with N.

When I'm with him, I barely even think about Bryan. I did at first, of course. I told N everything, and he listened. But how much is there to say? The subject, and my feelings, have exhausted themselves. Worn thin like an old rug until there's nothing left but the threads and you can see that, underneath all the pattern and the colour, it was meaningless to start with.

Sam is still ignoring me. It's almost impressive, the way she manages to pretend I'm not there, that she can't see me, even when we're standing at the same bus stop and making the same journey twice a day, sitting in the same classroom and moving along the same hallways. I'd love to tell her about N, just to see the look on her stupid face.

But I won't. I can't.

Besides, it's nice, having a secret. Even the thought of it is delicious, sweet on my tongue; the words I'll never whisper. The one thing I have that's mine, truly mine. Just for me.

I got detention this week. Mrs Pankhurst, geography coursework – or lack of, at least. I know I should care more than I do, but it's geography, for god's sake. Who cares about geography? It's no good to anyone unless you're lost.

Which I am. I see the irony of that, believe me.

Maeve was so upset, as if it's the end of the bloody world. How can I make her understand that handing in my geography coursework is not going to be the thing that makes or breaks me?

Anyway, it's my first detention like *ever*. I've been the model student my entire life; everyone's allowed to slip up once in a while. But I've disappointed them; I could see it in the downturn of Maeve's mouth, the slump of her shoulders. So now I'm grounded this weekend – Eric says it's a chance to catch up on my schoolwork. As if that makes any difference. I've no one to see, nowhere to go.

When I told N about getting detention, he just laughed. He says I'm a rebel without a cause. It's the name of some old film, apparently. A classic, starring James Dean, who was quite hot back in the day. N knows loads about old films, old bands. He used to be in a band himself when he was a teenager, and he loves to listen to music.

I think he was just trying to impress me, but I find it sweet that he cares enough to want me to think he is cool. *Was* cool.

Whatever.

N says I've got my whole life ahead of me, and I'm going places – he can see it. He would have liked to leave Seahouses too, but it's complicated for him; he got married young and is stuck in a loveless marriage.

I think of that word – loveless. How tragic. Not enough

emotion for hate, or resentment, just a *lack*. A void where the love should be. A black hole of nothingness.

I listen to him when he talks. *Really* listen. Not offering advice or suggestions. Just listening. I like how he speaks to me, how he tells me things. Tells me his secrets.

N said he'll take me to see a cool band one of these days. A *gig*, he calls it. In Newcastle, where no one would know us, although he doesn't say that last part out loud. Not Beyoncé at the arena, like I suggested, but a proper band. His eyes were glittering as he said this, and I could tell he was really excited at the prospect.

It would be a club, somewhere, he says. A club where it's dark, and people don't listen to the band from seats but from a dancefloor. He asked me if I would dance with him if we went to a club like that and I teased him by pretending to think about it before I said yes, I would.

He liked that. I could tell by his smile, and the way he squeezed my hand even tighter; the little skip that appeared in his step.

I like that I can do that to him. That I can make him happy, simply by agreeing to dance with him. That we have this thing between us; me, and him. Just ours. Just us.

Our secret, whatever it is. Whatever that means.

22

Now

DIANA WAS WAITING BY THE DOOR TWENTY MINUTES AHEAD OF time.

Not that Izzy was ever early. Punctuality, Diana had noted, was not one of the girl's finer qualities.

Last night, Izzy had called Diana to say that finally, she had found a possible address for Kelly's aunt. It might be a long shot, but for now, it was the only lead they had.

She checked her bag again, making sure she had everything they might need for their excursion. An old A to Z of Newcastle, her notebook and a spare pen, an umbrella, even though the fair weather showed no signs of turning. Her handkerchief, a headscarf and sunglasses in case a disguise was called for, a torch with spare batteries, a small pair of scissors, rubber gloves and a freezer bag – a rudimentary detective kit but one which Diana hoped would serve its purpose, if needed. Her passport – the chances of cross-border travel were negligible, but one could never be too well-prepared – and her over-sixties bus pass. A packet of Murray Mints for the journey, and she was set.

From his photograph on the mantelpiece, Lionel caught her gaze. Diana might have imagined it, but in the shadows cast by the mid-morning sun that streamed through her living room window, a look of caution flashed over his handsome face. A look that urged her to be careful.

There was always a risk in such operations, Diana knew that. But her greatest concern was that Kelly's aunt might have moved away. What were the odds that the woman still lived at the same address all these years later? Still, they had to try. They owed it to Kelly to get to the bottom of this. Particularly her, who had let the girl down all those years ago.

Her resolve steeled. She would not fail Kelly for a second time.

And then there was that pesky inspector with her curt warning to stay away from the case. Diana would happily have left them to it, if only she had the slightest iota of confidence that they were giving this investigation the full attention it deserved.

Yes, police forces across the country had seen their budgets cut, and modern policing was like modern education: driven by results, statistics, with diminishing care for the people behind the figures. The untold human suffering, which could not be quantified by numbers on a spreadsheet. All the more reason, in her opinion, to lend a helping hand.

Finally, at three minutes past nine, she heard the growl of a car engine in the back lane.

. . .

The A1 was quiet, thank heavens; Izzy was a cautious driver, faltering at multiple opportunities to overtake slower vehicles.

The single carriageway widened to two lanes and then three, as forests and fields gave way to suburbia. Several new housing estates had sprung up on the northern outskirts of the city since the last time Diana had made the journey to Newcastle; homes and shops and offices encroaching into the space that used to be countryside. She watched the changed landscape from the passenger window, remembering when all of this had been wide open spaces.

Izzy turned off the motorway, and the car wound through increasingly narrower streets until a sign proclaimed they had arrived in Scotswood. From here, at the peak of the hill, narrow rows of terraced houses cascaded towards the river which glittered at the base of the valley.

A tough area, some would say. Not unlike the district on the other side of the city where Diana had spent two years at a comprehensive school as a newly qualified teacher. Another so-called rough area, where one might expect life to be harsher, crueller, blighted by crime. Only, Kelly's tragic demise had not happened here but in Seahouses; beautiful, tranquil, rural Seahouses. The terrible thing had not occurred in the place that many would consider the bad part of town, but in their own village. It was not places, per se, that were bad, Diana mused. It was people, and bad people can be found everywhere.

Scotswood used to be home to the workers of the shipyards that lined the banks of the Tyne. Now, the cranes that once dominated the landscape had disappeared, replaced by shining new buildings that housed industry of another kind.

A woman dressed in a brightly coloured salwar kameez

pushed a pram past a boarded-up pub. Diana thought of the generations of families that used to work and live here, and she idly wondered where they were now. Had Kelly's aunt remained, or had she departed, like so many others, to be replaced by a new working class seeking opportunity in the city?

Change, Diana knew, was inevitable; whether any of it could be called progress was another question entirely.

'There,' she said, pointing to the street sign. Dunelm Street. Entirely unnecessarily, given that Izzy was studiously following the satnav, but it felt good to contribute.

They followed the road at a crawl, Diana counting the door numbers until they reached thirty-two. Izzy parked and the pair of them took a good look at the house, Diana's fingers crossed tightly behind her back.

The property appeared to be well-maintained; that was a positive sign. Someone lived here. An upstairs window was open, and the curtain fluttered in the breeze. For the first time since they had left Seahouses, Diana felt a wrench of anxiety. She fought against it.

'Let's give this a try,' she said, her fingers still crossed, her eyes still on the house.

Izzy helped her from the car, and Diana felt a crunch in her back as she stood, straightening out the cracks. It was even warmer here than at the coast. The scent of tarmac, heated by the sun, tinged the air.

The doorbell worked; that was another good sign. Diana's heart galloped as the sound of footsteps from within grew louder. From behind the door, a chain clunked. Diana's mouth was dry.

The woman who answered was most definitely *not* Dawn Reynolds. Diana exchanged a glance with Izzy, her heart sinking.

'Yes?' the woman asked, clearly puzzled at the strangers on her doorstep. Then a hesitation. 'Are you the council tax people? Because I called and explained...'

West African, Diana presumed. Her accent was heavy, musical, and Diana was sure that she would have rather enjoyed meeting this interesting stranger had she not, in that moment, felt so bitterly disappointed.

'No, sorry, we're...' Izzy stuttered, then composed herself. 'We were looking for someone. Dawn Reynolds?'

'Sorry, can't help you there, I'm afraid.' The woman leaned against the doorframe. 'Friend of yours?'

'Something like that,' Diana mumbled.

'You sure you have the right address?'

From inside the house came the fragrant smell of cooking; meat and spices and something unfamiliar and exotic. Diana would have liked to come in for tea, to rest her body and compose her mind before the return journey. *A wasted trip.*

'Yes. Well, this is the address we have for her.' Izzy sighed, her shoulders dropping. 'I'm terribly sorry to have bothered you.'

The woman waved off the apology and smiled generously, exposing a gap between her front teeth. 'No bother at all. I hope you find your friend Dawn Reynolds.'

They turned and walked back to the car, a weariness threatening to overcome Diana. She felt it in her knees, her back, her neck, a tiredness that might consume her. She raked their dilemma over in her mind, wondering how else they might find Dawn. Her momentary distraction meant she barely noticed the woman walking up the hill towards them. In fact, Diana might not have noticed her at all, had she not set her shopping bags on the ground by Izzy's car.

'Did I just hear you say you're looking for Dawn

Reynolds?' The woman's voice was surprisingly deep for someone so slight. Her face was heavily lined, her eyebrows plucked to two thin arches.

'Yes,' said Diana. 'Do you know where we might find her?'

The woman glared at them, her dark eyes narrowing to slits. 'Depends. Who's looking?'

'We're not police, nothing like that.' Diana immediately knew she had protested too quickly and softened. 'I knew Kelly. Her niece.'

The woman picked up her shopping bags. 'In that case, you'd better come with me.'

Dawn Reynolds had not gone far. The woman, who introduced herself as Brenda, maintained an incessant chatter as she led them to the adjacent street, but Diana barely caught a word of it. She thanked the heavens for such fortuitous timing.

'Here we are. Number forty-nine.' Brenda nodded to a house on the other side of the street. 'She's working nights, so she should be in.'

'Honestly,' said Izzy, breathless from the uphill walk laden with half of Brenda's shopping bags. 'I can't thank you enough.'

'Do you want me to come with you? Dawn doesn't like... Well. It's understandable, but she doesn't have a lot of trust for people she doesn't know.'

Diana shook her head. 'You've been most helpful.'

'It's no bother, pet. I saw the news. It's terrible what happened to the lass. They should have left her with Dawn – I could have told them that at the time. That poor bairn.'

Brenda's eyes glistened, and Diana nodded sadly. If

only... if only. So many if onlys. She pushed her regret to one side as they crossed the road, her hand folded in the crook of Izzy's elbow.

The paint on the door was peeling. From somewhere inside came the tinny sound of laughter and audience applause. Yellowing net curtains hung at the window.

Diana took a deep breath. 'Ready?' She didn't wait for Izzy's response before knocking at the door.

Izzy didn't know what she had expected Dawn Reynolds to look like, but it certainly wasn't this. She was young, for a start. Possibly around Izzy's age. And there was no family resemblance to Kelly. Izzy searched her features for some similarity to the image of Kelly she'd seen in the photographs, but found nothing. Her complexion was milky-white, and her dark hair hung around her shoulders in soft waves.

Dawn scowled at them through the gap in the door, open no more than a fist. 'What do you want?'

'I'm Izzy Morton and this' —Izzy gestured to Diana— 'is my friend Diana. We're here because of Kelly. It was my house where they found...' She couldn't find the words to finish her sentence, but she pictured that hole in her garden. The football with two eyes that now had a name, a history. A family.

Dawn's frown deepened, her eyes narrowing. 'You never answered my question.'

Izzy took a deep breath. 'Diana knew Kelly. We're trying to find out what happened to her. We want to know what went on back then.'

Dawn seemed to consider this for a moment. She gave a small, reluctant nod. 'Come in.'

The house was modest but clean, and Izzy could detect the smell of freshly washed laundry. They followed Dawn through to a living room. A widescreen television was mounted on the wall above an electric fireplace and a lilac nurse's uniform hung from the top of a sideboard.

'The police have been. And the papers.' Dawn sneered. 'Offering money to tell my story. I told them where to go.'

Izzy shuddered. She'd had similar offers after Amy's murder. The thought had nauseated her – as if the story of her family's suffering was so salacious it was worth paying for. That there was a price to be put on misery.

Dawn continued. 'So, if you're after anything like that, you can forget it.'

Diana took a seat on a faux-leather couch. 'Nothing of the sort, my dear.' She smoothed a crease on her skirt and spoke softly. 'I was a teacher. I taught Kelly at St Helen's in Alnwick. She was a wonderful woman, your niece. Incredibly bright. Ever since I found out what happened to her, I've been wondering how, why?'

'It would never have happened if they hadn't taken her away in the first place.' Dawn wiped away a tear. 'And not once have they apologised.'

'It's unjust, my dear.' Diana whispered. 'And that's what we want now. Justice for Kelly.'

'Well, I'm not holding out much hope for that. I know what they think of her. Of us. Don't make the same mistake I did – they're not on my side. Kelly's side. Even now.'

'What do you mean?' Izzy couldn't hide the concern from her voice.

Dawn huffed a sigh. 'They're not taking it seriously. The police aren't investigating – not properly. I just know it. They're asking all sorts about Kelly, about boyfriends and running away, making out that she was some kind of teenage tearaway. Insinuating that she might have brought this on herself, you know?'

Dawn sat and Izzy took the chair opposite her. 'Please... tell us about Kelly. About what happened to the pair of you.'

'Why should I? Why should I trust you?'

'I was her teacher.' Diana's eyes glittered now, wet with sadness. 'Not only did I see her every day; I cared about her. And I'm wondering what I missed, back then. What clues she might have left behind. Someone did this to her, and I want to see that person answer for their crimes. I'm certain that, somewhere in here' —she tapped a knuckle to her temple— 'there is an answer. And you, quite possibly, hold the key to unlock it. Please, just tell us anything you can.'

Dawn hesitated at this, then sat back in her armchair and drew a deep, sorry breath. 'My sister, Linda – Kelly's mam – she was a lot older than me. Kind of like a second mother. She was a good woman, but she had a horrible time of things. Kelly's dad was violent. Domestic abuse. You know.' Dawn shrugged.

'Then one day, he disappeared for good. They moved back in with me and Mam. Kelly was only three years younger than me. More of a sister than a niece. Everything was good for a while. Then Linda fell in with another bad lad. Got her into drugs and all sorts. But Mam kept Kelly straight. Kept the pair of us healthy and fed.

'Linda had got herself into a sorry state, but she was turning things around. Getting herself sorted for Kelly. She got clean and got rid of that piece of scum that had dragged her down. And then just when things were looking up, he killed her.' Dawn's eyes grew wet.

'They said it was an overdose, but Linda hadn't been using for a while, and someone gave her the drugs, didn't they? That bastard. He just couldn't stand to see her getting on with her life without him.' She brushed away tears with the back of her hand.

'She had everything going for her, our Kelly. Clever. Good at school. Much better than I was. Even after Linda died, she kept going. Top of the class, that one. And Mam was determined that we would have a better life than Linda. Told us both to stay away from drugs, from wrong'uns. But then Mam died.'

Dawn stared out of the window, her gaze misting, fixed on some unseen point. When she spoke again, her voice was tight. 'We lost the house. I was only eighteen, but I was ready to do anything. I dropped out of college and got a job, got us a council flat. I would have managed, you know? But social services weren't having any of it. It went to court and everything, but they took Kelly away in the end.'

Izzy fought back the urge to cry. Tears wouldn't help anyone, now. Not Dawn, not Kelly. 'You did everything you could.'

'Eighteen years old. I tried; I really did.' Dawn choked back a sob. 'But I had nothing, certainly not money for a good solicitor or anything like that. It's why Kelly wanted to be a lawyer – so she could help families in the same situation. She never held any of it against me, though. We kept in touch. She was with a couple of families before social services found her a place in Seahouses. She said it wasn't so bad, and she was happy there. *Seemed* happy. And then one day she showed up here.'

'I remember,' said Diana. 'She ran away for a week.'

Dawn scoffed. '"Ran away". Ran *home*, more like. Turned up on my doorstep one night, out the blue. Had some madcap plan about hiding out at home until she turned eighteen. Social services came, of course. Kelly hid under the bed, but they found her. Threatened to have me arrested for kidnap or some crap.'

'Did she say why?' Izzy asked. 'What had happened?'

Dawn shook her head. 'She just kept saying she couldn't go back there. It was only a few months until her birthday, and I told her to go. I mean, I could see how much trouble I could get in, and it was only for a little while longer. She was going to come back as soon as she turned eighteen. She even left some of her stuff. *Just a few more months.* That's what I told her.'

'They took her back and then, three weeks later, she disappeared again. I got another visit from social services; they turned the place upside-down. It took me two days to convince them she wasn't with me. Then, out of the blue, they decided she had run away. Properly, this time. There was a postcard from London to the foster parents, but that made no sense. Why would she write to them but not me? I told you, she wasn't angry with me. I kept pushing them, kept pressing. I told them Kelly wouldn't just vanish like that without at least a phone call. Surprise, surprise, they wouldn't listen. They never do. They never even looked for her, not properly. Not like they should have. All these years... I always wondered. I think about her all the time. She's always on my mind. And I've always had a terrible feeling that something bad happened to her.' Dawn choked back a sob.

'She was pregnant when she was killed, you know. That's what the police are saying now. Far along enough that she would have known herself; Kelly wasn't daft. That means she was already pregnant that week she came here. And I keep thinking, was that the reason she wanted to run away? But why wouldn't she have told me that?' Dawn shook her head. 'She would have told me. Kelly knew she could have told me anything. I would have helped her, she knew that. No, there was something else bothering her.'

'And they don't know who the father was. No boyfriend on the scene, apparently. Which, I swear, they're using against Kelly. Like it reflects badly on her, means she was up to no good. They're making out that what happened to her was her own fault, somehow.' Her eyes met Diana's, then Izzy's. 'Every day, I ask myself, *why did I let her go?* I should have fought harder for her. Kept her here, kept her safe.'

'My dear,' said Diana, her eyes glistening. 'You did everything you could.'

'But it wasn't enough. *I wasn't enough.* Me, the one person in the world who should have had her back. I failed her.'

23

Diana was deeply troubled.

She had understood Kelly had a 'difficult background' – that was the phrase they would have used back then. In all likelihood, the exact words Bernadette Fearon had uttered as she briefed the staff of St Helen's on the new arrival in the lower sixth that term. But until the circumstances of the girl's life were laid out in front of her, Diana had not quite comprehended the extent of the difficulties Kelly had overcome. In her eyes, it made the dear young woman all the more remarkable.

The aunt – Dawn – was a mess. What a wretched thing to go through. Losing her sister, then her mother, and then finally, poor Kelly. What an appalling state of affairs. And Dawn was right – the system had failed them repeatedly. The system that Diana had been part of.

And darling Kelly. It was clear; Diana could see that she had been shielding her aunt from the truth. What had happened in Seahouses back then? What secret had been so terrible that Kelly had dared not whisper it even to her closest confidante? The woman who was practically a sister to her? Evidently, this was about more than a falling out with a friend, a breakup, or even an unplanned pregnancy.

The police had not looked for Kelly when she disappeared. Social services had written her off based on nothing more than a postcard. They had ignored Dawn's pleas. It was despicable. The girl had been forgotten; her secrets buried in a salty grave.

Recovered from the ordeal of telling her story, Dawn set about making tea. Diana gratefully accepted the chipped mug and took greedy gulps of the hot, sugary liquid.

It wouldn't do to tell Dawn about the breakup with Bryan Shaw, the row with Samantha, or that the pair had got together. That Bryan's family firm had been responsible for the construction of the conservatory under which Kelly had been buried. It would not bring the woman any peace. What Dawn needed, what they all needed, was for justice to be served.

And Diana was now quite certain that the police – that silly lady detective, who wore the ghastliest shade of lipstick and unfailingly smelled of stale cigarette smoke – were still not doing their job.

In the pit of her stomach, her anger hardened. She pushed it to one side, taking another sip of tea to calm herself, and tried to think rationally. Where to go from here? Where was the next clue?

'You said that Kelly left some things here when she went back to Seahouses?'

'Yeah. Well, not here. My old flat. But I brought them with me.' Dawn chewed at a nail. 'Even though I had a bad feeling, there was always a part of me that hoped she might come back one day.'

'Might we take a look? Just to see if there's anything that

might give us some indication of what was going through her mind?'

It didn't take Dawn long to locate the box of Kelly's affairs. Diana sighed, unable to ignore the parallels with the box of Kelly's things left behind at the Barretts'. Possessions, pieces of her, held in safekeeping by those whose hopes of her return had been cruelly crushed.

Dawn folded her arms across her chest, hugging herself. 'I haven't been able to bring myself to go through it since I got the news. I'm not sure I could bear to, to be honest.'

'Why don't you take a breather?' said Izzy. 'We won't take long, and we'll put everything back exactly as it was. You can go through it when you're feeling stronger.'

Dawn hesitated only for a moment before agreeing.

Diana was glad when she left the room, leaving them to it. It wasn't so much that she craved privacy for her and Izzy to search through Kelly's possessions; rather, it was the weight of the woman's grief. Her regrets – Dawn's many regrets – were a dark rain cloud that stirred Diana's own guilt and made it difficult to concentrate on finding a way forward. It was a black forest, a thicket of thorny brambles, through which she knew they had to forge a path. Find a clearing in the darkness.

There were no photographs or mementos this time, just some books. Diana remembered once again Kelly's insatiable appetite for reading. She brushed the cover of a fabric-bound edition of *A Midsummer Night's Dream*, exploring the ridges of the embossed title with her fingertips.

The words of a monologue came to her, and she recited it out loud. 'Sweet Moon, I thank thee for thy sunny beams; I thank thee, Moon, for shining now so bright—'

What comes next?

The phrase which had been on the tip of her tongue just a moment ago had vanished. Diana panicked, scouring her memory.

For shining now so bright...

But try as she might, there was nothing. Just an emptiness where once a tapestry of language had hung; words that she knew by heart.

Izzy was watching her, a frown of concern knotting her face. 'Are you feeling all right, Diana?'

Diana's pulse galloped, and she fought against her fear.

Granny Agnew.

'I'm perfectly fine, dear. Just forgotten my lines, is all.' She tried to laugh, but her voice shook when she spoke.

And then, because of the distress of that morning, her sorrow for all that had happened, or through sheer fright, Diana found that she could not remember the name of the girl they were searching for.

It was like vertigo – as if Diana was peering down into an infinite, eternal, black hole of nothingness. A void. Her heart fluttered in her chest, and she took a deep, steadying breath.

When Izzy spoke, her voice sounded far away. 'Come on, have a drink of water.'

Then there was a glass in Diana's hand, and if it wasn't for Izzy guiding her, Diana might have forgotten how to lift it to her lips. A tear trickled from the corner of her eye, rolling down her cheek.

'The dear girl...' Her mouth was dry; the words cracked on her lips.

'Kelly?'

There it was. Kelly. *Kelly.*

Diana closed her eyes. It was happening. The very thing that had terrified her for years. The night was closing in on her, a blackness that threatened to envelop her. Swallow her whole.

'Perhaps this is all too much?' Izzy's voice was clearer again now.

Diana was back in the room. She glanced around them, re-familiarising herself with her surroundings.

'I can do this myself if you want to take a moment?'

Diana felt her heart rate slowly return to normal. 'I'm fine, dear, I promise. Just a dizzy spell. It's passed, now.' She bravely mustered a smile for her sweet, kind friend.

She would not tell Izzy the truth. She wouldn't tell Jennifer or Sandra, nor would she see a doctor. Diana resolved, there in Dawn's living room, to live with this privately for as long as she possibly could. And she would see justice for Kelly, even if it was the very last thing she did.

Conscious that Izzy was monitoring her closely, Diana retrieved another book from the box, doing her best to give her friend the impression that she had recovered. It was a notebook. School work? She opened the page and read over Kelly's handwriting.

Not a notebook.

'Oh my,' she said, her voice faltering as her pulse picked up again. 'Kelly kept a diary.'

Izzy's eyes widened. 'Are you serious?'

But of course, Diana would not joke about something like this. Her old friend offered her the book and Izzy took it, her breath catching.

Kelly's handwriting was neat, lines scrawled in black ink in an unmistakably teenage hand. She had dated each page. Blood thundered in Izzy's ears now, and she skipped through to the last entry, her head buzzing with the possibility of what this could mean. 'February 2003.' She gasped, the realisation hitting her. 'That's when she ran away.'

She flicked back through the pages, her eyes scanning the first entry. 'And it starts in March 2002. Just after she arrived in Seahouses.'

Izzy didn't know where to begin. Kelly's diary entries were long and detailed, and it would take hours to read through the entire thing. Even days, perhaps. Her eyes danced over the pages, catching only a line here or there.

'Here – she's written about Bryan, about them getting together. And here, this is about Sam.' She bit her lip, her eyes flitting over the words on the page. 'Kelly says Sam deliberately turned the other girls against her. She didn't understand why, but overnight, they all stopped speaking to Kelly.'

'I remember,' said Diana. 'They ostracised her.'

'And here... She's talking about going for a walk with N. N? Who is N?'

This was strange – Kelly had used names throughout her entries, and yet one person was designated by just an initial. Was this the mystery older man that Sam had alluded to? Izzy scanned the pages. N this, N that. Walks on the beach. Holding hands. She felt the blood drain from her face.

'She was hiding his identity,' said Diana, carefully. 'N was someone she should not have been with. A married man, perhaps?'

'Whoever it was, if anyone found out about them, Kelly knew he would be in trouble.'

'We can't give this to the police,' Diana said, as if anticipating Izzy's next suggestion. 'Not until we've had time to go through it all ourselves. Not until we know who N is.'

Izzy considered this. It had been harrowing, listening to

Dawn's account of how the system of social workers, police, and courts had let them down again and again. The odds had been stacked against Kelly from the start, no matter what she and Dawn had done.

One thing was certain – whatever had been bothering Kelly was in this diary, somewhere. The threat of a migraine throbbed at her temple.

'It's evidence.' She spoke slowly, thinking as she went. Allowing the thought to fully form. 'But that doesn't mean we have to hand it over right away. They don't know we have it, after all.'

And if they had been doing their job properly, they would already have the diary by now.

Izzy heaved a sigh. She knew what Jake would advise her to do in this situation. What she *should* do. And she thought of what DI Bell would say if the police knew they had stumbled across evidence in a murder investigation and withheld it, and what the consequences of that might be.

Then she thought again of how badly Kelly had been failed. Of a vulnerable teenage girl who had been allowed to fall through the cracks. That an entire village had forgotten her, allowed her secrets to be buried.

'Three days, and then we have to give it to them.'

Diana nodded in agreement. 'Deal. And what about Dawn?'

'We'll tell her we found it, of course.' She saw immediately that Diana was not convinced. 'We have to, Diana. I insist. It's a matter of respect – we need her permission. But something tells me she'll have more faith in us than she has in the police.'

Diana shrugged, mulling over the sad truth to Izzy's words.

Just then, Dawn came back into the living room. 'Find anything interesting?' she said.

Izzy clutched the diary, wondering how to break this to her. And suddenly unsure whether Dawn would, in fact, allow them to keep it.

'Kelly was keeping a diary. The whole time she was in Seahouses. She names people – people we know.' Izzy set the book down on the table between them and watched as Dawn regarded it cautiously, her eyes sheening with tears once more. 'We should give this to the police, but I'd ask you to let us go through it first. And I promise that we'll use it to find whoever hurt Kelly. Whoever did this to her – his name is probably in here. And if it is, we'll find him. It's your decision, but that's my promise.'

Dawn brushed a strand of hair away from her face, tucking it behind her ear. 'All I ever wanted was what was best for Kelly. Nobody would listen to me – not then, and not now.' She locked eyes with Izzy and spoke firmly. 'I just want to know who did this.'

Izzy nodded. 'So do we.'

With the diary tucked away safely in her handbag, they bade farewell to Dawn. Diana gripped Izzy's arm even more tightly on the walk back to the car, and Izzy deliberately slowed her pace to a shuffle. Her friend's episode earlier had terrified her, and at one point, she had thought they might have to call for an ambulance. It could have been the heat, or the upset of the morning, but Izzy had an unnerving feeling that there was something seriously wrong.

Diana had tried to gloss over it, and the discovery of the diary had created a timely distraction. As Izzy helped Diana into the car, she recalled in frighteningly vivid detail the look on the older lady's face in the moment Shakespeare's words had escaped her. And she could have imagined it, but it had seemed that, for a second, Diana hadn't been able to remember Kelly's name. Her eyes had gone vacant, as if she was lost, as if she had suddenly found herself in a strange place.

Alzheimer's, or dementia – Izzy wasn't even sure if they were the same thing. The worst thing was how frightened her friend had been. True terror was impossible to disguise.

Izzy sensed the weight of Diana's fatigue as the car wound northward through the city, listening as her breathing slowed.

As she pulled onto the motorway, she threw a glance at her passenger, now comfortably snoozing next to her. Izzy knew she wouldn't be able to bear it if – *when* – anything happened to the old lady. Their unlikely friendship had been one of the unexpected good things to come out of her return to Seahouses. Another link to Amy, and one that she wasn't ready to see severed.

The diary. She thought back to the snippets she had read. Who could N be? And what had happened to make Kelly think running away was her only option? Hiding out at Dawn's house would have meant missing her exams, forgoing her plan to go to university. What was so terrible that she had been prepared to throw it all away?

The answer was in there, somewhere. Kelly's words, her truth, captured and preserved. Her secrets no longer buried.

24

Then

It's the Christmas Ball in a couple of weeks. I've been studiously ignoring the posters that have appeared all over school. It's an event for St Helen's Sixth Form and the boys from Alnwick Grammar. A mixer, they call it. It's all any of them can talk about. Although, of course, not with me.

They'll all be there in their fancy dresses and suits. Teachers from both schools watching on from the side-lines, chaperoning them. Corsages and high heels. Hair styled in rollers and fixed up with hairspray, trying to catch Mr Tait's eyes. Flowers in the boys' buttonholes. The swish of polyester, one glass of champagne per guest. Plenty of mistletoe, no doubt; sixteen pounds per ticket. Limos to take them home.

I bet Bryan looks gorgeous in a suit.

Obviously, I'm not going.

Besides, I'd rather save my money. I got another job – nothing special, just cleaning at The Ship on Saturday and Sunday mornings. It pays £3.60 an hour. Minimum wage.

Two hours each day. I work before the pub opens, so I don't even get to see any of the customers. It makes me wonder what Sunflower Woman and the Colonel are up to. I spend my shift alone, wiping the surfaces, mopping down the floors, clearing out the bins and ashtrays, doing my best to ignore the stench of piss in the men's toilets.

And there I was thinking there was nothing worse than the smell of fresh cow carcass and Kyle's stares.

Whatever. It's not like I have anything better to do with my weekends, now.

There could be extra hours in the run-up to Christmas, and I'll use the money to get Dawn something nice, like a bottle of perfume or a pair of fancy pyjamas – something I know she would never buy for herself.

Lisa, my case worker, has told me I can go home and stay overnight. Dawn can only get one day off work, but it's better than nothing. Jackson will be around. She says this like it's a good thing, and I can't bring myself to correct her.

She's stressing about getting a turkey, of all things. I phone her twice a week for thirty minutes and Dawn wasted the best part of half an hour going through the ins and outs of frozen turkey versus fresh. What if they're sold out by Christmas Eve, and how long would it take to defrost? And I couldn't help but smile at her flapping. We both know I'll end up doing it.

My room is ready for me, even if it is only for one night. Dawn's bought a new cover for the duvet and the back window has been fixed. I'll put a desk in there, eventually. When it's my official home. When I'm finally at university. Whenever that might be.

I just hope she's got me the phone she promised. Although who would I ring besides her? I could phone N, I suppose.

I missed the deadline for history coursework. Mr Tait gave me a two-day extension, and even then, I still couldn't make it. I spent hours staring at the blank page, the pen poised in my hand, but the words, the arguments, the perspectives I'd spent weeks preparing – none of it came to me. He says he's left with no choice but to adjust my grade, and it means I'll have to score over ninety percent in the exam if I'm to get the B I need.

N says I'll be fine, though, and I shouldn't worry about failing this year. It's all the girls' fault; all the stress they put me under. *What they did to me.* He makes it sound as if I stopped speaking to them. As if I cut them out, not the other way around, and he says this like it's a positive thing; as if I made the right choice. That I'm too good for them, and I should never speak to any of them ever again. N says I've got more potential in my little finger than most of those girls have in their entire bodies.

As if to prove his point, he put his little finger in my mouth. Just the tip.

I think he was trying to be sexy, but I ruined it by bursting out laughing. He was in a huff all the way back, and I felt awful. It's hard, watching a grown man sulk like that. *So hurt,* no matter how much I apologised. I hurt the one person in the world who truly cares about me. Shows what kind of person I am, doesn't it?

I wanted to make it up to him, to show him I *do* care; that I do appreciate how much he's been there for me these past couple of months. So today, I took him to the spot that I used to go to with Bryan. It's hidden in the dunes – you have to know how to get there, and it's far from the main path. I knew no one would be down there, not on a day like this.

N is a much better kisser than Bryan. He has proper facial hair, not like the sad little fluffy slug that Bryan was attempting to grow on his top lip. He doesn't taste of strawberry bubble-gum. N tastes like mints, and the sea. His arms are strong; I feel safe in them. Wanted. Needed.

I shouldn't compare him to Bryan, but I do. Bryan was always in a rush, a frantic dash to nowhere in particular. N takes his time, asks me if I'm OK. If I feel good. N knows exactly where he wants to go.

N asked me if I wanted to stop, and I said no. I knew where it was going – where he was going – and I wanted to see where things lead. To feel something, anything, in place of the emptiness.

I always thought my first time would be special. I don't know what *special* means. Candles, maybe. Soft music. And it was special, in a way. The sound of the sea echoing all around us, sheltered from the wind down there in the dunes. I lay on my back, looking up at the shape of the sky.

Afterwards, N noticed I was shivering and told me that body heat is the best way to keep warm. It's what explorers do, down in the Antarctic or up on Everest – they huddle together to survive the cold, their bodies sustaining each other just by being close.

I like the thought of that. Two people, keeping one another alive.

He says he is going to take me away somewhere. A five-star hotel, with soft sheets and those little fancy slippers and chocolates on the pillows. I've never been anywhere like that. N says I would have to wear my skinny jeans and the jacket he likes. What he doesn't say: that these are the clothes that make me look older.

What will they say at reception, I wonder? When we check in to this imaginary five-star hotel? Me and N, asking for a room. Fake names. *A double bed.* I can just picture their faces. Imagine what they might whisper once we're out of earshot.

Which makes me wonder if I've lost my common sense? Because I know that this is wrong. Don't I? And not just because of the age gap. No. It's more than that.

Sam has this daft expression; *this is wrong on so many levels.* And yet, still, I'm doing it. I'm *with* him. We're not a proper couple – not like I was with Bryan. It's more than that, yet at the same time, less.

Me and Bryan. That seems so childish now, when I think about it. What I felt for him. What he felt for me. We were kids. *Are kids.* Except I've grown up about ten years in the past two months.

I know that me being with N is wrong, but I'm still doing it. It's like touching something hot, knowing it will burn. Why am I doing this? And why don't I want to stop? Just thinking about it makes my head spin.

25

Now

THE DAY WAS STILL YOUNG WHEN IZZY WOKE.

Apricot light streamed in from the gaps where the curtain did not quite meet the edge of the window. *Blackout blinds.* Another thing to add to her list. Another week was almost over, and her list was no shorter than it had been on Monday.

She turned and curled into Jake's back, and he stirred as the cool pebble of her nose met with the ridge of his shoulder. She inhaled deeply, drinking in his scent.

Kelly's diary was stashed in Izzy's drawer, under an old cashmere sweater of Amy's, now dotted with moth bite-sized holes. Another item she couldn't bear to see discarded, even though the smell of Amy had long since faded from the fabric. She dozed as the birds outside roused, their chorus rising, serenading her back to a sleep that was fitful, interrupted by images of a lost girl buried in salt. Between the folds of her dream, Kelly's ghost whispered to her.

Who was N? And what had Kelly been so desperate to hide?

Last night, as she had dropped Diana at home, the old lady had given her a file. Izzy had been surprised to learn that her former teacher had kept records of pupils' performances. Not for every year group, she assured Izzy. But it was enough to make Izzy wonder if, subconsciously, Diana had always known she might need to revisit these particular reports again one day. As if she had somehow suspected, on some unseen level, that the sudden disappearance of Kelly might eventually be explained in the essay and exam marks and the attendance registration.

Izzy hadn't had time to look at it before bed. Jake had been eager to hear about the trip to Newcastle and their meeting with Dawn Reynolds, and Izzy hadn't wanted to – *couldn't* – tell him yet about the diary.

Instead, he had listened anxiously as she described Diana's mental blip. That's how she'd phrased it – a blip. Like radio static, or a power cut, or the Wi-Fi dropping out.

'Probably just the stress of the situation,' Jake had offered. And Izzy had agreed, despite her gnawing concern that it was something much, much worse.

She woke again a couple of hours later to the sound of the shower. The bed was empty, and Izzy rolled onto her back, her hand reaching for the cool spot on the sheets where Jake had lain. Before long, he emerged from the bathroom, droplets of water glistening on his collarbone, the hairs on his torso and arms sodden and glossy. She drank in the sight of him, trying to imagine him on their wedding day.

No, not their wedding day – on their honeymoon. Bali or the Maldives. *Afterwards. Afterwards* was the part she was looking forward to. *The only part.*

She watched him dress, moving around their bedroom as he retrieved underwear, a clean shirt, trousers, socks. Again, her mind flitted to Kelly's diary in her drawer. The ghost of the girl hidden under their patio, now hidden under the ghost of Amy.

The ghosts of lost girls, piling up in her bedroom.

'Did you say you were going to work on the plans for the house this morning?' Jake said, pulling her back to the moment.

'Yes,' Izzy lied. The truth was, the renovation was the last thing on her mind.

Her new home, with the ambitious renovation she had taken on single-handedly. *Their home.* Projects that she wouldn't – couldn't – even think about, not yet, not until she'd pored over Kelly's diary. Not until she'd found out what had happened to her.

'You sure you're OK?' Jake asked.

She couldn't remember him asking in the first place. 'I'm fine,' she fibbed again, smiling sweetly.

Once Jake had left, Izzy got to work.

The kids would stay with Mike this weekend, which alleviated some of the pressure on her and Jake – there was nothing to be planned for tomorrow night's dinner, and there would be none of the stress of the Saturday Schedule.

It was ironic, she realised, that the kids had more complicated social lives than she did these days.

She made herself a coffee and took it back upstairs to the spare bedroom. On Jake's desk, she spread out the reports on one side – a fan of paper, comprising the attendance register and the academic marks. Izzy sipped at the coffee and opened the diary.

From across the decades, Kelly spoke to her. Izzy heard the naivety in her words, undercut with a humour and insight that belied the girl's age. Kelly's initial impressions of the Barretts made Izzy laugh, and her astute observations of the genteel lives of her classmates were soured by a sadness over how much she had lost.

She seemed to be remarkably resilient; Izzy wondered how she herself would have fared if she and Amy had been taken into care. If they had been sent away to live with a new family, attend a new school, away from their friends.

She sighed. Amy, most certainly, would have coped best.

Kelly was describing the beginnings of her friendship with Samantha now. How naïve and unworldly these small-town girls had been compared to her, and yet, how badly she'd wanted to fit in. And here was Kelly's account of her blossoming romance with Bryan. Kelly seemed to have fallen for him fast, while never taking her eyes off the clock. The time until she could leave Seahouses seemed to be never far from the girl's mind.

Here – here was N. Izzy sat up straighter in her chair.

It started out innocently enough – walks along the beach, the squeeze of a hand offered initially in reassurance and soon, as something else.

Dawn had been right; Kelly was not stupid. It was obvious that he was older: the illicit meetings, the way he would drop Kelly's hand if anyone passed them during their walks... Kelly had known that her relationship with this older man was completely inappropriate.

Izzy squirmed. *Inappropriate*. That was an understatement and a half. And yet, Kelly had been OK with it. Despite her intelligence, she had been happy to accept the advances of someone who should clearly have been off-limits.

Izzy leaned back and closed her eyes as she raked over

the names in Kelly's diary. No one beginning with N. And no one else had merited a codename.

She read on. Soon, and with a sickening predictably, the friendship with N morphed into something deeper. Something worse.

Much worse.

First, there were crude attempts at flirting – mostly on his part, but not unwelcomed by Kelly, who, by this point, seemed to be quite isolated.

'You poor thing,' Izzy said aloud. From the pages, between the lines, she felt the bitter smart of Kelly's loneliness.

Was that it? Did loneliness drive this young woman to gratitude for this grotesque affection?

Was that why he preyed on her?

Suddenly, Izzy could see it. A young woman at the end of her rope, who had tried and tried and tried and still, at the end of it all, had failed. A man who had seen her desperation. A predator that had sensed her weakness.

The coffee was like acid in her stomach, and Izzy took deep breaths, her heart rate racing.

He had preyed on her. *Groomed her.*

She made a note of the date on the page and went back to the school reports. And yes, there it was. Kelly had hit straight As throughout the autumn term, and had scored a respectable eighty-three percent for English Literature in the Autumn mocks. But by December her grades were slipping, and by February she was consistently in the Ds and Cs, with some blank gaps on the page and even a couple of crosses. "Coursework not submitted," read one of the comments.

She flicked over the attendance register, her eyes scanning Kelly's line. Once more, Izzy could see precisely where it had started to go wrong.

Was it too much of a stretch to link the two? N had come into Kelly's life, and she had given up on school. Or had she given up already, and N had been there just as she hit rock bottom? Izzy gnawed on her lip, turning the question over in her mind.

Her stomach growled, and she glanced at her watch. It was already past noon, and even though her discovery sickened her, she needed to eat. She abandoned the work and went down to the kitchen, failing to notice the floorboards, or the tiles, or the hideous wallpaper that routinely kept her awake at night.

Cause and effect. Who could say what had happened first? All Izzy could see was that there was a clear correlation between Kelly's grades slipping and her progressing relationship with N.

She munched on a slice of buttered toast without tasting it and made another coffee.

Back upstairs, she resumed reading. There were scant few mentions of Bryan or Sam by this point. Kelly's mood darkened as the weeks progressed, consumed by black thoughts, and even her hope for the end – her eighteenth birthday – seemed to dissipate.

Her days were consumed by N; when she wasn't with him, she seemed to be agonising over their relationship. N told her what to do, what to wear, what to say to people, and Izzy got the distinct sense Kelly regretted ever becoming involved with him.

And there it was – the day that things had really started to go badly wrong. Kelly found out she was pregnant.

Izzy cross-referenced the entry with the attendance register, her pulse thundering in her ears. The words blurred on the page in front of her, ink melting into the paper. Her mouth was dry, and dark spots began to cloud the periphery of her vision.

The week she ran away.

She was still shaken when Jake arrived home.

'Sorry I'm late – I got held up on the probate.'

Izzy hadn't even noticed the advancing hour.

'That old dear who donated her estate to Alnwick Garden. It's causing such a row with the family.' Jake shook his head.

She'd had to lie down that afternoon, stilling herself in the cool of their bedroom. Staring at the ceiling, willing the threat of a headache to pass. Trying to piece it all together. The shards of a promising young woman who had fractured, fragmented, and the man who had picked up the pieces, reforming them into something other.

Someone had taken advantage of Kelly – preyed on her when she was at her weakest. But he wasn't the only one to blame. Her friends – Sam, and Bryan, and the others – had deserted her, condemning her to a loneliness that made her reckless.

And then there were the Barretts – the so-called family she should have been able to depend on in the absence of her own. Despite their dedication and discipline, they had neglected Kelly, allowing her to become a victim when they should have been protecting her.

The entire system: the courts, the police, the social workers, and even the teachers at St Helen's – Izzy fought a fresh wave of nausea as she realised that Diana, too, was implicated in Kelly's downfall – they had all let her down.

Allowed her to slip through the cracks.

It took a village to raise a child, and an entire village had failed this one girl.

Now, the diary and the school records were safely stashed in the drawer of her wardrobe, hidden under Amy's sweater. Tucked away again until Izzy could face looking at them once more.

Jake eyed her cautiously. 'Did you get the plans finished?'

The renovation. Another day gone, and no progress to show for it. She shook her head.

But Jake didn't prod or pry.

He sighed, forcing a smile. 'Come on. Let's get you out of here. You need some fresh air and a change of scene.'

Another thing she loved about him; the way he could sense when to let her lie and when to push. She pulled a cardigan over her t-shirt. 'Pub?'

'Exactly what I was thinking.'

He was right, she thought. A change of scene. People. Talk. Anything other than sitting here, stewing over Kelly. Wordlessly, she followed him downstairs and stepped out into the street.

The heat of the day lingered even as the shadows elongated, straining against the strength of the sun as it dipped towards the hills on the horizon. They paused at the junction of Main Street as a coach turned in the narrow corner, ferrying day trippers back home.

'The Castle?' Jake asked.

Izzy shook her head. Although there were few days in the year warm enough to take advantage of the one pub in Seahouses with outside seating, she felt the pull of The Ship. Her dad's favourite pub.

Edward Morton had liked to joke that it was his home-from-home, but as a young girl, the suggestion had struck

Izzy as something more. As if part of him would always remain here. Sometimes, sitting there, she could almost imagine he was at the bar, squeezed in at the front of the crush. His familiar and comforting presence at her shoulder, his words in her ear, the warmth of his hand on hers.

Walking into The Ship was like hearing the lyrics of an old song, a tune that she had never forgotten, no matter how hard she had tried. No matter how far she had flown from this place. Like Seahouses itself. This pub, the ghosts of her father, of Amy, always pulling her back.

Gina, the landlady, flashed Izzy a friendly smile. Were they friends? Gina had been friends with Amy, and Auntie Sue seemed to like her. Perhaps Izzy should make more of an effort. They were close in age, and Izzy had always got the feeling that Gina – with her big hair, gel nails, and glamorous outfits – might have once had dreams beyond a place like Seahouses. That would be at least one thing they had in common.

They found the corner table was empty, and Jake gestured for her to sit first. 'Tonic water?'

Izzy nodded. Occasionally she missed the taste of wine, the zesty kick of a good gin and tonic, but she knew from bitter experience that for her, alcohol and sorrow did not sit well together.

She watched as Jake made his way to the bar and did her best to ignore the eyes that flitted to her corner. Everyone knew about the Salt Girl, and Izzy had no doubt they'd all been speculating about it ever since the story broke. Scouring over Kelly's sorry demise, looking for a salacious story.

How many of them had been here when it had happened? How many of them had been looking the other way as an innocent girl slipped between the cracks?

Izzy was lost in this thought as a couple of women entered the bar and was sufficiently distracted that she failed to notice one of them was Sam Shaw.

'Izzy.' Sam approached her table, her eyes narrowing into a glare.

A hush descended, and Izzy shifted uncomfortably on the banquet, the leather creaking beneath her.

'Hi, Sam...' Izzy's voice was quiet.

'Don't "hi Sam" me. I know what you've been up to.'

Izzy's heart pounded; how did Sam know? Or rather, *how much* did she know? Could she have found out, somehow, about Kelly's diary?

Sam snarled. 'I told you that whatever happened to Kelly had nothing to do with us. But you've been going around raking up the past as if...' Izzy noticed Sam's hands were clutched into fists at her thighs. 'Making out to anyone who'll listen that I stole Bryan from her or something.'

Izzy desperately scanned the faces at the bar, searching for Jake.

'Look at me when I'm talking to you.' Sam's mouth was reduced to a tight line.

There was silence in the bar now.

'Listen, Sam, I don't know what you heard—'

'Oh, I heard, all right. What, you think my husband doesn't tell me everything? Like how you came around to see him, asking him about me and about what happened back then? We don't have secrets, me and Bryan. Which is how he knows I did nothing wrong and how I know' —Sam edged closer to Izzy, so close that Izzy could smell her perfume— 'I know he had nothing to do with it.' She ground the words out through a clenched jaw.

Just then, Jake appeared at Sam's shoulder. 'Samantha, is it—'

'Don't touch me!' she hissed.

Jake held up his hands. 'I was just going to say, if you want to talk about it, why not sit down and join us?'

Sam took a step backwards, her eyes still locked with Izzy's.

'Leave me alone, you hear? Leave me and my *husband*,' she spat, 'out of this.'

26

Then

Another two detentions this week, and we're only in the second week of term. I had to explain to Mrs Wheeler that I couldn't make her Wednesday night sit-in because Mr Tait had already booked me on History. She says I might not even make a C at this rate, and I wanted to tell her I don't care; more than that, I wanted to tell her it doesn't matter. None of it matters. But how could I?

I actually kind of like her. She's nice – for a teacher, at least. It's the disappointment I see in her eyes that hurts the most.

I hardly mind detention, anyway. At least it means I'm not on the bus with Sam and that lot. Gets me out of a journey at the front, feeling their stares on the back of my head and hearing their whispers, their giggles hidden behind their hands. So utterly pathetic, the lot of them.

And it means one hour less at home with the Barretts, which is always a bonus. Some days I can't stand the stupid board games they make us play, the forced fun and all their dumb little sayings. It takes all my effort not to scream, to smash the place up, to whirl around the smallest bedroom in the house like a hurricane. Destroying what little remains.

One hundred and thirty-four days. That's how long until my birthday. How long I have left before I can escape.

I thought the Christmas holidays dragged on forever, but January feels like purgatory. The sun doesn't properly rise until we're on the school bus, and it's dark again before the end of final period. The evenings at home are almost unbearable, and I count down the hours until I can go up to my bedroom. Detentions are at least something to do. Another hour to myself.

I'm thinking about Mam more and more these days. Let's face it: I've got plenty of time on my hands. Nanna always said she was bright at school but had no common sense. You need to have both: school sense and common sense. One is no good without the other. Clearly, Mam didn't have enough sense to recognise the danger that came for her, the threat that she let into her heart and her bed. I can see that now.

I find myself wondering if she is with me. If she's up there, just beyond the clouds, looking down on me, or sitting at my shoulder like a guardian angel.

She's not doing a very good job, if she is.

N tells me not to worry about it. I can always go to college and re-sit my A levels, if that's what I want to do. It doesn't sound like such a bad plan. It means I'll delay university a year, but that's fine. I'll still be able to go back home, back to Dawn.

I'm gutted that we missed Christmas together. Especially after everything Dawn promised me. It's not like I wanted much – just her, really. For the two of us to be together at home. *Just the two of us.* But the care home offered her extra shifts, and it was time-and-a-half, and she's trying to save up for when I come back so that we can redecorate my room...

I stopped listening to her after a while. I'm tired of all her excuses.

N and I no longer talk about me going back. In the beginning, he used to say he would come to visit me in Newcastle. It was just talk, though, really. Let's face it: Dawn would throw a fit if he showed up on her doorstep. I think he cottoned on to that eventually.

Now, he gets annoyed whenever I mention going home, so I don't. Instead, we talk about me catching up next year without specifying where. As if my life will carry on – our life, our *thing*, whatever it is – will continue in some parallel universe.

He got me a phone. The phone that Dawn promised me for Christmas. She lets me down, N picks me up. That's how it works. Just like when Sam and the girls cut me out, he was there to catch me. There are so many pieces of me these days. I'm a broken cup, shards of porcelain on the floor, and he is gluing me back together.

We don't talk about Dawn anymore, either. N says she's never there for me when I need her. I don't want to agree with him, but that thought is there now. It hangs between me and Dawn during our weekly phone calls, which are getting shorter. I don't think she has noticed.

Having my own phone means N can always reach me. I wake to a flurry of messages from him, telling me how much he wants me. How much he needs me. 'You can never leave me,' he says.

The knowledge that someone desires me, depends on me – it's a new and unexpected sensation. That there's this thread between us, binding us together.

The phone is another secret between me and N. No one else can know about it, which means I can't even text Dawn. When I'm at home, I hide it in my jewellery box, then transfer it to my schoolbag each morning. I only take it out to text him once I'm safely hidden in the school toilets.

I see the girls whispering about me when I re-emerge from the cubicle. Let them talk. As if I care.

We have fallen into a comfortable pattern: I text N in the morning, at lunch break, at the start of study period. His replies come instantly, telling me where to meet him later, what to wear.

It makes it easier to plan our walks. Although we never seem to get very far. We have our spot in the dunes and N heads straight there, leading me by the hand. His hands are always warm.

It's so cold out, and there are hardly any people on the beach most days. All the sensible people are at home, avoiding the bitter winds that whip at the sea and bite at my nose, my ears. Other places. Sometimes it makes my teeth chatter. What I would give to spend a night with N in a nice, warm bed. I reminded him about his suggestion of a night away in a hotel, but he says things are too complicated just now.

And everything is about to get much, much worse.

I might not have even noticed. But Maeve does a weekly shop in the big supermarket up at Berwick, and she left a box of tampons in my room. And that's when I realised my period was late.

I bought a test in the chemist at Alnwick, praying the pharmacist wasn't someone who might know me. Praying I'd got it wrong.

Two pink lines told me I hadn't.

I don't want to tell N – I don't want to break the spell,

destroy the magic of whatever this is, this beautiful yet precarious thing we have together.

One hundred and thirty-four days. The sand in the timer stands still, but I'm not worried about how I'm going to make it to the finishing line, or how I'm going to get through these last few months.

I'm wondering how this is going to end.

27

Now

THE HOUSE WAS QUIET BY THE TIME IZZY WOKE.

Sleep had come in frantic bursts, the argument with Sam replaying in her mind over and over. She couldn't even remember the exact words Sam had said. Only the look in the woman's eyes.

Pure malice.

She could see why: Sam's marriage – her entire life – had been built on betrayal. A house of sand. Tug at the foundation, and the whole thing threatened to topple down. Izzy and Diana's visit to Bryan had clearly been enough to stir up things which had gone unsaid since their teenage years. Izzy wondered, now, what he had told Sam.

She had a vague, dream-like memory of Jake kissing her as he left earlier that morning. Untroubled, as he always was. He'd downplayed the encounter with Sam on their walk home last night, saying that such petty rows were inevitable in a small village. In a place where everyone knew everyone, there was always going to be someone who felt that the line between neighbourliness and meddling had been crossed.

There were new messages in the family group chat: Mike suggesting a barbecue that night and the others, including Jake, agreeing.

She paused on her way down the stairs, listening to her house. *Their house.* The creaks and echoes of emptiness, the stone of the walls and the timber frame of the roof responding to the warming sun. Finn would be back next week with a couple of lads to start the orangery. Izzy knew she should appreciate the peace and quiet while it lasted, but found the silence oppressive. From outside, somewhere in the shade of the back garden, came the coo of the wood pigeon.

The coffee machine whirred to life. Izzy leaned back against the ugly tiles of the wall as she waited for it to brew and thought over everything they had on Kelly.

It was now obvious that she had been involved with someone else by the time she was killed. The relationship between her and Bryan had fizzled out some months before, and her friendship with Sam had ended abruptly around the same time.

Izzy pinched the bridge of her nose between the tips of her fingers.

Halloween, Sam said. *October.*

That meant Kelly had been isolated for a couple of months before N came into her life. Had that triggered her depression? Lit the fuse on her downward spiral?

And Bryan – where did he fit in all of this? Had he known about the mystery older man? Sam mentioned that there had been rumours about Kelly, and Bryan had also suspected she was seeing someone else. Had he been worried about his former girlfriend, or consumed by jealousy?

Then there was Sam. She had betrayed Kelly, turning the others against her and claiming Bryan for herself. All these years later and she was still insecure in her relationship. Had she been worried, back then, that her treachery might catch up with her? Worried that it would be enough to break her and Bryan... Worried enough to want to bury it?

Izzy needed to clear her head.

Running always helped her to think straight. The kids had told her that Amy referred to it as her 'mum time', and although Izzy could think of far more relaxing pursuits, she had eventually decided that her sister had been on to something. She dressed quickly, lacing up her trainers and slopping on a baseball cap, locking the front door behind her.

The tide was out, and the beach was already busy. On the sand below, a boy chased after a black Labrador. She turned onto Seafield Road, following the path that ran along the top of the dunes, and the strait of St Aidan's unfurled before her, a stretch of rose-coloured tarmac road that disappeared at the base of the castle five kilometres away. She slowed, trying to fall into the pace that would allow her to focus. A fresh breeze blew in from the sea, the salt air burning in her lungs.

There wasn't much left to read in the diary; she could finish it before Jake got home that afternoon. Something had been stopping her from tackling the last few entries. The sad inevitability of Kelly's last words, perhaps? Or perhaps it was the desire to keep Kelly with her for as long as possible? Whatever it was, Izzy knew how this story finished and she didn't want the end to come until she was ready.

The question gnawed at her, a fist squeezing her stomach. *Who was N?* And what would possess a bright young woman to put it all on the line for him?

True, Kelly had been depressed for a couple of months, ostracised from her school friends and unhappy at home with the Barretts. N had befriended her at her weakest point.

And then it struck her: N's timing was not fortuitous, happenstance, or coincidence. He had known Kelly was vulnerable.

Izzy stopped running, catching her breath. Catching the meaning of this as the thought fully formed.

They had already known each other.

Like a true predator, N had stalked his victim, watching as she became more isolated. More vulnerable. He had watched as Kelly fell apart, circling her from above, and then he swooped, sinking his fangs into her like carrion.

He was someone Kelly already knew.

This would narrow the field of suspects considerably. For who? For the police? It was already Friday; she and Diana had agreed to hand over the diary after three days.

Tomorrow. She had only twenty-four hours left to work out who N was.

White clouds uncurled across the vast sky, chased by the warm breeze, and Izzy took a moment to refocus before setting off again, centring herself.

She felt her heartbeat slow to normal, and listened to each of her limbs in turn, just as her mother had shown her. *Mindfulness.* Listening to her body to take her mind off other things and allow her to see what she was missing.

Because there was something, wasn't there? Something

in that diary. Kelly's secret, hidden, waiting for her to find it. There had to be.

And if there wasn't?

Izzy turned and jogged back towards Seahouses, the sun in her eyes now. Perhaps the answer wasn't *in* the diary, but *was* the diary itself.

She reached the top of Harbour Bank and the light turned green as if it had been expecting her. The diary...

Why did Kelly leave it at Dawn's?

Kelly had been writing in it every day and had left nothing out – except N's real name, of course. Presumably, if N had already been known to her, it wouldn't have taken anyone long to work out who he was. There had already been rumours.

Izzy thought again about what Dawn had told them. The box of Kelly's things, the possessions she had left after that week she ran away. *Ran home.* Whatever.

Kelly had known that she was being taken back to Seahouses, so why would she leave her diary? And what about the other books? That random assortment of textbooks, exercise books and jotters. Perhaps their purpose had been to conceal the existence of the diary?

It was rudimentary, but Kelly would have been desperate – she'd had little notice that she was leaving. She hadn't wanted to take the diary back to Seahouses, and she hadn't wanted Dawn to find it. Without a better option, she had hidden it in plain sight.

Why couldn't she take it back with her?

Izzy thought again of the last few entries in the diary. The darkening mood at home, Eric and Maeve's disappointment in Kelly. *The Barretts.* That had to be it. Kelly had been terrified they would find out about N. But why?

Could N have been someone they knew?

She ran back to her street and kept going, passing her house and continuing to the end of the road, then looped back onto Clyde Street.

Eric Barrett was washing his car in the driveway. Izzy stopped, waiting while her heart rate and breathing slowed. He didn't see her as she approached and she watched him, wondering how he and Maeve failed to realise what was going on, back then. *What they should have known.*

Kelly had been good at keeping secrets; that much was clear. But she had been living under their roof. She wasn't their biological daughter, but they should have seen that something – many things – had troubled the young woman that lived with them.

Alerted by the sound of her footsteps, Eric looked up.

'Izzy.' He smiled, setting the sponge into a bucket of sudsy grey water. 'Good to see you again.'

'Likewise.' She tried to sound friendly, casual. 'Do you have a moment?'

He wiped his hands on his shorts self-consciously. 'Certainly. I was just about to take a tea break, as it happens.' He gestured for her to follow him inside, and she obliged.

'Maeve,' he called out. 'We have a visitor.'

Maeve appeared at the doorway to the kitchen, wide-eyed, unable to conceal her surprise.

'Please, come on through. I was just working out in the garden.' She gestured to her floral overalls by way of explanation. 'Shall we sit in the living room?'

Izzy suddenly felt conscious of her damp running vest, the sour smell of the sweat on her skin.

'We can sit out in the garden, if that's all right with you.'

She couldn't help but notice Maeve's sigh of relief.

The Barretts' garden was as neat and orderly as the interior of their house. The lawn was freshly mown, and a well-tended vegetable patch nestled in one corner. Izzy's eyes were drawn to the gate that led onto the cut between the gardens.

From here, she could see her own house. She'd never viewed it from this angle. Even at this distance, Izzy could make out the scar on the brickwork where the old conservatory had stood. She took a seat at the teak patio table, angling her chair so that she was facing away from her house, and pushed thoughts of the conservatory and Kelly's salty grave from her mind.

Maeve, ever the consummate hostess, emerged with a tray of iced tea. The glasses immediately began to sweat, crystal droplets of water beading in the heat. The weather forecast said there might be a storm later that night, but Izzy couldn't imagine this heat ever ending.

She took a sip and wondered where to begin.

'Diana and I went to see Dawn Reynolds.' She clocked the momentary puzzlement that flashed over Maeve's face. 'Kelly's aunt, in Newcastle,' she added quickly.

'Yes, of course. I'm surprised she hasn't come here herself.' Eric looked troubled. 'I would want to see the place for myself, if it was my family. Still, you can't predict how people will respond in these situations.'

'Indeed...' said Maeve, her mouth pinching into a tight line. 'And we must not draw conclusions from that.'

Izzy felt a pang of sympathy for Dawn. But who knew what the Barretts had been told? They had no way of knowing, she realised, how hard Dawn had fought to keep Kelly.

'You're right.' Eric shook his head and sighed. 'Judge not, and you shall not be judged.'

Izzy did her best to ignore this. 'We wondered – Diana wondered – about the week that Kelly ran away in February that year. If she might have told her aunt what was bothering her.' She paused, wondering how to explain what she knew without revealing the existence of the diary. 'It seems that Kelly was in a relationship.'

'Yes.' Maeve frowned. 'We already told you that. We knew she was involved with a boy—'

'Not Bryan Shaw.' Izzy spoke quickly. 'There was someone else. Someone after Bryan.'

'Oh?' Eric exchanged a troubled glance with Maeve. 'I doubt that very much. If memory serves me...'

'He was an older man.' Izzy avoided their eyes. 'Married. Someone that she had to keep secret.'

'Heavens above,' Maeve muttered, lifting her eyes skyward.

'It's not... I mean...'

'Now, come on.' Eric tutted. 'That's a terrible thing to suggest.'

'That's... It's, er, not my suggestion,' Izzy stuttered. She felt her face growing red and spoke quickly. 'Her friends, and Dawn, well, they thought—'

Maeve scoffed. 'I doubt very much the aunt would have known a thing like that and not said something. They never seemed close, anyway. And Sam and those other girls had a falling out with her. You said so yourself. Besides, do you think we would have allowed such a thing?' Maeve's voice softened. 'I can imagine that there are rumours and all sorts flying around about dear Kelly, god rest her soul, but you can't put store in any of that.'

Eric laid a hand on his wife's. A show of solidarity. 'You must understand, we provided a good home to those children. A loving home. We took care of them, protected them. Yes, that means running a tight ship. Kelly might have been troubled, but I can assure you, she was never caught up in anything as unsavoury as what you're suggesting.'

Izzy took a deep breath. 'But just imagine, for a moment, that I'm right? She would have gone to great lengths to hide it from you.' She did her best to still her features to a neutral expression. 'No one would blame you for not noticing.'

She wasn't sure that the last part was entirely true, but she needed them to see; to at least consider the possibility.

'Kelly was mature for her age.' Maeve sighed, her eyes sheened with tears now. 'We did our best for her, but perhaps our best wasn't good enough this time.'

'Say for argument's sake, she was seeing someone – and keeping it secret. Is there somebody, anybody at all you can think of? Anyone, an adult, that she was particularly... close to?'

A look of incredulity passed between Maeve and Eric, the magnitude of this dawning on them. The horror of what they might have missed.

Izzy changed tack. 'I understand that you were strict with Kelly.'

'We were strict with all of them.' Eric leaned forward, as if to stress the importance of his point. 'We needed to be. After what those children had been through, they needed the discipline and the routine. They needed to learn that care means boundaries.' He laced his fingers through Maeve's. 'And I can assure you, every child who passed through our door received nothing but the best care.'

'Izzy.' Tears brimmed in Maeve's eyes now, and Izzy sensed that their conversation was coming to an end. 'This is a godly home. We would both go to the ends of the earth to protect the children from harm. Boyfriends and such were out of bounds and the kind of thing you're suggesting is, frankly, unthinkable. Yes, Kelly might not have liked our rules. But if she had been in any sort of trouble, we'd have been the first to know.'

Izzy sighed, resigned. She could see it now. Rules that were set with care but created an impassable friction. The attempt to build a loving home, only for it to feel oppressive to those who lived within its walls.

Kelly would never have been able to tell the Barretts that she had become involved with an older man, or that she was pregnant. There was no way she could have told them what kind of trouble she was in. It was why she hadn't been able to risk bringing her diary back to Seahouses.

And it was probably, thought Izzy, the reason that Kelly had seen only one way out.

Her escape plan, though, had failed.

28

Back at home, Izzy resumed her reading of Kelly's diary. There were just a couple of entries left, and she was still holding out hope that one of the last pages contained some clue, some hint, as to who N might have been.

She took a pitcher of water out into the back garden and settled herself just feet from where Kelly had lain, willing the girl to tell her something. *Anything.*

A spider was spinning a web between the tabletop and the leg. A net in which to catch its prey, just as N had preyed on Kelly. In the pit of Izzy's stomach, furious indignation smouldered. She exhaled slowly, breathing out her angry thoughts and forcing herself to focus on Kelly's words.

The entries were no longer daily – Kelly would skip a day or two, here and there. Izzy imagined long evenings at the Barretts' when taking the diary out of its hiding place would have been too risky. Kelly couldn't take the chance that one of them caught her writing and discovered her secrets.

Kelly had written her final entry at Dawn's house. *The week she ran home.* There was a sadness to the words on the page now. But Kelly had not despaired. Even with the odds stacked against her, she seemed determined to find a way out. She had been strong and resilient, right up until the end.

Izzy brushed away the tears that fell without warning as she turned onto the final page, absorbing Kelly's last words. The page opposite was blank. A solitary tear landed on the paper, turning it translucent.

There was no finality to Kelly's story, no poetic sign-off. She'd written that last entry in the belief she was coming back to the diary, with no way of knowing that social services were about to cart her back to Seahouses.

Back to the man who would end her story for good.

Straight into the spider's web.

The anger was a raging fire now, and Izzy could no longer fight it. Hot tears coursed down her face. It was senseless; that's what it was. She sobbed in fury at the man who had done this to Kelly and the system that had allowed it to happen, and in outrage at the village that had turned its back on a girl, looking the other way as she had fallen through the cracks. Mostly, she cried for Kelly: a girl who had deserved so much more. They had all failed her.

She didn't hear the front door open, nor Jake's careful tread along the hallway and through the living room.

'Good afternoon, gorgeous.'

Izzy was startled by his sudden presence; she laid a palm to her chest, willing her racing pulse to slow.

'Hey...' Jake softened in concern. 'What's all this?' His eyes settled on the diary in front of her.

'It's Kelly. She left her diary behind at Dawn's place.'

Jake's eyes widened, but he said nothing.

'Diana and I took it away. Just to see if there was something... well...' Izzy shrugged.

'And is there?' Jake asked.

Izzy took a deep breath. 'She was seeing an older man. Just like Sam suggested. But she only uses a codename for him: N. And there's no clue as to who he could be. Just that he was married, and he got her pregnant...' She choked on the words, and fresh tears fell.

Jake leaned down towards her, wrapping an arm around her shoulder and kissing the top of her head. 'Darling, I'm so sorry. That can't have been easy reading.'

'And I know what you're about to say. I know this is evidence. And we're going to hand it over to the police. It's just...'

'I get it,' said Jake with a sad sigh. 'You don't trust that they'll take it seriously.'

Izzy sniffed. 'It's been three weeks already and they seem to be no further forward. Diana and I just thought—'

'You don't need to tell me. I know Diana Wheeler well enough. She'd have fancied cracking the case herself and handing the results of her investigation to the police. Solving the mystery and leaving them all wondering how she did it.'

'It's not that.' Izzy considered this. 'Well, it's more than that. She feels... responsible, I guess? Like she should have known what was happening to Kelly? Like she could have stopped it...'

'That's a terrible guilt to live with.'

Izzy nodded. 'We agreed we would try to work out who N might have been, but there's nothing to go on. It's hopeless.'

'Nothing is ever hopeless.' Jake glanced at his watch. 'We're due over at Mike's in an hour. Let's see what Sue thinks. Two heads are better than one, and all that.'

She had forgotten the invitation to a family barbecue

that she had skim-read that morning. Spending an evening with Auntie Sue held some appeal, though. And perhaps Jake was right. Izzy had been so focused on the diary, looking for clues between Kelly's words, that she had overlooked the obvious. Everyone knew everyone in Seahouses; surely, someone could work out who N was?

'I'm not sure it's barbecue weather,' she mumbled. 'The forecast is for a storm tonight.'

Jake dismissed her concern with a wave of his hand. 'What would a barbecue be without a side-serving of the great British weather? I refuse to go unless we're expecting at least three centimetres of rain.'

She smiled at this; at his ability to find the sunshine behind every grey cloud.

Far out at sea, the sky was turning slate. They drove to Mike's, expecting a wash-out before it was time to go home.

'I love it when it's like this,' Jake said, as they parked outside the house.

'Like what?'

'Changeable. You know. Bright sunshine one moment, dark and stormy the next. How the day can completely transform, as if by magic. And no matter how extreme it gets, you know it will always swing back again.'

Izzy felt the breath snag in her throat. *Changeable.* The weather, her temperament. Unpredictable, except in its unpredictability. Perhaps it wasn't just that she and Jake were opposites which made them a good match. It was that she was the wild weather, and he knew that no matter which way she swung, she would always come right back to him.

They let themselves into the house. Even after all this

time, Izzy could still sense her sister here. The shape and smell of Amy; her voice, her spirit, infused in the bricks and mortar. Amy, she knew, would never leave this place.

'There you are.' Emily was alone in the kitchen, mixing a large salad at the old oak table that took up half the room. 'The others are out the back.'

'Need a hand?' Jake offered.

Izzy skirted past them and slipped out into the back garden. Mike was optimistically stoking charcoals on the barbecue while Izzy's mother and the three children were engaged in what appeared to be an energetic dance routine in the middle of the lawn.

'Look, Auntie Izzy!' cried Betsy, waving to her. 'We're making a TikTok!'

Izzy waved back and took a seat next to the table beside her aunt, who regarded her with a raised eyebrow.

'It's the new thing on social media, apparently,' Sue explained.

Izzy suppressed a smile. 'Sorry I missed tea in Bamburgh.' She bit her lip. 'I've had quite a busy week.'

'The renovation keeping you occupied?' Izzy could tell from the tone of her aunt's question that Sue already knew there was more to it.

'Actually, I've been looking into Kelly's disappearance. Trying to...' She didn't want to say it: *investigate*.

'I don't suppose Diana Wheeler put you up to that, did she?' Her aunt flashed her a knowing look.

Izzy nodded. 'She feels bad, Auntie Sue. Like she missed something back then. Like she could have stopped it.' Her aunt said nothing, leaving Izzy the space to continue. She lowered her voice. 'Kelly was pregnant when she was killed. And we know she had been involved with a man – an older man.'

'Ah. I see...' Sue's smile dropped.

'Kelly left a diary at her aunt's, hidden amongst some books she left behind. This older guy, he *groomed* her. And when he got her pregnant, he was furious with her. Kelly was clearly concerned enough for her safety to run away. She wrote it all down.'

Sue hugged her arms across her chest. 'Any idea who he was?'

The day was darkening now; the colour draining from the garden.

'She only gives him a codename.' Izzy shrugged. 'We noticed straight away that something was up because everyone else was named. "N". That's all she said.'

'Someone whose name begins with N... There can't be too many people.'

Goosebumps speckled up Izzy's forearms. 'And my guess is that it's someone she had known for a while. Someone who had seen her fall out with her friends and break up with Bryan. Someone who knew how unhappy she was at the Barretts'.'

Just then, the rain started. A fat drop landed on Izzy's shoulder.

'Oh dear.' Sue looked up at the sky. 'I tried to warn him...'

Mike dashed over to join them, a grill fork in his hand. 'It'll pass in a minute, don't you worry. We can keep dry under here in the meantime.' He chanced a glance upward and a look of uncertainty flashed behind his eyes. 'So, Jake tells me you're starting work on the new conservatory next week?'

Izzy did not remind him it was an orangery. What was the point? 'I've got Finn and a couple of guys coming in.'

'Not Shaw's?'

Izzy tried to disguise a shudder at the mention of the name. Even if Kelly had been seeing another man, it was Bryan Shaw's family firm that dug the hole. Bryan was not off the hook. Not yet.

'I bumped into him the other day.' Mike carried on, oblivious to her discomfort. 'Old Nicholas Shaw.'

An icy chill snaked down Izzy's spine. She exchanged a glance with Sue and saw the realisation as it dawned on her aunt's face.

'Wait a second.' Izzy's heart was hammering now. 'Who's Nicholas Shaw?'

'Bryan's old man.' Mike's expression was puzzled, as if this answer was obvious. 'They did most of our building work, back when Amy and I first got this place.'

Izzy's scalp prickled. 'Nicholas Shaw is Bryan Shaw's father?'

'That would be the one,' muttered Sue, with a sad shake of her head.

'I need to go.' Izzy stood in panicked haste, the chair legs scraping against the flagstones of the patio, nails on a chalkboard. 'I'll be back soon,' she said, as she dashed to the door.

Diana was staring at the crossword.

She had stared at it for twenty minutes before she gave up on timing the activity, sparing herself the indignity and unnecessary added pressure. The time it took wasn't important, after all; only that she got there in the end.

Now, only three words eluded her. Diana scoured the dictionary of her mind, pushing her brain to connect the dots.

Once upon a time she had been able to complete *The Guardian*'s crossword in her sleep. Well, perhaps not quite in her sleep. But now, despite being wide awake she felt groggy, her mind hazy. Mist over the fields in the morning, gathering in the spaces by the hedgerows and next to the stile. She imagined old farm equipment left out in the rain, the hinges and joints and mechanisms worn by the weather. Rusted and rotten.

It could be down to having spent the best part of the past two years alone, she mused. Plenty of people were reportedly still feeling the effects of isolation. If she was only suffering from some minor bouts of memory loss, well, that wasn't so much to complain about, was it? Diana liked to believe she had fared rather well in lockdown; although she had so badly missed the girls, at times. Even Jennifer. Heavens, even the grandchildren.

Or perhaps it would have happened anyway. It wasn't loneliness that had triggered Granny Agnew's demise.

The trick, she knew, was to think about something else – anything else – in order to distract the brain. Focus elsewhere, temporarily, to subconsciously find clarity in what was presently a blind spot.

How bizarre, she thought, the ways in which the mind could work. How it *should* work. And yet, deep down, she knew this wasn't just a side-effect of isolation. It was her body betraying her. A secret code, hidden in her DNA. Her fate written in her blood, just as it had been for Granny Agnew.

Diana's heart sank with the most dreadful realisation that the answer to this conundrum would quite possibly never come, even if she were to look in the opposite direction.

Besides, the only other subject she seemed capable of focusing on was dear Kelly.

The trip to Newcastle three days ago had exhausted her,

leaving her both physically and emotionally depleted. Izzy had to help her from the car, and it had taken all Diana's strength to lift her key to the door and step over the threshold into her cottage.

She had handed Izzy the folder from 2003 – which included Kelly's attendance records and exam scores in that last term before she vanished – and, at one moment, had considered asking her friend to help her up the stairs to bed.

But Diana was a proud woman. She could think of few things worse than becoming a grotesque old lady who needed help with brushing her teeth.

She was holding out hope that Izzy would find something of import in that wretched diary. Diana's greatest – indeed, her only remaining desire – was to see whoever hurt that girl caught and brought to justice.

From his perch atop the mantelpiece, inside the gilded frame that had been a wedding gift, Lionel returned her gaze. Was that disappointment she saw in his expression? Those eyes that had once sparkled with mischief and vitality. Did Lionel see, from wherever he was, how badly Diana had failed the girl?

A knock at her door startled her. More of a frantic pounding than a friendly alert. It creaked as she opened it.

'Izzy.' Diana wished she had known to expect company; she would have smartened up. She always suspected that Izzy, unlike her darling sister Amy, placed much importance on appearances.

'I think I've got it.' The younger woman struggled to catch her breath between the words, and Diana sensed that she'd had the most terrible fright. A cup of sugary tea would calm the girl down and steady her nerves. Diana ushered her inside.

'The diary.' Izzy retrieved the notebook from her handbag. 'I was at Mike's, and he said something, so I called at home...' She took a steadying breath. 'Sorry, I'm babbling. The diary. Kelly was definitely seeing someone – an older, married man. The one she refers to only as N.'

'And you have worked out who N is?'

'It's Nicholas Shaw. Bryan Shaw's father. He ran the business—'

'Yes, I know who he is. And your assumption that he is the perpetrator is based on... What, exactly?'

'His name begins with N. Kelly knew him – she dated his son. And the way she describes the relationship... how it, er, progressed. Diana, N was someone who *knew* Kelly. Someone who knew that she was unhappy and isolated and exploited it.'

'And you believe that Nicholas Shaw could have done that? Conducted an illicit affair with Kelly and then killed her?'

'Yes! He's the only person that fits the profile. It has to be him.'

Diana could sense Izzy's exasperation and did not want to ask how much time, exactly, she had dedicated to thinking about this puzzle. It seemed to her that the girl had snatched at the first available straw and clutched it with all her might.

'Perhaps you're on to something...' She sank back into the armchair and steepled her fingers. 'Or perhaps this N might be someone else entirely. I think we need to spend a little more time—'

'No. No, Diana.' Izzy shot her a warning look. 'We said we'd give the diary to the police this weekend. We can't keep it any longer.' She lowered her voice to an urgent whisper. 'We're withholding evidence in a murder investigation.'

Diana shrugged, resigned. Clearly, on this point, her friend was not for turning.

It was dark now, the day prematurely cut short. The storm was already upon them.

Izzy misread Diana's silence as agreement. 'I'm calling the police right now and we're going to tell them everything.'

Diana nodded. It was easier to acquiesce, and far be it from her to put up a fight. Izzy would find out the hard way, if it came to that.

For the truth, Diana had learned, was almost always more complicated than it initially seemed.

29

THE INCIDENT ROOM FOR THE SALT GIRL MURDER WAS A sorry state of affairs. Pamela Bell tossed her jacket onto a pale blue chair and sank into the seat opposite with a sigh.

The pastel colour scheme had been a mandate from regional HQ to redecorate meeting rooms in calming, relaxing colours – hues that studies had shown were conducive to good teamwork and creative thinking. But then some budget line had been cut before the job was finished, and Room Three at Alnwick Police Station was mired by a burgundy carpet against which the cleaners seemed to be fighting a losing battle against the crisp crumbs permanently trapped between the fibres.

It wasn't as if there were many of them around to be induced into creative collaboration, anyway. After the initial excitement – she hated to think of it that way, but Pam was a pragmatist – the teams had been reassigned to other cases. Less complex cases with more likelihood of favourable outcomes. Quick wins for the victims of crime. Results that would bolster some line on a graph at HQ. One or two officers had been moved at first, then a flurry.

A bloody exodus, more like.

Pam sighed. It was more than three weeks since they had found the body. The vic that the papers had called the Salt Girl. So far, they had an ID on the body and nowt much else to go on.

There had been the usual calls from fantasists and conspiracy theorists, as well as several individuals claiming to be the murderer. None of them took long to check out. Now, even the nut-jobs' calls had dried to a trickle.

The parents – the foster parents, that was – were distraught, sure enough. They had been too easily fooled by the story that Kelly had run away, but Pamela couldn't hold that against them. Social services had been ultimately responsible for the girl's welfare.

The girl's old case worker, a woman named Lisa who had retired several years ago, said she'd wanted to leave the file open, but the department had been under-staffed and under-funded, and when they'd received a postcard from Kelly, she had reluctantly shut it down. Happened frequently, according to Lisa, especially when a child got close to eighteen.

And the friends, including the ex-boyfriend – Pam had quite fancied that one's chances, initially – were all pleading ignorance. Kelly, as far as they were concerned, had simply vanished.

Somehow, no one had felt singularly responsible for finding her.

If it were another child, another time, perhaps there would have been a more thorough investigation. The police would have looked more closely at that bloody postcard, for one thing. *An own goal.* They had kept Kelly on the missing person's list, but without social services or a family braying at the door, the case had been allowed to gather dust.

The whole sorry fiasco was a big, bloody mess.

Finally, forensics had managed to come up with a DNA sample from the pregnancy. It would help, but only if they had someone to test.

Again, Pam thought of the ex-boyfriend. He didn't seem the type, but then again, did any of them? Thirty years of policing had taught her to keep an open mind.

They would need a warrant for a paternity test, though, and here Pam was on shaky ground. If Bryan Shaw failed to be a match, the real father – and possibly the killer, whether that was the same person – could be alerted to the fact they had DNA from the pregnancy and flee.

The temperature had dropped this evening, the heat-wave finally breaking. Pam stood to close the window just as the first drops of rain fell. A storm was blowing in from the sea. She was in for a long night.

And why the salt? It had some significance – everything had some rhyme or reason, no matter how warped the killer's logic – but what? She shuddered.

They needed something more concrete, but that required old-fashioned police work. Boots on the ground.

She sighed. Hers were the only pair of boots in sight.

The phone on the desk rang, startling her.

'Incident Room.' Her voice echoed in the emptiness, and she was conscious that it was too quiet in here. She shuffled some papers, hoping it sounded like activity. 'How can I help you?'

'I'd like to speak with DI Bell.' The caller's voice was familiar. *Too familiar.*

Pam's mouth drew to a tight line. 'Speaking.'

'Diana Wheeler here,' Diana said, as if Pam hadn't already figured that out. 'I – we – may have turned up some evidence.'

Now there was a bloody surprise. Pam had almost been expecting as much ever since the afternoon she caught Miss bleeding Marple paying a visit on the Shaws.

Pam leaned back against the wall. The periwinkle gloss paint had yellowed with age and as the result of more than one sneaked cigarette. More than one smoked by Pam herself.

Calm, calm, calm.

'I see. Do you want to talk about it?'

'Face-to-face would be preferable. There's something we need to show you.'

Pam rolled her eyes. Well, she supposed, it wasn't as if there was much else going on tonight.

'I'll be there in twenty minutes.' She picked up her jacket, ready to brave the rain.

The roads were deserted and the drive to Beadnell took no time at all. She pulled up outside Diana's cottage, remembering the last time she had been here. It was too much of a coincidence that whenever trouble brewed in these quarters, Diana Wheeler never seemed to be far away. Besides, Pam had never believed in coincidences.

'Good evening, Inspector.' Diana greeted Pam with a smile and gestured for her to enter.

The cottage was warm, and a cloud of steam indicated a freshly boiled kettle.

'Isabelle.' Pam kept her voice cool. 'We meet again.'

Izzy Morton gave a noncommittal shrug, and Pam thought of Amy. They looked alike – had looked alike – and Pam thought back to a time when it was the other sister roped into one of Diana Wheeler's amateur investigations. The woman truly did fancy herself as some kind of private eye, preferably surrounded by a gaggle of women to do her bidding.

Pam accepted a seat at the small dining table and Izzy poured tea.

'We ran into Dawn Reynolds, Kelly's aunt.' Izzy was avoiding eye contact, and Pam had the distinct impression that the two of them had agreed the younger woman would do the talking. 'And she mentioned she kept some of Kelly's old books. We found a diary from her year in Seahouses.'

Izzy placed the book on the table. It wasn't obviously a diary; no lock and key, or anything like that. Pam wondered how come they had 'run into' Kelly's aunt, and just how much time they had spent going through this alleged diary before deciding to alert her to its presence. She stilled her features, hiding her annoyance, and let Izzy continue with her rehearsed explanation.

'Kelly had become involved with a man in the months leading up to her death. An older, married man. We heard there were rumours at the time, and the diary corroborates this. She was groomed by a man she codenamed N.'

'I see...' Pamela managed. 'And do you have any idea who N was?'

'Nicholas Shaw.' Izzy spoke firmly, now. 'Bryan Shaw's father. He was the one who built the conservatory. We have the paperwork from the house to prove it. And Kelly knew him – she says in one of her earlier entries that he was a nice guy. I've read the whole thing and there's no one else who fits the profile.' She took a deep breath. 'I believe Nick Shaw exploited her, and when she got pregnant, he killed her. It's all in there. The pieces fit.'

Pam took the diary from Izzy. The book was a little over two-thirds full. She flicked through it, skimming the lines of neat handwriting. Here it was: Kelly was writing about Bryan's dad. And here – and here – was N.

Her stomach twisted in revulsion. No matter how many cases of child abuse and exploitation she dealt with, it never got any easier. Pam bit the inside of her lip hard enough to draw blood. She skipped to the last entry. The opposite page was blank.

The poor lass. *What a sorry old mess.*

Pam closed the book and set it on the table in front of her. She took a slow breath before she spoke again. 'How do you know the diary is credible?' She picked up her teacup, forcing herself to stay calm. 'How can you even be sure it was Kelly who wrote this?' She leaned forward in her seat and kept her voice impassive.

Izzy and Diana exchanged a worried glance. Finally, they were thinking this through. Seeing, once and for all, that there were good reasons to leave the detective work to the real detectives.

'In fact,' said Pam, 'how do I know you haven't fabricated this piece of so-called "evidence" yourselves?'

Izzy swallowed. 'We wouldn't do that...'

'You're telling me that you stumbled upon a critical piece of evidence in a murder enquiry.' Pam shrugged. 'It's my job to question what your motives are. What skin you have in this game.'

Izzy was incredulous. 'How can you...? It was my garden where they found her. *My home.* Of course, I want you to catch whoever did this. That's my skin, right there—'

'My dear.' Diana laid a hand on Pam's. The old lady's palm was cool, her skin papery, and her eyes grew moist as she spoke. 'I failed Kelly all those years ago. She crumbled before my eyes, and I missed it. And when she vanished, I was one of the many who were content to take the explanation at face value. Now, I want to see justice.'

Pam took stock of her. The woman must be almost ninety by now. A tiny bird-like thing, with a wispy halo of cloud-white hair fixed back in a low knot at the nape of her neck. She could imagine Diana had been quite a looker, back in her day.

Pam's stomach growled, and she realised she had missed lunch. She'd been too preoccupied, and without much of a team – all right, any team – working alongside her, there had been no one to remind her when mealtimes rolled around.

It was almost impressive what these women had achieved. Not that she would ever permit Diana Wheeler the satisfaction of acknowledging as much. But Pam had to admit, they had got further than she had. Perhaps people were more willing to open up to a neighbour than the police.

She sighed, shaking her head. The badge did put people off.

This was not the time to let frustration cloud her judgement – she needed to act on facts, and facts alone. N had got Kelly pregnant, and his response to the news had frightened her. Had she been right to fear him?

'I'm going to pay a visit to Nick Shaw.' Pam spoke carefully, her voice measured. 'If anyone asks, you found this diary and gave it straight to me. Without reading it cover-to-cover before you bothered to call. Is that clear?'

Izzy nodded meekly. 'Crystal.'

'And if there is any other evidence that you suddenly remember or happen across, please be sure to let me know.'

She bade them farewell and dashed back to her car. Rain

slicked the pavements to an oily shine, and beyond the harbour, the sea was a black void. Pamela locked the doors and picked up the radio.

'Control room, this is DI Bell requesting attendance of a unit in Seahouses. I'm bringing a suspect in.'

'I was getting worried,' Jake said to Izzy when she finally arrived back at Mike's.

The barbecue had officially been abandoned some time earlier, the hamburgers and sausages cooked under the kitchen grill instead. Even from the warmth of Amy's kitchen, she felt the aggression of the storm outside as the night battered the coastline.

Sue was loading the dishwasher. 'Where on earth did you get to?'

Izzy took a seat at Amy's old oak table, her stomach suddenly knotting in hunger at the smell of the food. 'I went to Diana's. We called DI Bell out and told her everything.'

A shadow of concern flashed across Jake's face. 'You're not in any trouble, are you? Was she all right about... it all?'

'Yes.' Izzy shrugged. 'In the end. Although she clearly doesn't appreciate anyone stepping on her toes.'

Sue dried her hands and joined her. 'I'm afraid the police and Diana have history, as far as toe-stepping is concerned.'

'Here. Saved you some.' Jake set a plate down in front of her, and she gratefully accepted a burger that was still warm. 'Sue told me about Nicholas Shaw.'

Izzy nodded; her mouth was too full to speak.

'Are you sure about this?' Sue said, her face creasing in a frown. 'He always struck me as being an all right bloke.'

Izzy swallowed. 'He was the only person called N in the whole diary. Kelly knew him, and he knew when to pounce. All the pieces fit.'

'My goodness.' Sue had paled. 'So, will they arrest him?'

'Sounded like she's going to speak to him.' Izzy glanced at Jake for confirmation.

He nodded. 'They'll want to get a DNA sample, and they'll need a warrant for that.'

'Heavens...' Sue muttered. 'It'll be all over the village by morning.'

'What are you so worried about? That man deserves everything that's coming to him.' Izzy couldn't hide her annoyance.

Finally, just when they had worked out who N was, her aunt seemed more concerned about the upset an arrest might cause than what he'd done to warrant it.

She thought back to the diary. It had been quite obvious all along. The answer had been staring them in the face. If only she knew her neighbours as well as Diana or Sue did, or even Amy, she would have connected the dots from the beginning.

But why hadn't Diana made the connection to Nicholas Shaw?

Her memory, thought Izzy. *Her memory is going.*

And then Izzy remembered Diana's response when she'd presented the suggestion. Her old friend had been hesitant to call the police. Was it because she wanted more time to work on the case? To keep Kelly's diary to themselves, even if only for a little longer?

Or was it something more?

She saw, then, what she'd missed earlier. What she had overlooked in her haste. *Diana's doubt.*

Diana had doubted Nicholas Shaw was their man. Why? Izzy tried to shake it off.

N. Nicholas Shaw ticked all the boxes. It was obvious.

Wasn't it?

30

ACCORDING TO THE NEWSREADER, LAST NIGHT'S STORM hadn't done too much damage.

Izzy carried the radio into the kitchen, waiting for the rest of the headlines, anxious to see if the police had released details of an arrest in the Salt Girl case. She chewed on the inside of her lip.

A storm – it was almost laughable to call it as much. Nothing like the spectacles she had seen in Hong Kong, where lightning set the sky ablaze, and thunder rattled the windows. The first time Izzy had experienced a typhoon, despite instinct pushing her to be afraid, she had sat at the window of her living room, marvelling at the might of nature as the wind furiously raged outside.

She sighed. Even the weather here was flat. Missing that spark, that flair. Grey.

Although, she remembered a second later, that last storm had been strong enough to blow the old conservatory in on itself.

The news segment ended, and the presenter skipped

into a bouncy nineties track with no mention of the girl found buried under Izzy's garden.

DI Bell was probably still working on Shaw, Izzy mused, shuddering as she imagined the detective's interrogation techniques. Or perhaps they were waiting for the results of his paternity test. It was surely only a matter of time until the evidence spoke for itself.

Jake was out at his every-other-Saturday personal training session in Alnwick, something he had taken up as a way of getting in shape for their wedding. Izzy had insisted that she loved him exactly the way he was. Even now, she thought of the curve of his collarbone, the smooth arc of his shoulder blade and the soft, pale skin on the underside of his forearm. She knew every angle and line of his body with a cherished familiarity.

It was true, he wasn't her usual type. Before, in her old life, Izzy had gone for men with gym-honed muscles, faux-casual hair, and thick wallets. Exotic accents, sometimes. Invariably sun-tanned. Men who were seeking the same goals she was: adventure, status, novelty. Bright lights, bigger and better things.

She cringed as she thought back to some of her previous relationships. No wonder none of them had lasted terribly long.

Jake had been precisely everything she had not been looking for, and he had walked into her life at the exact moment she had not been looking. It had taken her sister's death to force Izzy to reassess how far, exactly, her dreams had taken her. And when she had, she'd come up short.

She thought of Amy, now. How Amy would have set a date for this damned wedding; would have got the renovation going. How Amy would have known how to handle the fall-out from the girl buried under the conservatory.

A lump rose in her throat, and Izzy wiped away tears that came out of nowhere. They said it got easier, and perhaps it did, but whenever the grief came, it was still a wave that knocked her off-centre. A bottomless sea.

She stood in the silence of her kitchen and let it wash over her, waiting for the swell of sorrow to pass.

It was a good ten minutes before she felt ready to move again. Izzy picked up her shopping basket and slipped on a baseball cap, ready to resume her day.

The heatwave had picked up where it left off and was predicted to continue for at least another week. Yesterday's inclement weather was already long forgotten, judging by the river of tourists idling along Main Street. Streams of people were breaking away and spilling down Harbour Bank.

There was a small queue outside Carter's. Izzy joined the end of the line at the bakery and pulled her phone out of her bag, mindlessly flicking through Pinterest while she waited. She had almost zoned out of her surroundings, absorbed in her phone, until the chatter up ahead caught her attention.

'... they arrested him! Last night!'

Izzy ducked her chin to her chest and peered out from beneath her baseball cap, but it was impossible to see who was speaking.

'Yes,' the voice was saying. A stage whisper. 'Nick Shaw. Something to do with that lass they found.'

There was a gasp from further ahead in the line. 'You're kidding...'

'That's what I heard. Joanne is furious.'

'What's this?' Someone else had joined the conversation now, the news spreading along the queue like a flame, igniting their attention.

'It's true. Celia told me.'

'Heavens above...'

'Aye. There were three police cars outside their house for over an hour.'

A tut. 'Whatever is this world coming to...'

Izzy felt her ears growing hot, a flush burning in her face. She imagined these same people standing in line almost thirty years ago, whispering about her mother's breakdown. They had found glee in gossiping about it, but not one of them had jumped in to help.

She abandoned her place in the queue, forgoing the bread she'd intended to buy, and walked back along Main Street with her head down. *This is how it starts,* she thought. By the time the radio and television and newspapers got wind of it, the story would be common knowledge in Seahouses.

She was staring intently at her feet, taking long, purposeful strides, and didn't see Sam Shaw approach her until it was too late.

'You.' Sam spat.

Izzy took stock of her. That artfully blow-dried hair had been left to its own devices and hung at her shoulders in careless, uneven waves. Sam's face was make-up free, and the dark hollows beneath her eyes told Izzy it had been a long, sleepless night.

'You're behind this, aren't you?' Without the gloss, Izzy could imagine the plain teenager who had once paled in Kelly's shadow.

'I didn't... I mean, I don't know what you're talking about.' Izzy made a move to pass Sam, but the other woman blocked her path.

'Oh, I think you do. The police said they'd had *new evidence* from an acquaintance of Kelly. It's you and that bloody Mrs Wheeler. I know what you've been up to.' Sam took another step towards her until there was no more than a fist between them.

'But I... It's just...' Izzy stuttered, lost for words. Afraid to back down and afraid to stand her ground.

Sam's eyes were cold. 'I told you before: this has nothing to do with us. Not with me, not with my Bryan, and not his dad. And I'm warning you one last time: stay away from my family.'

With that, Sam stormed off, and Izzy watched her hurried gait as she wove through the crowds before disappearing from view.

Izzy exhaled, a long, slow release, her pulse hammering in her ears.

'I'm telling you, Jake, she was furious with me.' Izzy shuddered.

'Perhaps she's angry with herself.' Jake sank back against the ugly sofa beside her, his hand still on Izzy's. His thumb traced a circle on her palm. 'Who knows? Maybe Sam always suspected it was Nick that Kelly got tangled up with and she turned a blind eye back then.'

'Well, she seems to be turning all her anger on me right now.'

But was Jake right? Was Sam's rage because her father-in-law had been exposed, or because of her guilt at covering up for him?

So what? She mused. *Who cares what Sam or any of them think?* If Nick Shaw had committed a crime, he needed to pay for it. And if Sam had known... well, she would have to live with the consequences.

'He's protesting his innocence, of course,' said Jake. 'I

checked in with a pal earlier. According to Nick, he had nothing to do with Kelly.'

'How convenient.' Izzy leaned back, closing her eyes again.

Running into Sam this morning had left her drained, unable to focus. Another day lost to time, her to-do list no shorter than it had been yesterday.

'Come on.' Jake stood.

'Come where?'

'I'm taking my fiancée out for the evening.'

Izzy rubbed the corner of her eye with her thumb. 'I don't know...'

'Nonsense. We're going to the pub for a couple of drinks, then we're going to get a takeaway on our way home. Besides...' He leaned down towards her, his lips brushing her forehead. 'My fiancée abandoned the grocery shopping this morning, and we have nothing in for dinner.'

Izzy grimaced. 'Fine,' she sighed. 'I'll just go and change...'

'What for? You're perfect as you are.'

She glanced at the mirror. She was still in the same shorts and faded band t-shirt she'd been wearing since that morning.

Once upon a time, Izzy wouldn't have worn this to take out the bins just in case she ran into any of the well-heeled neighbours at her polished Hong Kong high-rise. Her hair hadn't been professionally coloured for months, but the sun had left it streaked with natural caramel highlights. She had twisted it into a low chignon for her Saturday errands, and the salt air had given her the kind of carefree beachy waves she used to pay good money for.

She looked... healthy. And happy. Sort of.

'Let's go,' she said – before she changed her mind – and picked up her purse.

Jake laced his fingers through hers as they walked through the village. Overhead, starlings danced in the buttery dusk light, arching wildly as they swooped and soared through the warm evening air.

The pub was busy; she could hear the din of chatter from out here on the street as they approached. Izzy took a deep breath and followed Jake inside.

This place. So many memories. *Too many, sometimes.* She pictured two little girls in sandy wellies, clutching their dad's hands, then her and Amy as teenagers, sipping clandestine drinks that they hadn't been old enough yet to purchase.

The echoes of her father and her sister were ingrained in this pub, in this village. Shadows of her loss lurked in the nooks and crannies, tucked into the corners and scattered across the open spaces. Impossible to escape.

Now, Izzy felt the weight of stares on her back as she trailed in Jake's wake. She stuck close to him, keeping her eyes down, ignoring the hushed whisper that rippled through the bar. Words spoken about her, like the leaves shivering in the wind.

'All right.' Jake's voice was breezy. 'What are you having?'

'Maybe we should just get that takeaway and go home...' she mumbled.

'Why? What's the matter?'

She leaned into him, close enough to smell the cologne on his neck, and whispered as loud as she dared. 'They're all talking about us. About *me*.'

'Nonsense,' Jake scoffed, scanning the bar. 'Just relax.

You've nothing to worry about.'

But Izzy felt the temperature change, the pressure dropping. A barely perceptible increase in the air's density, and the imagined warm breath of those whispers concealed behind hands.

Her heart drummed, an urgent pounding in her chest. The police taking Nick Shaw in for questioning was a cyclone brewing, and she was at the eye of the storm. After all, it was Izzy who dug up the conservatory. Izzy who had probed, asked questions, dislodged the secrets that had been buried here for twenty years.

'Evening,' Gina greeted them. Izzy might have imagined it, but even the landlady seemed stand-offish.

'A half of IPA and a Diet Coke please, Gina.' Jake handed over a ten-pound note.

Gina nodded in response and began to pour. 'I take it you heard about Nick Shaw?' she asked, almost under her breath.

Almost, but not quietly enough.

The man next to them at the bar, an old guy in a threadbare t-shirt, angled his head to hear better.

Jake replied loudly enough for any onlookers to hear. 'I understand he's assisting the police with their enquiries. I'm sure he's being very helpful.' He grabbed Izzy's hand and tugged her away. 'Come on. Let's see if there's a table in the snug.'

The back room of the pub was, mercifully, only half-full, and there was no one Izzy seemed to recognise.

'OK.' Jake held his hands up. 'So, they're all talking about it. Big deal? It's huge news around here. Everyone knows Nick.'

'It's a big deal if they think I'm responsible.'

'Izzy.' His gaze met hers. 'Only he is responsible for

whatever he's done.'

She shrugged. 'Whatever he *might* have done...'

'You're not second-guessing yourself now, are you?'

Izzy reached up to the nape of her neck, kneading the spot where she could feel the pressure growing, a tension that was already spreading along her shoulders. 'It just seems like they've been holding him for a while with no news.'

'I'll check back in with the team tomorrow. Maybe they'll have something from the lab by then.'

The unease was gnawing at her, now. It had begun as a feeling of being off kilter, as if a step in the wrong direction or even a gentle gust might cause her to stumble. Now, it was a thick, cloying knot, a lump in her throat that made it difficult to swallow.

What was she missing?

Her mind drifted to Hannah, of all people. Her niece was mature for her age, too. Just as Kelly had been. Teetering on that brink between being a child and a woman, that perilous and delicate tipping point when you were neither one nor the other.

It would be hard for a teenage girl to hide a relationship with a man twice her age, even if that relationship comprised little more than walking along the beach and illicit forays into the dunes. How had Kelly managed to keep such an enormous secret?

But there was something else, something that cut to the heart of who Kelly had been. What could have motivated her to start an affair with her ex-boyfriend's father? Had Kelly been capable of that?

Izzy thought again of the things she had written about Bryan. She hadn't been fixated on him, or even bitter. There had been no thoughts of revenge, no desire to get back at him. No animosity at all, really. Even if there had been some pull on Nick's part, and even if Kelly had been desperately, devastatingly lonely, there would have been some push, too.

Dumping a boy and then getting together with his father just a couple of months later – something about it didn't add up. It didn't sound – *it didn't feel* – like Kelly.

'Sip up, love.' Jake's voice snapped her from her reverie.

'Jeez, sorry.' Izzy shook her head. 'I was miles away.'

He shrugged. 'Tell me all about it on the way home.'

It was still balmy, the warmth of the day lingering, reluctant to leave. The last of the fishing trawlers skirted the harbour wall, slowing to a chug as it approached its mooring.

She looped her arm through the crook of Jake's elbow, anchoring herself to him. 'What do they know that I don't?'

'What do you mean?'

'None of them believe Nick could have done something like that. That, back there,' — Izzy gestured in the direction of the pub — 'it's because they don't think he did it. They think I've got it wrong.'

'Well, none of them have read Kelly's diary. Besides. People are full of surprises.'

'Yes, but…' She shrugged. 'Yeah. Maybe you're right.'

Her phone rang, a chime from inside her purse. It was a mobile number she didn't recognise.

'Hello?'

'Isabelle. It's Pam Bell.'

Izzy heard the weariness in the woman's words. She stopped walking, fixed to the spot.

'I need to speak to you. And Diana.' Izzy heard voices in the background, a door closing. 'Tomorrow morning, at Diana's place. I'll be in Beadnell by ten.'

DI Bell hung up without saying goodbye.

31

DIANA DID ENJOY A GOOD FUNERAL.

This morning's paper had contained an obituary for her old friend Edith Goldsworthy, and Diana was already picturing the service in her head.

She had maintained a decent correspondence with Edith – Christmas and birthday cards, and phone calls every other month. They'd been part of the same gang at school and had continued to meet up as part of the old girls' group until just a few years back when Edith's mobility diminished her ability to venture far from home.

The group had been dwindling, by then, and Maureen Finkle had given up on organising the day trips and flower-arranging classes and luncheons when numbers became too low to merit the increasingly arduous task of organising such activities. Then Maureen died – breast cancer, Diana heard on the grapevine – and that put a stop to any further get-togethers. None of them had the energy, or the heart, to carry on after that.

A brief illness. The sanitised, censored explanation Maureen's daughters had offered in her obit.

It had seemed, to Diana, to be something of a game. At one point, at least. Each time, the thought fleetingly came to her. *Another one.* But she was still here. The race was still on. Who would be the last woman standing?

Only, the game became less entertaining the fewer players left on the field. How frightfully unfair. It might feel like cheating death, but who really wins in the end? You could be the last woman in the race, but you would cross the finish line alone, and there was no fun in that.

She hoped that Edith's daughters were planning to incorporate some violin music into the service. Edith had played so splendidly back when they were girls. She should send the daughters a sympathy card and remind them of this.

The roses were struggling in this heat, the edges of their petals curling and browning in the ferocious sun. Diana knew she should prune them, lop off the heads of the worst-hit, a sacrifice to save the others. But she had never been able to bring herself to take her secateurs to Lionel's pride and joy.

Not quite accurate – *she* had been his pride and joy. She could see that now.

She sank into the weather-worn loveseat in the secluded front yard of her cottage, relieving the pressure on her ankles, and admired the blooms. As she watched, a wilted petal tumbled to the ground where it lay, almost translucent, sweating in the midday sun.

Decay, she realised, was as much a part of life as the joys of spring, the enrapture of summer, autumn's delights. Diana had blossomed and bloomed, and now, in the winter of her life, the rot was setting in. She could feel it in her knees, in her hips, in her eyes. Each morning, it was taking her longer and longer to stand, to make the short journey to the bathroom for her daily ablutions. She could feel it taking a piece of her, day by day, week by week. Nature reclaiming what was rightfully hers, and, like all living things, Diana would eventually return to the eternal infinity whence she came.

She just hoped she could accomplish it with some grace. *Dignity*. Was that too much to ask?

The sound of a car engine echoed down the empty lane. A familiar growl. She should speak to Izzy, remind her about global warming, remind her they were merely custodians of the earth, and the planet was not theirs to destroy.

But she would do that another day. From the expression on the young woman's face, Diana knew she had news on the case.

The case. Perhaps Diana had just one fight left in her, and she resolved to make it count.

'DI Bell is on her way over,' said Izzy, without pausing for formalities. She offered a hand and Diana gratefully accepted it, her knee cracking awkwardly as she stood.

'In that case, my dear, you had better make tea.'

The girl looked wretched; Diana could see the worry scored across her features even in the cool gloom of her kitchen. She eyed Izzy as the kettle boiled, hoping the girl would know to bring out the good china without having to be prompted.

Izzy rubbed at her eyes. *No make-up again*, Diana noted.

There was the sound of the gate creaking and footsteps on the path. Izzy answered the door to the detective, a woman who had achieved the unenviable feat of looking even more worn out than her.

'Good morning, ladies.' DI Bell greeted them with a nod and joined Diana at the table.

'I assume there has been a breakthrough, Inspector?' Diana asked.

Izzy set down the tea – the correct cups, for once.

The detective's eyes met Diana's. 'I've sent Nick Shaw home. His paternity test was negative, and anyway, he has an alibi for the week Kelly disappeared. We've released him without charge.'

Izzy sank into the seat opposite Diana, her mouth dropping open. 'But it was him. I mean, he built the conservatory – he dug the foundations. He knew Kelly. It had to be him. He was N.'

DI Bell shook her head. 'He wasn't even personally involved in the construction project – some of his labourers did that job. And he has the paperwork to prove it.'

Izzy raked a hand through her hair. 'What about Bryan? If it wasn't Nicholas—'

'The DNA test would have shown if there was a familial link.' DI Bell sighed. 'Neither Nick nor Bryan fathered Kelly's baby. And when she disappeared, Nick was on a stag do in Mallorca. The lads checked and, as far as alibis go, it's ironclad. We have nothing.'

Not quite nothing, Diana thought, but kept this to herself.

'I know.' Izzy gasped. Diana could sense her desperation. 'Maybe the father was someone else, but Nick mistakenly *thought* it was his baby and set the whole thing up...'

'Izzy, I interviewed the man personally for several hours. He's innocent. There's nothing linking him to any of it apart from the fact that Kelly briefly dated his son several months before she was killed.' DI Bell couldn't disguise the disappointment in her voice.

'Still, this is progress.' Diana added a sugar cube to her tea and stirred.

DI Bell's eyes met hers; Diana could see her searching for some understanding. Checking that the *old dear* was keeping up.

'It means you can rule one man out. Besides. We – you – have the diary now. We know much more than we did a week ago. And memories have been stirred. Someone out there knows something, even if they don't realise it. Now, all it will take is some good old-fashioned house-to-house enquiries—'

'We won't do that.' DI Bell's shoulders sagged. 'They – the Chief Superintendent, specifically, won't authorise more resources.'

'That's preposterous,' Diana scoffed. 'You have the DNA sample; you can test every man in the village. Find out who the father was. Even if he wasn't the killer, it would certainly point us in the right direction.'

'That's also not going to happen. Without another suspect and a warrant, it would have to be a voluntary programme, and the Guv won't sanction it.'

The policewoman appeared to be close to tears now. Diana exchanged an anxious glance with Izzy.

'It's man-hours that we simply don't have.' DI Bell splayed her hands on the tabletop. 'They don't see a win here. This type of case can take years to crack, and I have to be honest: most historic murders go unsolved.'

Something inside Diana wilted at that moment. A curling petal on a decaying rose.

'So, what are you saying?' Izzy spoke slowly.

'It's just me.' DI Bell really did start crying, then. Hot, angry tears, rolling down her cheeks. 'God, look at me.' She scoffed at herself, then shrugged. 'I'm the only detective assigned to the investigation, and that's only because I insisted. Nick Shaw... he was our best lead.'

Izzy handed her a tissue.

'And without you, we wouldn't even have the diary.' DI Bell blew her nose. 'I'm at my wits' end.'

It took courage, Diana realised, to expose one's feelings like this. Anyone could play a game of bravery but admitting weakness – that required true strength.

She laid a hand on DI Bell's and met her eyes. 'Let's be clear on one thing, Inspector: you're not alone.'

'Really? Certainly feels like it...'

'Nick Shaw wasn't the only lead that Izzy and I have.' Izzy threw her a questioning frown, but Diana continued. 'We're part of this community. We know these people, and they divulge things to us that they would never share with you. If you're happy for us to keep... *investigating*' —Diana couldn't help it – her fingertips tingled in anticipation— 'we'd be happy to keep digging.'

'Off the record?' DI Bell asked, a note of timidity to her voice, now.

'Always.' Diana fought the urge to smile and instead offered her most solemn expression. 'You have my word.'

Izzy seethed all the way home, a thunderous storm of a mood that she was unable to shake, even after twenty minutes of the mindfulness exercises her mother had forced her to learn.

It had been days since she had properly looked at the renovation plans. Tomorrow the builders would be back to start on the orangery, and Izzy still hadn't finished the design for its interior. She needed to figure out the underfloor heating, sockets, light fittings... Soon, Finn and the boys would tread through the house with dirty boots and creating a din that would make it impossible to concentrate.

And now Diana had signed them up to be some sort of voluntary police support unit.

In the cool of her kitchen, Izzy stared at the ugly tiles and did her best not to think about the bare floorboards in the hallway, or the living room, where shredded remnants of that god-awful paisley wallpaper clung tenaciously to the walls.

What was Diana thinking? Fancying herself as some sort of amateur detective and dragging Izzy along with her for the hell of it. As if she didn't have enough on her plate.

She wondered again what Diana had meant when she'd told DI Bell that they had another lead. *What other lead?*

'We know these people,' she'd said. 'They divulge things to us.' *Yeah, right.* Izzy was barely on first-name terms with her neighbours, let alone knowing them well enough to initiate a friendly chat about the dead girl in her garden.

What had happened to Kelly all those years ago? *Who did that to her?*

Someone had buried a terrible secret, and somehow, Izzy had been landed with the responsibility of finding them.

She'd never asked for any of this. She hadn't even wanted to come back to Seahouses. She hadn't wanted the kids, hadn't wanted to settle here, hadn't wanted to make her life in this village where cruel rumours and gossip curled through the streets like the wind. It was as if fate had guided her along a series of wrong turns, each one leading her blindly to this.

What had she ever done to deserve this? Any of it?

She stomped up the stairs, her feet landing in satisfying thuds against the bare wooden treads.

It was all such a mess.

All she'd ever wanted was to protect Amy's children, to shield them from the cruelty and evil of the world. Protect them in a way that Kelly had not been. It was a simple thing; it should be instinctive. So why could she never seem to get it right?

At the door to the girls' room, something made her stop. None of the kids ever commented on the state of the house, but Izzy had noticed that even Betsy – who had a very lax grasp on even the most basic hygiene concepts – wouldn't walk barefoot on this carpet.

Izzy could see why. It might have been dark pink, once upon a time. Now, it was faded in patches, dotted with old spills and the shadowed imprints of previous generations of furniture.

At the window, a pair of sun-bleached curtains hung limply.

The fireplace was original, though – a feature the estate agent had been keen to highlight. But ill-fitting MDF wardrobes stood in the recesses on either side, not quite filling the spaces and leaving ugly gaps around the edges where, Izzy imagined, spiders lurked.

And that carpet.

She wanted to scream. The urge swelled within her, and she choked it back, swallowing hard. The threat of tears pricked at her eyes and she balled her hands into fists, digging her nails into her palms.

Suddenly, Izzy couldn't tolerate it – any of it – for another second.

She didn't have all the answers – but who did? Wasn't that what parenting was all about? Fumbling in the dark, navigating the unexpected and the challenges you never asked for, guided only by a drive to do the best you could in the here and now? Doing everything in your power, even if you didn't know where to start?

This room. She could start with this room. Right now.

She tugged Hannah's bed out from its place next to the window and yanked at the carpet. It lifted easily and with a satisfying rip, revealing grotesque squares of green underlay that had been laid goodness knows how long ago. She pulled at one, gingerly lifting it by the corner.

It was sticky to the touch, and Izzy imagined that it had absorbed decades of moisture – the breath and dreams of everyone who had ever slept here. Their skin and hair and emotional debris, embalmed in this bloody carpet.

The girls deserve better.

With a grunt, she dragged Hannah's bed across the floor and continued to peel back the carpet, folding it on itself into a roll. She hesitated, her hands on her hips, catching her breath.

She needed tools.

It took forty-five minutes to dismantle the beds, ten minutes to move the wardrobes, and another twenty to rip the carpet out completely. The underlay filled two bin liners. She carried it all out to the skip at the bottom of the garden, heaving under the strain, her t-shirt clinging to her back.

It was heavy but satisfying work. Izzy opened the bedroom window, and the breeze tickled her skin, now slick with sweat.

She was surprised to find that not only were the floorboards original, but that hideous carpet had been hiding the most beautifully tiled hearth. She gazed at the intricately patterned squares, admiring the craftsmanship.

Next, she ripped down the curtains, then used her

screwdriver to prise off the cheap plastic curtain rail, too. It came away with a gratifying snap.

She wiped the sweat from her face with the long edge of her t-shirt. *The wardrobes.*

It would be easy enough to disassemble them piece by piece, but Izzy didn't have time for that. Besides, she wanted the satisfaction of ripping them to shreds. Jake's sledgehammer would do the trick.

She retrieved it from the shed and took it back to the bedroom, arcing it in a wild swing before sending it crashing into one of the wardrobe doors. The flimsy material splintered on the first blow, and a smile spread over her lips.

She pounded it again, a brutal and violent hit. A second panel broke neatly in two, a crack forming instantly down its centre, and within a few blows, the entire thing lay in jagged tatters on the floor.

Izzy brushed away a tear with the back of her hand and started on the second wardrobe, feeling a strength in her arms, her back, her shoulders. She swung the hammer high and smashed it down, relishing the destruction, exhilarated by her power to destroy.

The scream came out of nowhere; it started deep in her stomach and grew to a rumble in her throat, and she didn't give a shit if the neighbours heard.

She thought of Kelly, and of Amy, and of Seahouses, and the cruelty of fate, tears and snot mixing with sweat. She thought of the kids – *her kids* – and how, even if she didn't know what she was doing, the *instinct* to protect was good enough. Made her good enough.

Finally, she stopped, her rage spent. She let the sledgehammer fall to the floor, then sat down next to it on the naked floorboards. Her breath, ragged, echoed in the empty room. A tear spilled and landed in the dust, a single drop blotting into the grain of the wood.

Izzy took a moment to admire her work, the room that had been bothering her so much, now stripped back to nothing.

A blank canvas, ready to begin again.

32

Then

I'M IN SO MUCH SHIT. I CAN'T BELIEVE HOW BADLY I'VE MESSED everything up.

Last week, I finally told N. Safe to say he completely lost it.

His face turned the craziest shade of red and he said nothing for ages; just stood there and stared at me, trembling, his eyes as cold as the sky.

Then the shouting started.

He said it can't be his. Can you believe that? He actually accused me of having someone else on the go, which is so ridiculous I laughed out loud.

He didn't find it so funny. The red in his face deepened. He gripped my shoulders so hard that I imagined his fingers leaving a line of bruises.

"This is serious, Kelly! This is my fucking *life* you're messing with!" That's actually what he said.

And what about my life? How much do I count for in all of this? Or the life that's growing inside me?

At that moment, I hated him.

I've been so stupid.

Part of me thought he would be happy. *Could* be happy. Like, this would be the excuse he needs to finally end his so-called loveless marriage.

Hope is a terrible thing, sometimes. It blinds us to the reality that's staring us in the face.

Eventually, he calmed down. He says I'll have to *take care of it*, and I knew right away exactly what he meant by that. I swear to god, I thought I heard my own heart break. Somewhere, on the other side of the universe, a star extinguished.

That really happens, you know. Stars – they burn up and die, a light going out, like someone flicked a switch. The bigger the star, the more powerful the death; a violent explosion that leaves a black hole where something so beautiful once existed. An emptiness, sucking in anything that dares to come too close.

Take care of it.

He says there are special clinics where you don't have to give your real name. They don't ask questions. I could be in and out and be home in time for supper.

Funny, but N seems to know a lot about this sort of stuff.

Even though these clinics are supposedly anonymous, he won't take me; won't even give me a lift to Alnwick, just in case we're seen.

He was thinking it through, speaking the thoughts out loud as they came to him. I would have to take the bus there, and he would give me the money for a taxi home.

Logistics. Practicalities.

N says they'd send him to jail if anyone knew we were physically intimate (his choice of words). If I had the baby, they would want to know who the father is and if they find out it's him, he'd get a prison sentence. According to him, there's no other choice.

But what makes N think I choose him?

I felt sick.

I lied to him that I would take care of it.

We've been avoiding each other ever since, and this is buying me more time. Then yesterday I passed him on my way home, on the opposite side of the road, coming out of the butcher's. He must have crossed over when he saw the school bus stopping. He carried on walking to the pub, pretending not to see me.

I'm sure if I went through with it – if I did *take care of it* – everything could go back to how it was before. But would I even want that?

The bigger question: what will he do once he finds out I didn't *take care of it?*

I can't stop thinking that I've got this tiny person, an entire life, inside me. What does it matter where it came from? And over the past couple of days, I've had this weird feeling that it's a girl. It's as if I can feel her, as if I can hear her spirit whispering to me when I lie in bed at night. A little star, blazing. A light in the darkness.

Mam was my age when she had me. That is most definitely irony.

Obviously, I'll do things differently. The plan must evolve. I'll still go to university. Eventually.

Tonight, I snuck out while the Barretts were at evening prayer. Escape, I know, is my only hope.

I got the coach down to Newcastle and took the bus up the hill. Dawn was surprised to see me, but not shocked. It takes a lot to shock her. I suppose she's seen it all by this point. She made me beans on toast and didn't ask too many questions.

I haven't told her about the baby yet. She's working tonight, so I'll tell her in the morning, once I've had a good night's sleep, and she is too weary from her shift to be too livid. There's no way she'll let social services take me back once she knows the truth. I just have to find the courage to tell her. The truth – at least part of it – is my key to freedom.

Dawn will go ballistic, but she'll calm down eventually. She can never stay mad at me. And she'll help me look after the baby. I know she will, and no one ever needs to know about N. I'll keep that secret with me forever. Anyway, it's only three months until I turn eighteen, and after that, I'm free.

It's strange to be back here in my room – the room that should have been but never was mine. At least I'm here now. Instead of a desk, we'll have to get a cot. It'll have one of those little mobiles hanging above it, something with lambs or teddy bears. Perhaps I'll still be able to get a job. It'll have to fit around Dawn's shifts, but I can do it. I know, now, that I can do anything. I will do whatever it takes to make this work.

I've got it all figured out. When they turn up, I'm going to hide under the divan, and I'll make Dawn swear on Mam's grave to pretend she hasn't seen me. They'll think I've run away, and soon enough, they'll give up on looking for me.

Because I'm not going back to Seahouses. No way.

I've seen who he is now. N has revealed himself. And I can't believe I didn't see it sooner. See what I mean about hope? I had so badly hoped; I had actually believed he was something else.

I was an idiot.

This afternoon, I packed in a hurry, shoving whatever I could into the holdall I arrived with. I left most of my stuff behind in Seahouses, leaving my room at the Barretts' exactly as it was so that they think I'm coming back. I even left my egg timer from Nanna's kitchen, the one item I took from her house. It's not like I need it anymore. In my mind, all the sand has run through to the bottom. There is no more time for waiting. See? I ran out of sand in the end.

There's no going back.

I'll sleep well tonight, safe in the knowledge that no one will come looking for me before daybreak.

Tomorrow is a new day, and the day after that, another. That's what Nanna used to say. *Just take things one day at a time.*

Each morning is a fresh opportunity to start again. I'll get it right next time.

33

Now

Izzy woke at the first notes of birdsong and slipped carefully from their bed.

Jake was still deep in sleep, his perfect mouth parted slightly, the whisper of a dream on his lips. He didn't stir as he stretched into the space she had vacated.

Downstairs in the kitchen, she popped a capsule into the coffee machine and waited as the device whirred to life. She could imagine taking her sledgehammer to these tiles. Watch them crack and splinter to the floor, shards of ugly.

One room at a time, she told herself.

She flicked her laptop open and brought up the renovation plans, reviewing the work that she had done so far. Since last night, she had been able to visualise the entire house in perfect precision. The ideas simmered now, coming so fast that she struggled to keep up with her racing imagination. A feature lighting concept, here and there. Wall panelling, custom-built units for the family room, an

Italian shower in the ensuite. A floor-to-ceiling glass cabinet that she had saved on Pinterest and knew Jake would love. The last pieces fell into place at the click of her mouse.

'You're up early?' Jake said it like a question. He stood in the doorway of their living room, rubbing sleep from his eyes.

She looked up at him with a smile. 'Early bird, and all that. Coffee?'

'I'll get my own, thanks. Don't want to interrupt the genius at work.' He grinned, flashing those perfect teeth that Izzy knew were the result of genetic good fortune rather than the orthodontic artistry for which she'd shelled out a few thousand pounds.

He came back into the living room and joined her on the sofa. 'The girls' room looks amazing. I mean, the progress...'

'Don't worry.' Izzy didn't take her eyes off the screen. 'I'll have it finished this week.'

'I still can't believe you did all that on your own.'

Izzy couldn't help but wince. 'I can't believe it took me so long,' she mumbled.

The girls' room would be straightforward to complete, now. Once she had sanded the floors, painted the walls, and hung new curtains, the space would be transformed. She couldn't wait to see their faces when they stayed over on Wednesday. The built-in wardrobes would take a little longer. She would ask Finn to measure up when he arrived this morning, and she could order the units this afternoon.

She had planned to buy new beds, but the old ones would be perfectly fine after a new coat of paint. Gold, perhaps, to complement the fittings and finishes. Izzy opened the shopping list in her phone and added a note.

Next, she'd tackle Lucas's room, giving it the same treatment. Carpet out, floors sanded, fresh colour on the walls – sage green was very in, this year – and a large cream rug, although that was possibly asking for trouble when the occupant was a thirteen-year-old boy...

Her mind raced with the possibilities.

'There,' she said, with one final click. Her home, her future, in sudden clarity.

'Well, I'm in court this afternoon.' Jake yawned. 'Early dinner?'

'Early night, you mean?'

He kissed her, his eyes glinting as they met hers. 'It's as if you read my mind...'

Izzy would be tired again this evening; she already knew that. But tired in a good way, from the fatigue that came from physical exertion and mental accomplishment. Her muscles still ached from yesterday's adventure with the sledgehammer. It made a pleasant change to the weariness she had felt these past couple of months; the lethargy that came from being underpowered and overburdened.

She glanced at her watch. 'I'm going to get going,' she told him. 'I want to pick up the sander and get some samples before the crew arrives.'

Jake watched her leave, and she did her best to ignore the look of surprise on his face. It wasn't his fault, after all. In many ways, she had surprised herself.

The carpark at B&Q was deserted. Izzy pulled up in front of the shuttered store. Another five minutes until it opened.

Finally, she heard the sounds of life from the entrance: the clunk of the lock and the purr of the metal roller. A man in uniform overalls threw her a quizzical look as she wheeled a trolley towards the open door.

First, she picked samples of paint and wallpaper from the decorating aisle, then threw some brushes and a couple of rollers in the trolley.

An entire section of the store was dedicated to kitchens. Normally, Izzy would have marvelled at the choice on offer, the vast arrays of hobs and ovens, gadgets and unit coverings with knobs and handles in every colour and style imaginable. *Too much choice.* But today, she knew exactly what she wanted. She found a drawer handle that was close enough to her idea, and tossed it in. If it wasn't perfect, she would have something custom made.

She turned back on herself, steering the trolley towards the tool department. The store loaned sanding machines, for a fee, but she would need to buy her own gloves and goggles, and a dust mask, and—

Her trolley collided with another, the metal clanging together.

'Sorry,' she began. 'I wasn't looking...'

She stopped. She was face-to-face with Bryan Shaw.

'Bryan, hi,' Izzy said, trying to hide her awkwardness. Her heart fluttered. 'Look, I'm so sorry about what happened with your dad. I'm sure everyone—'

His mouth pulled into a tight line. 'It's OK. I didn't think... I mean, we never actually believed...' Bryan raked a hand through his hair and frowned. 'What the hell happened, exactly?'

The bright lights of the store made him appear less tanned than before and somehow, under the neon glare, he looked younger. Softer.

There was nowhere to hide. Izzy drew a deep breath, steeling herself. 'I really am sorry. But we found Kelly's diary. The rumours were right: she was seeing someone – an older guy – in the months before she was killed. We – I –

thought it might have been your father.' She gripped the handle of her trolley. 'Clearly, I got that very wrong.'

'No. Yeah. I mean, no, it wasn't him. Couldn't have been. But I understand why you... well. I understand. I can't stop thinking about her, too. Keep asking myself what I missed, what more I could have done.'

'She cared about you.'

'Did she say that?' Izzy saw something in his expression, then. Hope and loss. 'Did she say that in her diary?'

Izzy nodded.

'I cared about her, too. I loved her.' He ran a hand over his jaw, his fingertips brushing two-day stubble. 'At least, I think I loved her.' His eyes misted with unshed tears. 'My eldest daughter is fourteen. Younger than Kelly was, but I... Well. It hurts, doesn't it?'

'It should never have happened.' Izzy didn't want to think, now, about all the many ways in which Kelly had been failed. She hesitated a beat. 'I don't suppose you have time for a coffee?'

The café was at the back of the store, overlooking the garden department. The air was artificially warm and had a sweet, earthy smell. Bryan ordered two coffees at the counter without asking what she wanted and joined her at a small bistro table in the corner.

They sat for a moment, regarding one another. Izzy broke the silence first.

'I really am sorry about your dad. But there was the diary, and Shaw's built the old conservatory on our house...'

'I know. The police asked him about that. But he wasn't involved with the construction at your place. Back then, he had a whole team of workers. He didn't oversee every job personally. Dad reckons a hole had been dug for the foundations, then someone came along and buried Kelly in it, and filled it over. The labourers wouldn't have noticed a thing like that.' He emptied a packet of sugar into his coffee and stirred it. 'But none of that stops me feeling so guilty.'

Izzy sighed. 'It wasn't your fault, Bryan.'

'I know. I do know that, deep down. But I keep thinking, if only I had stayed friends with her... The poor lass didn't have anyone else. Or maybe if I hadn't got together with Sam so soon after we broke up...'

'She must feel bad, too?' Izzy ventured.

He nodded, avoiding Izzy's eyes. 'She does, believe me. She might have a funny way of showing it, but we're both... Well. Let's just say we're both wondering what we could have done differently back then.'

'Tell me about Kelly.'

'Ah, man.' Izzy noticed a spark in Bryan's eyes now. 'She was amazing. Even now, when I think back... So clever. And funny, too. And she just, like, didn't give a shit what anyone thought of her.'

'Isn't that kind of unusual for a teenage girl?'

Bryan shrugged. 'I suppose so. I never really thought about it like that. And I have thought about her over the years, even though we don't talk about her. Me and Sam, I mean. Although these past couple of weeks have dredged up a lot of old memories.' He let out a long, slow sigh. 'The truth is, Sam wasn't very nice to Kelly. She made up some stupid lie about Kelly stealing money from her to turn the other girls against her, and so that I... So that she might have a chance with me.' He grimaced. 'We were just kids. Daft kids. But Sam has had to face facts: if she had stayed friends with Kelly, if she hadn't lied to turn everyone against her, well... maybe Kelly would still be here. It's not an easy thing to come to terms with, believe me.'

'Your wife's not very keen on me, is she?'

Bryan grimaced. 'Seahouses is a small place and people have long memories. She knows that some people around here remember how she treated Kelly. That's almost as hard as living with the guilt of what she did. And she doesn't like to think she was my second choice, even though I don't see it like that.'

Izzy eyed him. 'How do you see it, Bryan?'

He took a deep breath. 'Kelly was depressed. I knew that, even though we weren't... close. By the end, I mean.'

'Depressed because of what Sam did?'

He shook his head. 'It started before all of that, even if she did a good job of hiding it. She wasn't happy in Seahouses, full stop. Living with the Barretts wasn't easy. They were just too full-on, you know? Trying too hard. It was all prayers before dinner and board games and family time.' He rolled his eyes. 'She used to make fun of them. Said they were like that couple from *The Simpsons*, you know, the neighbours? They were just old-fashioned, I guess. But it was more than that. She didn't like being in foster care, obviously. She wanted to go home, to live with her aunt. And she missed her mam.'

'She lost her mother years before she came here...'

'But it still hurts, doesn't it? You must know how that feels.'

Izzy knew only too well. Living with grief, with the loss of a loved one, was like living without a limb. The pain dulled over time, but the memory never lost its sharp edges and vivid colours.

'I know,' she mumbled.

'So, are you back here for good now?'

'I guess so. I just bought a house and I'm getting married.'

'Congratulations.'

'But I didn't want to.' Izzy blurted the words and quickly corrected herself. 'I mean, I didn't want to come back to Seahouses. It's not... Well. It was never my plan.'

'Really? What was your plan?'

'I don't know. Just... something else. I was always more of a big city person than a country girl. I wanted to see the world, live in a skyscraper. Be able to walk along a street amongst thousands of people without anyone knowing who I was.'

Izzy knew she should have felt self-conscious sharing this, but there was a simplicity about Bryan that made him easy to talk to.

He smiled. 'You sound just like her, you know. Kelly. Forever talking about leaving, that one. She just couldn't settle here. It was like Seahouses – even me – it would never be enough for her. She wanted to go to university and become a lawyer, then go off to work in London or New York.' He sighed. 'I always assumed she'd had enough and run away, just like she always said she would. And all this time...'

'All this time, she was right here.'

His eyes filled now. 'I let her down, too. I know that.'

'Bryan, is there anyone you can think of? Who had she become involved with, who might have wanted to hurt her? Who was she keeping secret?'

He exhaled with a whoosh of air, his mouth dropping to a small 'o'.

'That's what I can't understand.' He shook his head. 'I mean, there were rumours. And everyone knows everyone's business around here. So how come no one knows who Kelly was seeing? In a place like Seahouses, it's not that easy to keep a secret.'

'No,' said Izzy. 'It's not easy to keep secrets. Not unless you bury them.'

34

WHAT OTHER LEADS? IZZY TOSSED DIANA'S WORDS OVER IN her mind on the drive home, turning the thought this way and that.

The day was cloudless, and from here, she could see for miles. To her left, the sea appeared, snatches of navy infinity visible in the breaks between the trees. She wound down the window and steadied her breathing, taking long inhalations of the salt air. Soon, she could see Holy Island, the stump of its castle pointing skywards, a thumb of stone in the middle of the sea.

The builders would be there by the time she got home, but the prospect of noise and dust didn't stress her so much now. It would be progress. *One step closer.* She could work on Lucas's room in the meantime. Keep her mind and body busy. Their dream home finally taking shape.

And then maybe, just maybe, she could start to plan the wedding. It didn't have to be complicated – she could see that now. Just her and Jake, the kids – their family. Perhaps they could do it on the beach and go to the pub for a nice lunch afterwards. After all, it wasn't about a single day. It was about the future – the future they were building together.

There was more to life than the shiny things, the gloss and sheen of her old dreams. Izzy realised that everything she had ever wanted – everything she had *truly* wanted – was right here. The comfort of waking up each morning next to a man who cared about her. Watching her nieces and nephew grow, protecting and nurturing them. A job that excited and fulfilled her. The years stretching out ahead of them, like miles of golden sand. A dream she hadn't been looking for, but it found her all the same.

Perhaps Amy had the right idea all along. But her dreams had been cut brutally short, and now Izzy had to live life for them both.

And what about Kelly, and her dreams? The unfairness of it needled at her.

She would have to regroup with Diana on these *other leads*. What could she possibly mean? Dawn didn't know anything. The Barretts were clearly in the dark, the Shaws had been ruled out, and Kelly's diary had given them very little apart from that single letter.

Sam, perhaps? Izzy raked over the conversations they'd had with her, wondering what she might have missed, but came up with nothing.

Perhaps it was the old lady's failing mind fooling her. A cruel trick of the light on the holes in Diana's memory. Seeing things that weren't really there. A moth-eaten cashmere jumper, degraded and worn by time. A thing of faded beauty that Izzy couldn't bear to part with.

. . .

The young man offered Diana a seat, and she gratefully accepted.

Such a considerate boy – he even moved the chair into a shady spot on the deck, out of the sun, just for her. His mother – Diana could picture the woman but didn't push herself to recall the name – would be proud.

She watched the three workmen as they unloaded material and equipment into Izzy's garden from the gate at the bottom. A cement mixer, and metal rods of some sort. She hoped one of them might offer to make her a cup of tea, but she wouldn't ask. They were on the clock, after all, and had assured her that Izzy wouldn't be too long.

The earth was dry; Diana could see the cracks that had appeared around the boundary of the space they had excavated for the new foundations. She wondered whether they had cleared away all the salt or if some traces still remained in the ground. The thought grew sour inside her. *Dear Kelly.*

She rolled her ankles, which were already swelling in this infernal heat. She had packed a light lunch of sandwiches and a couple of apples, a flask of tea. A picnic for the road. They had a long day ahead of them, if all went to plan, and she would need to keep her energy levels up.

Her memory might be fading – gaps appearing here and there – but Diana had not lost her ability to read people. *Particularly women.* After all, teaching was not merely a profession or a vocation; it was a calling. Four decades in a classroom of girls had allowed her to fine-tune her skill for interpreting expressions and decoding emotions, hearing the words that went unsaid.

And the more Diana thought about this one particular girl, the more she wondered what she wasn't telling them.

It was their fault, perhaps. They hadn't been asking the right questions.

She heard the growl of an unnecessarily large car and the sound of the front door, and then Izzy appeared.

'Diana. Lovely to see you.' If Izzy was surprised to find Diana waiting for her, she hid it well.

Diana smiled at her friend. 'I hope I'm not interrupting your work, dear.'

She could see, quite plainly, that she was. Judging by the shopping bags, Izzy had been planning a day of home improvements. *Lord knows, it was about time.* But there were more urgent issues to deal with, far more pressing than the dreadful state of this house.

'Shall we go inside? Leave the boys to it?' Izzy exchanged a smile with the nice young man who had let Diana in, and Diana followed her back into the house.

'I was going to call you, actually.' Izzy bit her lip, chewing over the words. 'I'm just not sure about all this... helping DI Bell. I want to, obviously, but I don't know what more we can do. It feels like we've explored all roads and arrived at nothing but a dead end.'

It was true, in a way. But Diana saw things differently.

'In that case, dear, it's time to retrace our steps.'

Izzy frowned, her eyebrows knitting in a question. 'How? Where?'

'My darling girl.' Diana leaned forward. 'I think you and I need to take another trip to Edinburgh.'

Izzy pulled up outside Neena Choudhury's house and took a deep breath. She couldn't believe she was doing this again. *Indulging Diana.* Best to get it over with as quickly as possible and then she could get home, get back to the renovation work she was now desperate to tackle.

She glanced at her passenger, snoozing peacefully in the seat beside her, her mouth slack. As she watched, Diana stirred, her slumber interrupted by the sudden lack of motion.

'Ah,' Diana said, blinking the sleep from her eyes as she took in her surroundings. 'Here already.'

Izzy said nothing as she helped her friend from the car, noting that it seemed to require much more effort on Diana's part than it had just two weeks ago. In the corner of her eye, at the upstairs window, a curtain fluttered.

Neena came to the door before they'd even rung the bell, a quizzical expression on her face.

'Come in,' she said, with a quick glance about the street. 'I wasn't expecting to see you two again so soon.'

'We weren't expecting to be back.' Diana smiled sweetly. 'But the investigation is ongoing, and I'm wondering if you can help.'

'I'll do my best,' Neena said with a resigned sigh, as she led them through to the living room. 'Although I already told you everything I know.'

'Indeed, dear, you were extremely helpful. But we were going over old ground, and something occurred to me.'

Neena's brow meshed. 'OK...'

'You mentioned you had a friend in Seahouses.'

'Judith?'

Diana clicked her fingers. 'That's the one. What else can you tell me about her?'

'Judith...' Neena repeated the name, her expression growing more perplexed, and even Izzy wondered where this was going. 'This is the strangest thing. I hadn't heard from her in over twenty years and last week, I got a friend request from her on Facebook.'

Izzy's heart pounded, but Diana kept her cool.

'What a splendid coincidence. I don't suppose you have an address for her, do you?'

Neena threw a glance from Izzy to Diana, and back to Izzy. 'Why? What do you want from her? I don't think she even knew Kelly – they weren't living in Seahouses at the same time.'

Izzy's stomach knotted; Neena was right. The girls hadn't lived together, and had possibly never even met, not unless Judith came back to visit the Barretts after she left.

And yet... She had a strange feeling that Diana might be on to something.

'We're just connecting the dots. Judith and Kelly might not have crossed paths, but she walked the same road as Kelly just several years earlier. No one is better placed to give us an understanding of Kelly's circumstances. I'm hoping Judith can tell us what, if anything, we might have missed.'

This seemed to satisfy Neena.

'She's called Judith Weston now. Lives not far from here, over in Falkirk. We exchanged a couple of messages. She runs a bookshop with her husband.' Neena took out her phone and scrolled through it. 'Here it is. Quill's Books.'

Izzy made a note of the address. She could see Diana's logic, now. If N had been someone close enough to Kelly that he knew when to pounce, there was a chance Judith had known him, too.

A small chance, Izzy told herself. But what more did they have?

The journey to Falkirk took almost an hour, and Diana felt every minute of it, every bump and twist and turn in the road. She longed to climb out of that blasted car and would quite happily have lain by the roadside for the sheer relief of it. Soon, the pretty town came into view.

It took them no time at all to find the book shop. Izzy parked in a vacant spot on the opposite side of the road, and they watched the entrance, an easy silence settling between them.

This would have to be handled delicately. *Very delicately.*

Diana was not surprised to learn that Judith had sought to renew the acquaintance of Neena. The question was: why now? Had she heard about the Salt Girl in Seahouses and remembered her childhood friend? Or had the story stirred deeper, more significant memories?

A predator. That's what they called men like N. Terrible, wicked men. The news was full of such stories these days. And they all seemed to have one dreadful thing in common: their behaviour followed a pattern of repetition.

But now, women were fighting back. Diana had seen the protests on the television, women and girls holding placards aloft that proclaimed them to be victims. Screaming 'Me Too' at the top of their lungs.

There was an entire movement around it: women emerging from the shadows, shaking off their victimhood and turning their shame onto the perpetrators. Some of the world's most powerful men had faced their reckoning, and not a moment too soon, in Diana's opinion.

But for every woman who found the strength to call out her abuser, Diana knew that there were several more, silenced and afraid. Living in the shadows, surviving with the misconception they had done something to deserve it.

The timing of Judith getting in touch with Neena was not a coincidence; of that, Diana was certain. In fact, she was now quite sure Judith had been living with a secret – a secret she was afraid could be exposed by this investigation. A secret just like Kelly's.

She turned to Izzy. 'You should wait here. We don't want to startle her.'

Izzy nodded, and Diana could see she understood what was at stake, now. Izzy helped her down from the car, and Diana straightened, unlocking the kinks in her knees and her ankles, her back and her shoulders.

Only a few years ago, Diana used to affect a hobble, a way of lulling onlookers into a false sense of security, reassuring them she was nothing more than a harmless old lady. Sadly, it no longer required her acting skills.

A bell tinkled as she entered the shop. It was small, and crammed floor to ceiling with books. She seemed to have the place to herself. Diana inhaled deeply, savouring the musty smell of paper, ink, the memories of thumbs on pages. She idled over to the mystery section and went directly to Christie.

'Anything in particular you're looking for today?' A woman appeared from out the back, her arms laden with books. Mid-forties, Diana would have guessed, and ever so pretty. Her dark hair was streaked with grey and hung in elegant waves around her shoulders.

Diana flashed her a smile. 'I'm looking for Judith.'

Confusion flashed over the woman's features. 'That's me. Do I know you from somewhere?' Her accent was lightly tipped in a beautiful Scottish lilt.

'I don't believe we've ever met.' Diana eyed her cautiously. 'But I'm from Seahouses.'

Judith's smile slipped. When she spoke again, her voice was cooler. 'And why are you looking for me?' She stacked the books on the desk, rearranging them into two piles. Diana noticed the woman's hands had begun to tremble.

'You used to live there, didn't you?'

Judith was avoiding her eyes now. 'I did,' she said quietly. 'Only for a couple of years when I was a teenager. And that was yonks ago.'

'On Clyde Street?'

Judith stopped shuffling the books, and Diana saw she had paled. 'How do you know...' Her gaze darted to the door at the rear of the shop and came to rest on her feet.

'I'm trying to find out what happened to a young lady named Kelly Reynolds. Kelly was murdered.'

Judith drew a deep breath. 'I saw the news. Terrible business. But I don't know anything about her. Never even met the girl.'

Diana spoke softly. 'Ah, but I think you do know something, Judith. And I think you might have an idea of who could have hurt Kelly. If—'

'I don't know anything of the sort.' Judith's voice was a harsh whisper. 'And I don't like to talk about that time of my life. So, if you don't mind...'

Diana recoiled, but quickly regained her composure. 'Of course. How insensitive of me. Please forgive my intrusion.'

She selected a copy of *Crooked House* – an early edition, at a fantastic price – and placed the book on the counter. 'Just this, please.'

Judith punched the keys of an old-fashioned till without looking at her. 'Do you need a bag?'

Diana shook her head and handed over a ten-pound note. Judith followed her to the door, seemingly keen to usher her out.

Perhaps Diana had miscalculated just how much tact this sortie required. Her shoulders sank at the opportunity she had lost. But just as she was about to step over the threshold, the younger woman grabbed her by the wrist.

'I can't talk now.' Judith whispered, throwing a glance over her shoulder. 'But meet me at this place.' She pressed a square of paper into Diana's hand. 'I'll be there in fifteen minutes.'

35

The café wasn't too busy, and Izzy was relieved to see that there was a table free in the corner.

Away from curious ears.

Although what, exactly, did Judith want to tell them?

Diana had only been in the book shop for five minutes, but by the way she bounced back across the road with the posture and energy of a woman a decade younger than she had just moments before, Izzy could tell she'd had a breakthrough.

Diana took a seat while Izzy ordered a pot of tea for three at the counter. As an afterthought, she added a selection of pastries and shortbread. From what Diana had told her, Judith seemed to be very nervous, and Izzy was sure she would appreciate having something to do with her hands.

She took a seat next to Diana, and they waited in anxious silence.

After a moment, Diana straightened in her chair. 'She's here,' she said under her breath, and waved Judith over.

The woman was older than Izzy had imagined she'd be. In her mind, the Judith of Neena's story was a teenager. But the years had been kind to her. Her skin was smooth, unlined, and even in her loose cotton dress, Izzy could see that she was lean.

Judith glanced around, scanning the faces of the other customers. Satisfied, she weaved her way through the tables towards them.

'Who's this?' she asked Diana, gesturing towards Izzy.

'I'm Izzy. A friend of Diana's. It was my garden where they found Kelly.'

'Right. Of course.' Judith nodded, a sad dip of her chin, and took the seat they had left for her. 'I read all about it in the papers, and I've been following the story on the news. Awful, what happened to her.'

'Indeed,' Diana said glumly. 'Kelly was one of my former pupils. A formidable young woman.'

'And she lived with the Barretts, too,' Izzy added, and noticed Judith wince. *Baby steps,* she reminded herself, just as Diana had cautioned her. *Ease her into it.*

'Right, yes. Of course.'

Diana leaned forward. 'While Izzy pours the tea, perhaps you could tell us about your time in Seahouses.'

Judith hesitated, her eyes on the table, and began. 'I went into foster care when I was eleven. Parents divorced, Dad disappeared, Mum couldn't cope – mental health issues.' She shrugged, dismissing her troubled childhood with a single gesture, as if this was a story she had told many times before. 'It wasn't so bad. I was with a family in Berwick for a few years, and then I went to live in Seahouses. I think I was fifteen by then?'

She looked to Izzy, as if Izzy might be able to confirm this.

Judith continued. 'It was great. I mean, overall, I had a

happy childhood. But no one expects kids in care to say that, do they?'

It was true, Izzy thought. People imagined tales of hardship and struggle without a happy ending. Not women like Judith, who seemed to have done all right for herself.

'It was great, living by the coast. I miss it. We used to surf.' She smiled, as if picturing herself back out there on the beach.

'I used to surf as a teenager, too,' Izzy said, her voice softening.

Judith's eyes widened in surprise. 'You grew up in Seahouses?'

'Yeah.' Izzy sipped her tea. 'Born and bred.'

'You're a few years younger than me. That might be why I don't recognise you.'

Izzy shrugged in response. A gap of two or three years at that age might as well be a different generation, even in a village as small as Seahouses.

'You didn't go to St Helen's?' Diana asked.

'No. They kept me in school at Berwick. Less disruption, you know...'

Diana nodded. 'But you were happy?'

Judith shrugged. 'I missed my mum and my friends from home. But there are worse places to be. I'm not sure how much any of this helps you, though...'

'My dear girl,' said Diana. 'The police are at a dead end. There are no suspects in this case, no witnesses. No one even looked for Kelly when she disappeared.'

'What?' Judith looked wounded. 'Not even the Barretts?'

'They reported her missing, but were convinced she ran away,' Izzy quickly added. 'And social services, too. They even got a postcard from Kelly, sent from London a couple of weeks after she vanished. Although we know that, obviously, she couldn't have sent it.'

'My dear girl.' Diana's voice softened. 'Why are we here?'

Judith sighed. 'It's Paul, my husband. I just thought it might be easier to talk without him around.'

'Because there was something you wanted to tell us?'

Judith shrugged. 'I didn't know what you wanted to ask me.'

Izzy felt it, then. The atmosphere, the atoms in the air, the static. A tension, a spark. Judith knew something. At least, she worried she might know something, and hadn't wanted her husband to even hear the question.

'You had a boyfriend in Seahouses. Am I right?' Izzy held Judith's gaze.

'Something like that.' Judith shifted uncomfortably in her seat.

'An older man? Was he married?'

Izzy saw it – a flash of something behind Judith's eyes. But she quickly stilled her features once more, the mask firmly back in place.

Judith hunched forward, her elbows on the table, and brought her index fingers to her lips. 'I never told anyone about this, not even Paul.'

The hairs on the back of Izzy's neck stood on end, and goosebumps prickled her skin.

Judith's voice reduced to little more than a whisper. 'I was in love. At least, I thought it was love. He said he loved me, too. Used to talk about leaving his wife for me and promised me we would be together. I know it was wrong. Believe me, I can see that now.'

She exhaled, a whoosh of air. Her hands were shaking. 'I was sixteen. I thought I was so grown-up, so mature. The boys my age, none of them... they just didn't get it, you know?'

'How old was he?' Diana asked, her voice faint.

Judith seemed to be close to tears. 'Forty. God, I feel sick when I think about it now. I really do. In fact, all these years, I've tried damned hard *not* to think about it.'

'Here. Have some water.' Izzy offered a glass to Judith and noticed that her hand trembled now, too.

'Bloody hell.' Judith chewed on a nail, and Izzy could see she was fighting the urge to cry. 'You see things differently once you're older. Back then, I thought I was an adult. I almost was, in the eyes of the law. But now I can see that I was probably just a sad, scared child. Would I say he was in the wrong? Yes, I suppose. I was too, of course. But at that age... I'm not sure I knew any better. It was consensual, though, I can tell you that.' She scoffed. 'I hate that part the most. I was a willing participant.'

Izzy laid a hand on hers. 'That doesn't make it OK. What he did was wrong.'

Judith's mouth was a tight line. 'I'm not going to the police. It's ancient history, anyway.'

'Do you think you were the only one, dear?' Diana's eyes sheened. 'Because men like that...'

The tears came now, silver streaks down Judith's face. She shrugged. 'He was so gentle. So patient with me. And kind. It wasn't abuse.'

There wasn't time, Izzy realised, to debate this last point. 'Judith, this is important. Kelly was also involved with an older man. And we believe he murdered her.'

Judith stopped crying and stared at her, incredulous. 'No way. He's not like that.'

'Kelly was pregnant when she was killed.' Izzy was getting desperate. They were so close to finding who N was.

'Just give us a name, and we'll do the rest. We know it was someone in the village, probably someone who knew the Barretts very well. Someone whose name began with N.'

'N?' Puzzlement flashed over Judith's face, and then she remembered. 'Oh right, N for Ned. Ned Flanders. That's what the kids called him.'

'Sorry, dear,' Diana glanced at Izzy, 'but who on earth is Ned Flanders?'

'It's a cartoon character from *The Simpsons*—' Izzy stopped, remembering something Bryan had said. Something about Kelly's nicknames for her foster parents. The last piece slotted into place.

'Eric Barrett,' Izzy whispered. 'It was Eric Barrett. He was N.'

Pam Bell was pacing, covering the length of that empty pastel-coloured room in five decent strides, then heading back on herself in the opposite direction.

Last night she had stayed up late to finish reading Kelly's diary. In those small, dark hours, she'd understood why Izzy had been so sure that Nick Shaw was N.

If only it were that easy.

Now, they had no suspect, no match on the DNA, and no other clues. *And no team.* She glanced around the deserted Incident Room, just to confirm the fact that she was entirely and utterly alone in this.

The Chief Superintendent had given her until the end of the week. Quite generous, Pam considered, given the circumstances. At that point, she would be reassigned, and there would be precisely zero detectives actively working on the Salt Girl case.

Of course, the Guv didn't know about Diana Wheeler

and Izzy Morton. *How had it come to this?* Pam wondered for the umpteenth time. She, and this entire investigation – *her investigation* – depended on the resourcefulness and cunning of two local busy-bodies.

The phone rang, a shrill clang that brought her back to the moment. Pam grabbed at it, her heart still thundering from the interruption.

'Incident Room,' she said, and had to battle against the laugh that rose in her throat at the irony of calling it as much.

'DI Bell, this is Izzy. Izzy Morton.'

The line was grainy; Pam could hear the purr of a car engine.

'I'm with Diana. We're on our way back from Falkirk.'

'Falkirk? What are you doing up there?' There was nothing in any of the case notes, nothing in any of the witness accounts that mentioned Falkirk.

'I don't have time to explain right now, but it's Eric Barrett.' There was a clatter of static. 'Pam, did you hear me? It was Eric Barrett. He was having an affair with Kelly.'

'Eric Barrett?'

These two were surely pulling her leg. Again, Pam wondered what she'd been thinking when she had agreed to let them work the case.

She hadn't been thinking; that was the problem. She'd been bloody desperate.

Besides, she had interviewed the Barretts twice. They'd been even more distraught than Kelly's biological family. A nice church-going couple who had fostered dozens of kids over the years. Their background checks had been impeccable, and neither had so much as the stain of a speeding ticket to taint their records.

'Eric was N. It stands for Ned Flanders, you know, that guy on *The Simpsons*—'

'Yes, yes, I know who Ned Flanders is.' And Pam could see it. There was a comic resemblance with that moustache, but also the penchant for quoting the Bible, the pristine home, the permanently sunny demeanour. It was...

It was laughable; that's what it was.

'Is this a wind up?'

'Bryan Shaw said something which corroborates it.'

Pam winced. She'd hoped that Izzy might have more sense than to go back to the Shaws, especially after everything that had happened. *Jesus.* If anyone found out that Pam had actually sanctioned this, she'd be done for.

She sighed, pinching the bridge of her nose between her thumb and forefinger. Forty years in the force, and she'd be out the door with a boot in her arse.

'Bryan told me that the kids' nickname for Eric was Ned Flanders.' Izzy's voice was urgent. 'And just think about it – the salt in the grave. My mum said something to me right at the beginning about the salt, that it was the *ritual* of it. That the killer was performing an embalming, burial rites or something. Almost biblical, don't you think?'

There was a new voice now. 'Detective? Are you there?'

They must have her on speakerphone.

'Yes, Diana. I'm still here.'

'We found another girl, a witness. She was also fostered by the Barretts. Eric had an affair with her when she was sixteen. Surely, that's enough to make an arrest?'

Pam thought this through. It might have been enough for a warrant, if she had found and interviewed the witness herself.

Pam sank into a mint-green chair, her head pounding. Eric Barrett was as nice as pie. But he had the means and the opportunity. Did he really have it in him? Pam had learned that the ones who smelled like roses were often just as capable of evil as the worst of them.

So, they had a witness who claimed Eric had been in a relationship with her while she was in his care. It was a reasonable expectation that he could have done the same with Kelly.

Pam could see that, if it was true, he would be desperate to hide it. *To bury his secret.*

And there was the salt. If Kelly's killer had been in a relationship with her, he might have performed some kind of burial ceremony – an embalming, or what have you. Perhaps salt was the only thing Eric Barrett had to hand.

But going on third-party evidence like this... By the time Eric Barrett got himself lawyered up, he'd be claiming human rights abuses and bloody all sorts. It would never fly with a jury.

'If we could get a DNA sample...' She was thinking out loud.

'Perhaps you could get him to volunteer for a test.' Izzy's voice was tinny, disconnected. 'Say that it's just to rule him out. Ask him in front of his wife, so he can't refuse.'

'No way,' said Pam. 'If he's guilty, he'll never agree.'

She'd need a warrant, and Eric would bring in an army of lawyers who would fight this tooth and nail. And then they might never get their man. But if they could get a sample without Eric finding out...

'We need to get a sample from him, but he can't know it's happening.' Pam couldn't believe she was actually giving this air, saying these words out loud.

'I don't understand.' It was Izzy, again. 'I thought it had to be given voluntarily, unless there was a warrant?'

Pam shook her head, then remembered that they

couldn't see her. *Who the hell gave Izzy Morton a crash course in police powers, anyway?*

From outside the room, she heard footsteps in the corridor. She held her breath, praying one of the lads wouldn't decide that now was the moment to show an interest in the Salt Girl investigation. But the footsteps continued, passing the door to Incident Room Two, and faded to an echo in the bowels of the police station.

'No. I mean, yes, but there are exceptions.' She lowered her voice to a whisper, just in case the passer-by came back. 'We can do it covertly if there are reasonable grounds for suspicion. Which, in this case, I believe there are.'

Pam's stomach curdled with the premonition – no, the certain knowledge – that she might live to regret this decision.

She'd been tipped for great things, once upon a time. In the early years of her career, Pam had helped to bring down one of Newcastle's most deadly gangland bosses. She'd smashed a people-smuggling ring and solved one of the most complex white collar fraud cases that the region's force had ever seen.

How had it come down to this?

'I'll go to see them again. I'll tell them we... I don't know.' She was thinking on her feet. 'I'll say that we need to search the house again, or that we've had a breakthrough thanks to a new witness.'

Pam could hear for herself just how uninspired and, more importantly, how unconvinced she sounded.

'No.' Izzy spoke firmly, now. 'I'll do it. He only lives around the corner from me. He won't suspect a thing. I can get a sample, and Eric will be none the wiser.'

Pam exhaled, long, slow. Painfully. This – surely, this – was the line. And she had no choice but to cross it.

'Fine.' It was as if someone else was speaking the words now. As if she could see herself, alone in this room, deranged by this case. Sleep-deprived and detached from reality.

Wasn't that one of the first signs of madness? Failure to recognise basic right from wrong?

Pam sighed, a heavy, weary exhale. She had lost touch with right and wrong a long time ago.

'Just make sure—'

She stopped. The line had gone dead.

36

The sun glared even as it dipped towards the hills inland, bathing everything it touched in buttery light. Izzy tried to steady her breathing as she walked. She clenched and unclenched her hands, shaking off the threat of a tremble.

At the top of Clyde Street, she paused and inhaled deeply. Her pulse was hammering; she could feel it in her temple, in her neck, and she willed her racing heart to steady. She slowed as she approached the Barretts' house, wiping her palms against her shorts.

By the time she reached their door, her heart was racing. *You can do this,* she told herself. She drew a deep breath. *Just get in and out.*

Eric answered the door. 'Izzy, what a pleasant surprise.' He pushed his glasses back up his nose. 'Come in, come in.'

The sight of him made her breath snag in her throat. She quickly recovered, faking a smile, and followed Eric inside.

'I wanted to talk to you about the memorial service.' She had rehearsed this line, and now heard that it sounded false, too forced. She swallowed. 'Diana says there's been quite a bit of interest from the old St Helen's girls.'

Eric smiled; a warm, genuine smile. But Izzy now recognised it as a mask for his evil. *A wolf in sheep's clothing.* 'I think it's a splendid idea.' He hesitated. 'Maeve isn't home, I'm afraid. Just had to nip to church to grab something. She won't be long, though, if you don't mind waiting?'

He gestured towards the sofa. It groaned as Izzy took a seat.

Eric sank into the armchair opposite. 'How are you enjoying Seahouses?'

'Excuse me?' Izzy's mouth was dry.

A question flashed across Eric's face. 'You and your fiancé, you just moved in recently, didn't you? I trust you're settling in, finding your feet?'

'Right... Yes, sorry. It's... ah, great.' Izzy struggled to think of anything else to add, anything else to say. The silence permeated the space around them, hanging thick and heavy in the air. It was broken only by the tick of the carriage clock on the mantelpiece, and the hammering in Izzy's chest which was so forceful, she worried Eric might hear it.

Calm down, she told herself. *Stay calm.*

She lay her hands on her lap, afraid to touch anything, and afraid that they might start shaking again.

Izzy couldn't imagine what Judith or Kelly had ever seen in this man. But that was the problem, wasn't it? The girls hadn't seen something in him. Not like that, at least. Any desire had been manufactured, engineered. What those young women had felt was not chemistry, or attraction, but the result of a careful manipulation.

Eric had wormed his way in once he knew their weak spots. Preyed on them when they were at their most vulnerable, dragging them through the cracks.

A predator that had circled then swooped, sinking his claws in.

'Tea?' Eric asked, after what felt like an eternity.

Izzy nodded. 'That would be great, thanks.' The words cracked on her tongue.

He left her there in the stale silence of that ghastly room. It was all a façade, she realised, a veneer, a trick of the light. Scratch below the surface, and you would find the patina of evil.

The wolf disguised in sheep's clothing.

From the kitchen, she heard the click of the kettle and the clunk of ceramic as Eric went through the ritual of making tea.

'Actually, Eric, do you mind if I use your bathroom?' She called out, hoping he didn't hear something amiss in her voice.

'Upstairs, third door on the left,' a bodiless voice answered back.

Izzy crept up the stairs, battling against the rush of blood to her head. In her pocket were three freezer bags and a pair of tweezers – the best she'd been able to come up with at short notice, but hopefully, everything she needed.

The upper floor of the Barretts' home was just as she had imagined. Fusty and vapid. The wall was lined with photographs: portraits of Eric and Maeve on their wedding day, and scores of anonymous children.

Where were they all now? How many others, Izzy wondered, had found themselves ensnared in Eric's web?

She hesitated outside the third door. There were six doors in total, four of which were uniformly ajar. Which room had been Kelly's? She took a guess and pushed against the door at the end of the hallway.

It was a box room, the walls a faded blush pink, the

curtains bleached by years of sunlight. A narrow bed was pushed up against the wall furthest away from the window. Izzy sat, sensing the ghost of Kelly by her side, sitting in this same spot as she journaled each evening.

She pushed away the lure of sorrow. There would be time to grieve later.

Two doors down, she found Maeve and Eric's room. A double bed, and this surprised her. Perhaps the Barretts' marriage was not quite as loveless as Eric had made out.

Poor Maeve. Izzy's heart sank for the woman. As if the depth of Eric's betrayal wasn't bad enough, there would be the rollercoaster of a court trial and sentencing, all played out in the media. And, as Izzy knew from experience, the worst would be yet to come; the daily torture of wicked whispers, jibes hidden behind the hands of those Maeve had once considered friends. Stares in the street, memories and ghosts everywhere she turned.

No, Eric would not be the only one who would suffer when all was done.

There was a dressing table in the furthest corner, and a vanity standing against the wall closest to the door. His and hers.

Izzy paused in the doorway, listening to the sounds from below, checking that Eric was still occupied in the kitchen. Satisfied, she crept towards the vanity, her tread light. A hairbrush lay discarded on its surface. There was a definite tremble in her hand as she extracted the tweezers and a ziplock bag from her pocket. Izzy tugged some of the pale hair free and shook the sample into the bag, her pulse a metronome in her ears.

Eric was stirring the tea; the musical chink of metal against ceramic echoed from the floor below.

Izzy tiptoed back to the bathroom and locked the door

behind her.

In the mirror over the sink, she caught sight of her reflection. Her complexion had the pallor of the haunted, glossed with a sheen of sweat. She wiped her forehead with the back of her wrist.

A cursory google had told her what to look for. A used toothbrush was ideal, but she had decided it would be too risky – Eric would notice right away if it were missing. Besides, she had no way of knowing which was his.

She went straight to the bin and emptied its contents into the sink. Immediately, she spotted what she wanted.

A used razor.

After bagging it up, she flushed the chain of the toilet. She restored the bin and its contents, righting the room, leaving it just as she had found it.

She paused again at the door, holding her breath until she heard the faint echo of Eric's footsteps on the kitchen floor.

The coast was clear.

Izzy slid the bolt from the latch and took a tentative step out onto the landing. She barely registered the shadow in the periphery of her vision.

There was a grunt and a crash, the dull thud of something heavy against the back of her head. Searing agony thundered through Izzy's skull, reverberating down her spine. She stumbled forward just as the world went dark.

When Izzy woke, she was staring at the sky. She tried to move, but her head was heavy, and her limbs didn't respond.

She attempted to speak, to call out for help, but no sound came. Her tongue scratched against the roof of her mouth.

Her surroundings were coming into focus now. Not the sky, but walls. *Blue walls.* A boy's bedroom. She righted her head so that she was looking up at the ceiling. The floor crunched beneath her, and her neck ached with the effort of this one slight movement.

Her breath came in shallow, panicked gulps. She focused on her breathing, willing herself to calm. How long had she been out for? Her ears were ringing.

Through the fog, it came back to her, piece by piece.

The Barretts' house. A blow to her head as she left their bathroom.

She'd been caught.

She reached a hand up to touch the back of her head, but still, her arm didn't respond. Izzy could feel why, now. Someone had restrained her. She glanced down and saw that her hands had been bound together with duct tape. A tear escaped from her eye, running into her hairline.

The ringing in her ears was quieting and beyond it, she could hear that the house was still, silent. Was she alone?

She re-angled her head to better hear, and again, the floor beneath her crunched. Izzy glanced and saw that it wasn't carpet she was lying on, but plastic sheeting. She swallowed against the urge to scream.

The feeling was coming back to her limbs, the heaviness dissipating. The mist lifting from her brain, bringing reality into sharp focus.

Her legs were tied at the knees and ankles, her wrists had been fixed to the front of her torso. Although she couldn't move her feet or hands, this last restraint had been hastily tied. She tugged, feeling some give, and was eventually able to tease her arms free.

She brought her hands up to her face for an inspection. The skin on her wrists was white where the tape had been tightly fastened. She worked them, twisting her hands first one way and then the other. It hurt like hell, but she felt the bindings loosening.

There was movement somewhere in the house. A shuffle, and the creak of a floorboard in a neighbouring room. Izzy closed her eyes and allowed her face to fall slack just as the door opened.

'She's still out cold.' It was Eric, but there was none of his habitual cheeriness. In its place, Izzy heard something else. *Fear.*

'Good,' came the reply. A woman.

Maeve? Izzy's heart hammered.

'I don't think—'

'No, Eric. That's your problem. You never bloody think.'

Oh god, thought Izzy. *Maeve.*

She barely recognised the woman's voice. All that gentleness had disappeared and now Maeve's words were clipped with a cold brutality.

Eric was wounded. 'I had it under control...'

A sigh. 'No, you didn't. She was onto you. And once again, I'm the one who's forced to clean up your mess.'

'I said I'll take care of it.'

Maeve scoffed. 'Too right, you will.'

They were only metres away. Izzy imagined them standing together on the landing, just outside the room, peering in at her. Watching her.

Blood pounded in her ears. She needed to fight, but she was outnumbered.

'Maybe we could talk to her?' His voice was small. 'Explain, make her see that there's been some mistake?'

'Are you a fucking imbecile, Eric? Are you seriously that stupid? I can't believe we're having this same bloody conversation. Because this is just like with that girl all over again, isn't it? "I'll just talk to her, Maeve. I'll make her understand, Maeve,"' she mocked him, sneering. 'You'd have thought you'd have learned your lesson by now. Dear god, I married an idiot. It's not enough that you can't keep your bloody hands to yourself—'

'I've said I'm sorry, a million times...'

'But you never stopped, did you? Again and again. Carrying on with harlots, under my own roof! Let's be clear here. This is all your fault, Eric. If you hadn't fooled around with those girls, we would never have been in this god-forsaken situation. And it's not like you can bury this one in the neighbours' garden, is it?'

'I wouldn't have had to bury her if you hadn't killed her. And hiding her in that garden was your idea...'

'How was I to know they'd bloody dig her up?' Maeve hissed. 'And that salt. I don't know what you were thinking.'

'She had sinned, I was...'

'Oh, she sinned, all right. There's not enough salt in the sea to keep the devil from that one. And she tempted you to sin too, with her whoring. But you were weak, Eric. You are nothing but weakness!'

Izzy winced. Maeve's words were pure fury, now. Acidic barbs.

Maeve exhaled, a deep whoosh of breath. When she spoke again, her calm had returned. 'And now I have to get us out of another mess. So, listen to me carefully: here's what we're going to do. You'll carry her to the bath, and I'll cut her throat...'

Eric moaned.

'Quiet, you! She can bleed out in there. As soon as it's dark, you're going to pack her up into your car and drive across to Kielder. Go the long way round, not through the village. There are cameras.'

'And...' Eric stuttered. 'And then what?'

'You'll dump her in the reservoir. Weigh her down, make sure she sinks. They'll all assume she's run away.'

Izzy's stomach curdled. Would anyone really believe that? Would Jake and the kids, her mum, Auntie Sue, be convinced that she had left them?

'Maybe we could—'

'No, Eric! There is no other way!' Maeve gave a deep, guttural growl of frustration. 'Do you see what you've driven us to? You and your adultery with sinful whores?'

A sob escaped Eric's lips.

'And it's no use bloody crying about it!'

From below them, there was the chime of the doorbell.

'Don't answer it!' Izzy could hear the panic in Eric's voice.

Maeve sighed. 'You will answer it, Eric. You'll smile and stay calm. Just get rid of whoever it is.'

'But I...'

'Just bloody do it, all right?'

There was the tread of footsteps as Eric retreated; the sound fading down the stairs. Izzy listened, following the shuffle of Maeve's feet as she padded down the landing to a spot where she could better overhear.

Izzy cautiously opened her eyes, checking that she was no longer being observed. There was no time to lose.

She brought her wrists back up to her face and yanked her hands apart, ripping at the raw edge of the tape with her teeth. The binding loosened sufficiently to free one hand, then the other.

From below, she heard the front door open, swiftly followed by a thud. There was a cry. 'What the...' Then the clatter of furniture, and more shouts.

It took Maeve just seconds to run back into the room,

but Izzy was ready for her. There was no time to unpick the restraints around her ankles, but Izzy had rolled into a crouch at the side of the door. She registered the shock on Maeve's face as she found the plastic sheet empty.

Izzy sprung up at Maeve, barrelling the woman to the floor with the full weight of her body.

Maeve fell onto her back, clawing wildly at Izzy. Maeve issued a swift kick; it caught Izzy in the stomach, knocking the breath out of her.

They rolled over, and now Maeve was on top of Izzy. The woman had a surprising strength for someone so petite. She snarled, and a fleck of spit landed on Izzy's face, just as Maeve's hands found Izzy's neck.

Izzy could see, now, that she had completely misjudged Maeve. All along, that kindly, dowdy exterior had been a disguise for a brutality that ran deep. *Maeve was the wolf in sheep's clothing.*

She had brought those girls into her home even after she knew what Eric was capable of; she had killed Kelly to keep their secret and then she had masterminded the cover-up. Eric might have buried Kelly's body, but she died at Maeve's hand.

The thought stirred something inside Izzy; a primitive, raw anger. It boiled over, bubbling to the surface in a furious explosion.

It gave her a renewed strength – enough to free her right arm from beneath Maeve's weight. She sliced a palm directly up and jabbed the heel of her hand straight into Maeve's nose.

Maeve recoiled, the shock of the blow enough to make her loosen her grip.

Izzy seized the advantage, rolling over, so that Maeve was once more beneath her. She barrelled her hand into a fist and swung her arm back to strike just as DI Bell crashed into the room.

Maeve barely had time to register the detective's presence before DI Bell was on top of her.

'Maeve Barrett, I'm arresting you on suspicion of murder.' The detective held out her handcuffs. 'Now, do you want to do this the hard way, or should I just tase you and get it over with?'

Izzy rocked onto her backside, her body now trembling uncontrollably, her eyes wet with relief.

'Officer...' Maeve's fragile little woman act was on again now. 'It was Eric. He is abusive. He has been mentally and physically abusing me for years, and anything I did was through coercion. And then this woman attacked me in my own home! I had to defend myself.'

DI Bell tutted, a sorry shake of her head. 'I'd hoped for more from you, Maeve. You see, Izzy here is wearing a wire, and I've been sitting out front listening to the whole thing.'

Maeve glared at Izzy, her eyes narrowing as her mouth turned down into a sneer.

DI Bell slapped the cuffs on her wrists. 'Which means, of course, your little confession just now was recorded. If I might offer you a piece of friendly advice, Maeve, it would be to shut the hell up.'

DI Bell glanced at Izzy. 'You all right there?'

Izzy grimaced. 'You certainly took your time.'

'Here.' The detective handed her a pocket knife and nodded to the duct tape on Izzy's ankles. 'I almost sent the team in when you went quiet on me. But then the Barretts started yapping, and we didn't want to interrupt.'

'Did you get Eric?'

'Oh, we got him, all right. He tried to make a run for it,

but a couple of the lads were waiting for him out the back. They're ready to cart these two off.'

'And Jake?'

'Waiting downstairs. He's still furious that I agreed to let you do this. One of my lot had to physically hold him back, at one point. Hopefully, you can convince him not to sue the force. My guess is he'll just be glad to have you home in one piece.' DI Bell turned to Maeve. 'We'd best get you going, eh?'

Another officer arrived, but Izzy could barely muster the strength to acknowledge him.

She watched with detachment as DI Bell yanked Maeve to a stand. A thin trail of blood snaked from Maeve's nose to her mouth. She was a shadow of the beast she had been moments earlier. A shell, hollowed out and exhausted, her evil spent. A woman who knew she was beaten.

'All right, Rich. Let's get this one booked and pack her off,' DI Bell instructed.

Maeve hung her head and kept her eyes on the ground as she was led away.

DI Bell helped Izzy to her feet. 'You should see a doctor.'

Izzy shook her head. 'I'm fine. I just want to go home.'

Home. Home with her fiancé.

Home, back to the bed she shared with the man she loved, where the ghost of a lost girl could now be laid to rest, and where Izzy could finally build the dream that had found her.

DI Bell had to help Izzy down the stairs to where Jake was waiting for her by the door. He bundled her into his arms, her tears soaking his t-shirt, relief and freedom and love coursing through her veins.

Home.

EPILOGUE

It was a nice day for a funeral, if one could say such a thing. And if anyone could, it was Diana.

After all, old age conferred certain indulgences.

Dawn had asked her to speak at the service, and Diana had taken great pains to prepare a eulogy befitting the exceptional young woman she'd had the brief pleasure of knowing. She hoped it did Kelly justice, but deep down, Diana knew there were no words that adequately captured her spark or wit, her unique brilliance, or her courage.

She could no longer blame herself for what happened to Kelly. What chance had she stood faced with such dreadful evil? The Barretts had fooled everyone. Diana might have failed the girl back then, but finally, eventually, she had exposed the truth. And after all these years, Kelly would see justice served. All Diana could do now was hope that Kelly would forgive her. Because life, Diana knew, was too short to live with regret. Each day was a precious gift, and she resolved to make the most of whatever time she had left.

Among the knot of mourners at the entrance to St Cuthbert's, she spotted Izzy. Diana thought of Amy and knew how proud she would be if she could see her sister now. And of course, Izzy's darling fiancé. The girl had more than landed on her feet with that one.

She greeted Sue and Emily with kisses on their cheeks. The couple seemed to have fallen into a comfortable living arrangement with Sue's sister Anne, which Diana found delightfully modern. She hoped they might consider marrying, if only so that Diana would have the chance to attend a wedding where two women wore white and no one so much as batted an eyelid.

Indeed, a sizeable party had gathered for the send-off. Diana waved at Samantha and Bryan Shaw, both of whom waved back, Samantha looking very sheepish. Diana smiled charitably. All water under the bridge, now. She hoped.

The eulogy was folded up in her purse, but Diana was confident that she would not need to consult her notes. She had the entire thing committed to memory, and today, she was certain that it would not let her down.

The hearse pulled up, and a tear rolled down her cheek at the sight of the casket. *Dear Kelly.* What a tragic ending to such a promising story.

The Barretts were in appalling trouble. If rumour was to be believed – and around these parts, it often was – they had turned on each other under questioning. The police had charged Maeve with murder, and Eric had an entire list of crimes on his charge sheet, including several counts of statutory rape, thanks in part to the bravery of Judith who had come forward to help the prosecution.

The mystery of the salt continued to occupy the public imagination. The most credible explanation had been offered by a local historian in last Tuesday's *Evening Chronicle*. According to her article, the tradition of burying people in salt was rooted in Northumbrian lore. Followers of the ancient custom believed the salt would cleanse the dead of their sins and keep the devil away. Diana's best guess was that Eric – through a warped logic and deranged by fervour – had believed Kelly to be the sinner in this scenario and had been performing burial rites of sorts.

The historian would be appearing as an expert witness at the trial, and Diana was determined to live long enough to see it. She did appreciate a good courtroom drama.

But she wouldn't think about the Barretts today. Today was for Kelly.

Several strapping young men carried the coffin into the church on their shoulders; relatives of Kelly, Diana had to presume. Dawn followed at the tail of the procession, her head held high. At the entrance of the church, she met Diana's eye and offered a sad smile.

The crowd folded, narrowing through the entrance, and Diana stepped into the church.

Her gaze, as always, was drawn upwards to the spectacular stained glass window, illuminated by the July sunshine and casting mottled hues across the flagstone floor. Dust motes caught in the light, dancing in the air.

Diana inhaled the memory of centuries, of life's many sorrows and joys and fleeting brilliance, and knew that, though she may be no more significant than a grain of salt, it had all counted for something.

She reached out into the space beside her, where she imagined Kelly now stood, and felt the girl's hand meet hers.

There was already quite a crowd by the time Izzy and Jake arrived.

'Ready?' he asked.

She wasn't sure that she was, but nodded anyway.

They had waited until dusk, until the sky was streaked with spectacular pinks and purples and oranges, and only traces of daylight remained. The sea was fading to an inky blackness, the last of the light catching the waves as they rolled out towards the horizon.

The others were waiting for them at the corner – Sue and Emily, her mum, Mike, and the kids.

'Ready?' Auntie Sue asked, and Izzy smiled.

In truth, she would never be ready to say goodbye to Kelly, the girl that had haunted her dreams. Just as she would never be ready to say a last goodbye to Amy or Dad. They would always be by her side.

But tonight, they would give Kelly a spectacular send-off.

'Auntie Izzy, do you like my lantern?' Betsy held her effort forth for inspection.

The lanterns had been Diana's idea, and the entire village had embraced it. Every child in the local primary school had made one as a special craft project, and that afternoon, Izzy had seen them adorning shop windows along the high street.

'It's beautiful, dear.' She took Betsy's hand and smiled at Jake. 'Have you got ours ready?'

He nodded, holding up two paper lanterns. 'Good to go. I even remembered the matches.'

They set about lighting the small candles. Izzy, unsure she could cope with the added anxiety of a fire risk, had bought battery-powered tea lights for the kids.

Lucas huffed. 'You can trust me with a real candle, you know. I am thirteen.'

Izzy caught Hannah's eye, and the two exchanged a knowing smile. She saw more and more of Amy in her oldest niece with every passing day. It was a privilege, she realised, to be here, watching the three of them grow. To be at their sides as they navigated a world that could be worrisome and wonderful in equal measure; to protect and nurture and guide them as they discovered life and all the possibilities it held.

No one could ever fill the void Amy had left in Izzy's heart, but the children had allowed her to learn a new kind of love; something fierce and frighteningly powerful and instinctive – an instinct that Izzy had not realised she possessed. An instinct that she now understood would be enough.

And Jake.

Home wasn't simply a place, Izzy realised; it was the people you let into your heart and share your life with. And her home was with him. Her Jake. The dream she hadn't been looking for, but she thanked her lucky stars it had found her. It didn't matter that it was in Seahouses. It didn't matter where it was, as long as they were together. Their future – the future they were building – unfurled before her in her mind's eye, an infinity of golden sand stretching to the horizon.

She took a deep breath. 'Let's go.' They walked down Sea Street and turned onto Harbour Bank. 'Oh my,' Izzy said, tears pricking her eyes.

The harbour was awash with lights; they snaked down the bank and along the harbour wall, curving around the small beach and back up the hill to Crewe Street. A trail of stars, as far as the eye could see.

'There must be hundreds of people here.' The words snagged in Jake's throat. 'It's spectacular.'

But Izzy was speechless. All these people. *So many lights.*

An entire village, righting a collective wrong. Remembering the girl they had once forgotten, never to forget her again.

She hoped Diana had found a good vantage point. And then she thought of Dawn, and hoped that she was down there somewhere in the thick of bodies, admiring the view from the harbour with a lantern in her hand.

They stood there, lost for words, drinking in the sight.

'Three minutes to nine,' said Mike under his breath.

A bell rang, the cue for a minute's silence, and a hush descended over the crowd. The only sounds came from the black water as it lapped at the harbour wall, and beyond it, the gentle crashing of the receding tide. A tear rolled down Izzy's cheek.

The bell tolled again, and one by one, the lights floated skywards, a cloud of stars ascending to heaven.

Izzy watched through the blur of tears as her star rose alongside Jake's, and offered a final, silent goodbye to Kelly.

THE END

AUTHOR'S NOTES

It is customary at this day, in some parts of Northumberland, *to set a pewter plate containing a little salt* upon the corpse.

Salt, says the learned Moresin, is the emblem of eternity and immortality. It is not liable to putrefaction itself, and it preserves things that are seasoned with it from decay.[2]

Considered in reference to this symbolical explication, how beautiful is that expression, "Ye are the salt of the earth!" Reginald Scot, in his Discourse concerning Devils and Spirits, p. 16, cites Bodin, as telling us that "the devil loveth no salt in his meat, for that is a sign of eternity, and used by God's commandment in all sacrifices."

Observations on the Popular Antiquities of Great Britain: Chiefly Illustrated The Origin of Our Vulgar Customs, Ceremonies, and Superstitions

John Brand, 1775.

Seahouses is an actual place, although I have (once again) distorted the geography to better fit my narrative. I hope to recreate the atmosphere of this beautiful village and encourage people to visit our unique corner of the country. I can assure you, murder rates in Seahouses are far lower than my novels would have you believe.

In chapter four, I refer to news reports of the body of a girl being found. The body of thirteen-year-old Milly Dowler was found on 18 September 2002, several months after she went missing on her way home from school in Surrey. It was a crime that shook the country. I was nineteen years old and, like most people, had followed the story since her disappearance, hoping for news of Milly being found safely. I remember my father being particularly upset at her tragic and senseless murder; his concern for the safety of his own daughters heightened in the aftermath and for years afterwards.

I also refer to the Me Too movement. Thank you to all the brave women – and men – who fight to make the world a safer place for women and girls.

ACKNOWLEDGMENTS

I dedicate Salt Girl to all the teachers. To the ones who nurture, inspire, and protect us; thank you for everything.

Writing a novel is not a solitary pursuit and I'm grateful to my editorial dream team: Helen Seymour, Gabrielle Chant, and Rosie Walker. Thank you all for shaping this story.

A special thanks to Laura Boyle for the cover design. My lovely dad passed away while I was writing Salt Girl, and I'm so grateful I had the chance to show him this gorgeous cover before we said, 'see you later'.

Thanks to my sister Beth Edwards, friends Paul Johnson, Elise Rasmussen, Yvonne Iwaniuk, Rosemary Hendry; to my aunt Anne Simms and mum Brenda Clelland for cheering me on, in this and everything.

A special thank you to Walle and Dr Britta Folmer for advice on the science, history, and customs of salt in burials. I'm pretty sure you didn't believe me when I promised I wasn't plotting a real murder, but hopefully you do now.

Thank you to the people of Northumberland and all those who call this corner of the country home (even if it's a home-away-from-home), particularly those of you who have supported my books since the beginning. Special thanks to North East legends LJ Ross, Coastal Custodian, and all those who champion our voices.

As always, thanks to Igor; for love, encouragement, patience, and everything in between.

Most of all, thank you, dear reader, for joining me on this journey. Please don't forget to show your love by rating Salt Girl on Amazon and Goodreads; it's the best way you can support authors like me.

If you enjoyed reading Salt Girl, be sure to check out my other books. You can find me at katherinegraham-author.com.

ABOUT THE AUTHOR

Katherine Graham is the author of the Seahouses Mystery series. When she's not dreaming up grisly methods of murder, Katherine enjoys hiking, Cadbury's chocolate, and 90s R'n'B.

facebook.com/KatherineGrahamauthor

ALSO BY KATHERINE GRAHAM

One dead husband is a tragedy. Two is one hell of a coincidence. Book two in the Seahouses Mystery series.

What secrets is this seaside village hiding? Book one in the Seahouses Mystery series.

Ingram Content Group UK Ltd.
Milton Keynes UK
UKHW041900240723
425711UK00004B/199